Finding Sunset Peak

Daphne, Enjoy!

David

TULSA

ISBN: 978-1-954095-42-7
Finding Sunset Peak
Copyright © 2021 by David Rollins
All rights reserved.

No part of this publication may be reproduced, distributed, or transmitted in any form or by any means, including photocopying, recording, or other electronic or mechanical methods, without the prior written permission of the publisher, except in the case of brief quotations embodied in critical reviews and certain other noncommercial uses permitted by copyright law.

For permission requests, write to the publisher at the address below.

Yorkshire Publishing
1425 E 41st Pl
Tulsa, OK 74105
www.YorkshirePublishing.com
918.394.2665

Published in the USA

Finding Sunset Peak

By
David Rollins

Dedication

For my wife, Kim.

Acknowledgements

To Leonard and Lisa Taylor for their friendship and support of my writing.

To Cecil and Patricia Gray for their friendship and advisement.

To Coretta Albright for her friendship and support of my writing.

All my love to my wife Kim, my daughter Kaitlyn and my son, Nathan for their patience, love, and understanding of my desire to write.

Thank you, God, for this wonderful variable in my life.

Preface

Sunset Peak is a mountain located along the western edge of the Wichita Mountains Wildlife Refuge in southwest Oklahoma. The mountain is located in the public use area of the refuge and borders state highway forty-nine. The Oklahoma towns of Cache and Indiahoma are south of the refuge and Sunset Peak. The mountain is separated from the neighboring Charon's Garden Wilderness Area by a valley and a seasonal stream. It is a boulder-covered mountain that is accessible by hiking and climbing. The mountain is comprised of several other contouring mountains. Sunset Peak is distinguished by its granite chimney and contouring slopes easily seen from the highway.

Thick cedar groves blanket the western base of the mountain, hiding its cliff faces and rugged terrain. Oaks and fire-scarred forests are scattered along the mountain's outer flats and the top ridge. The strong tree branches make hiking difficult. All refuge wildlife can be found in the Sunset Peak area. The mountain's remote location has fewer visitors due to its unforgiving terrain and limited trails. This creates the ideal setting for the refuge animals to evade intruding people.

The view from the top of Sunset Peak extends toward the western horizon. An unobstructed view of the Great Plains and the distant Great Plains State Park is seen from the top of the mountain. The view continues westward toward Altus, Oklahoma, and the visible end of the Wichita Mountains at Quartz Mountain State Park. Sunset Peak is the last mountain to witness sunsets on the public use side of the refuge. It casts a shadow eastward that darkens the valley and rolling hills leading toward Caddo Lake and the granite-walled borders of the Charon's Garden Wilderness Area.

Prologue

No one thought much of Wil Brooks. He did not talk a lot and kept to himself. He tried his hand at painting, only to end each attempt in frustration. He often mumbled that art was not his talent, but those close to him knew he was searching for inspiration. He attempted to paint animals, objects, and some people. He copied various works of other American Indian artists to spark intrigue or motivation. But each plagiary found a dismal end in the trash. He enjoyed life and relished his self-proclaimed ancestry. He touted his background as one of the last existing members of the Wichita tribe that were native to the area. Rarely did he boast of his real name, Wild Wind, and kept it as his treasured identity.

Wil wandered through life silently asking *what if?* He appreciated history and the occasional read of old Oklahoma, the Plains Indians or local folklore. Life was simple, working where he could in small town Cache, Oklahoma doing odd jobs and seasonal gigs to compensate his early retirement from the tire plant. The slower pace engaged his thoughts in ways he could not afford while employed full time. Regardless of his sense of wonder or boredom, he kept his promise to his most prized possessions.

His wife and daughter were the loves of his life. The many years of yearning for time with family were not forgotten. The guilt of missing his young daughter's life made early retirement an easy decision. A robust incentive pay and no mortgage helped too. They each had their likes and dislikes for family things to do. But their common bond was hiking the Wichita Mountains Wildlife Refuge. They often mentioned how the Wichitas seemed to call to them. The threesome had a yearning for the granite oasis and roamed it with relentless joy. The countless fried chicken picnics, autumn campfires and drives up Mount Scott were but pauses of reflection to the bliss of off-trail family hikes. Every mountain, valley and rock formation were logged in their conquered treks as symbols of their timeless memories.

Wil learned that for some experiences in life you have to go out and find them. But sometimes, an experience finds you. And it may only happen once. He recalled the old adage of *be careful what you ask for,* but paid it little attention. Retirement suited him, but as the days became months, he realized he was not ready to ride off in to the sunset. Wil took pride that he had it all figured out. He simply needed to search his life and focus on happiness. That was when life showed up. And the variables that it brought with it were nothing he could have ever imagined.

Chapter 1

The late November breeze chilled the air. The last of the autumn foliage clung to their branches against the stirring wind. The summer shades of green faded to tan and brown with waving brush and rustling shrubbery. The woodland leaves blanketed the ground. Bare trees lined the slopes allowing a clear view of the terrain and surrounding mountains. Streams and ponds, parched from heated days, waited for the replenishment of cyclical rains. Seasonal creatures prepared for hibernation while the toughest thickened their fur and firmed their resolve for the coming cold. Blue skies became more commonly gray from the obscuring clouds and declining temperatures. Nature's next episode was underway and ushering in another winter for the Wichita Mountains Wildlife Refuge.

The fire crackled with fresh wood, creating an inviting warmth. The surrounding area had been picked clean of anything that could burn. Piled logs and broken drift wood from the nearby shore of Quanah Parker Lake provided sustainment for the night. A medium tent and concrete table with a rusted grill neighbored the rock-lined fire pit. Comfy folding chairs and an over-sized cooler full of treats hinted at another Brooks family get-away at the Doris Campground.

They gathered around the table and held hands. Wil opened with a prayer of thankfulness for the food and the time that they were sharing. Keeping his head bowed, he struggled to maintain composure. He prayed for his loved ones, but his heart held what he truly wanted to say. He cleared his throat and opened his eyes. His focus for words vanished. Wil stammered through the prayer with rising emotion and faltering control. He took a deep breath and looked at his wife. Tears welled as he surrendered to the moment.

Ayita rubbed his shaking hand. Her eyes calmed Wil's anguish. Their love for each other flowed between them and connected their souls with passion. She turned toward Laura, still bowing her head and waiting for her father's cue to end the prayer.

"Laura, honey." Laura raised her head. "What is your favorite Thanksgiving?"

"Are we still praying, Momma?" she whispered.

Ayita chuckled. "Yes, dear. But now we're sharing what our favorite Thanksgiving is. What's yours?"

Laura lowered her hands and immersed herself in thought. The eagerness to answer her mother's request became more than her ten-year-old mind could muster. "I liked that Thanksgiving when we had our neighbors over, and Grandma came. We had turkey, ham, dressing, mashed potatoes, cranberry sauce, sweet potatoes, and that green bean stuff Grandma made."

"You didn't like Grandma's green bean casserole, did you?" Ayita asked.

"Um, no, not really. And I didn't like her egg nog pie either. I wish she had made her chocolate pie again. I love that one."

Wil cherished his daughter. The joy in her recollection soothed the torment within him. "Why did you like that Thanksgiving so much?" he asked.

Laura responded without hesitation. "Because we were all together."

Wil tightened the hold on his wife's hand. Ayita interjected and urged for Wil's composure. "And thanks to your daddy, our family is out here together for Thanksgiving."

Laura pointed at their tent. "We've never gone camping for Thanksgiving."

"No, that's true. But that is what makes this Thanksgiving so special. This is one we will always remember." Ayita kissed Wil with a grateful touch.

"I think this Thanksgiving is my new favorite one. I like camping in the Wichitas and going on our hikes. I like riding my bike in the campground too. Most of all, I like daddy being home and all of us being together," Laura said.

"Amen," Wil replied.

"Yes, we are celebrating daddy's retirement from work, too. That makes today very special." Ayita caressed Wil's cheek and covered her slight cough.

"Let's get you into the tent so you can eat." Wil motioned toward Ayita.

"I'd prefer sitting by the fire. I'd like to warm up a bit." Ayita turned toward Laura. "Bring your plate and come sit with me, sweetheart."

Wil moved her folding chair near the flames and set a sparse selection of food on her tray. Ayita nibbled at the meager portions pretending to have an appetite. Wil hurried about the campsite making everything perfect. The fire roared while he prepared the tent for the night. The orange and violet swaths of evening sun faded against the clouds. Wil lit his gas lantern and hung it on a tree branch. The light overwhelmed the camp in a piercing white illumination. Wil turned down the brightness and glanced at Ayita. An angelic glow emanated around her. Her smile intermingled with the brilliant light revealing a heavenly presence with her delightful laugh. Wil observed the moment with a lasting hope to see her image in his mind forever. His effort to hide his agony released with tears as he lowered the illumination and walked into the shadows.

"Momma," Laura picked at her portion of green bean casserole. "When are you not going to be sick anymore?"

Ayita placed her tray on the ground and looked into her daughter's eyes. "Come sit on my lap." She held Laura closely and watched the flames dance across the coals. "Soon, mommy is going to be able to be with you in a very special place."

"Where?"

Ayita tickled Laura's chest. "Right here in your heart."

"How are you going to do that?" Laura giggled.

The dread that Ayita now embraced fulfilled the reason for their camping on Thanksgiving Day. She guided her fingers through Laura's long, flowing hair. "Remember how we talked about the spirit that is within every person?"

"Yes. We all have bodies with a spirit inside, and our spirit is who we are," Laura replied.

"Very good. Well, my spirit is going to have something very special happen to it. My spirit is going to be with you and daddy every day."

"How?" Laura asked.

"My spirit will be free from my body. It will be free to watch over you and love you just as I do now."

Laura expressed a serious tone. "Will you be sick anymore?"

"No," Ayita held her hand. "Spirits don't get sick."

"Does this mean you are going to die?"

Ayita leaned closer to Laura. "My body will go to sleep, but my spirit will be awake. You won't get to see me like you can now, but I will be with you. I'll have strength that I do not have in my body. And when you think of me and remember me, my spirit will be in your heart. I'll be a part of your life. Which is why I want you to be happy. It will be sad that I won't be able to hold you like this, but I want you to remember that I love you, and I will always be with you."

"Why can't I see your spirit?" Laura asked.

Ayita kissed Laura on her forehead as a tear streamed onto her soft hair. "You will someday, my precious girl. You will someday."

* * * * * * * *

The moon illuminated the narrow trail with a pale glow. Wil navigated the forest without regard. He stumbled across the terrain, not caring about obstacles or risk of injury in the dark. His emotions paralyzed any concern for safety. He wiped his tears to see the blurry domed top of his destination. Little Baldy Mountain rose above the tree tops. It glowed in the lunar hue casting its appearance as a massive boulder in the middle of the valley. The layered granite hill proved to be a challenging ascent against the darkness. Wil knew the rock formation well and hiked at an angle to the top. Labeled a mountain for its location in the valley, Wil cherished the rocky hill as Laura's first hike and conquered climb.

From the top of the rock formation, he observed the Doris Campground near Quanah Parker Lake. The scenic view of the refuge valley allowed a unique vantage point for spotting deer and roaming buffalo. The observation of the lake against the backdrop of the Wichita Mountains accentuated the camp. The many primitive and modern campsites dotted the area. The scattered campfires appeared as twinkling stars through the tree limbs. The smoke from burning mesquite and oak drifted across the valley. The smell provided a natural fragrance reminiscent of Wil's numerous family camping adventures.

He pushed his memories aside and rested against a small boulder. The fatigue from the evening caressed his thoughts and laden his eyes. He yearned for an emotional escape from the reality at the campsite. A meteorite caught his attention from the west. The streaking light changed from yellow to green against the night sky and vanished beyond the horizon. Wil watched the split-second spectacle end as quickly as it began. He thought of Ayita, comparing the celestial event to their lives together.

He shared decades with his beloved wife, but now the years felt as momentary as the shooting star. He ended his working career early to be with Ayita and to enjoy life more. The lessons of time and age were revealed with expressed clarity that he had never known before. The variable of health, or its deterioration, made the simplicity of those lessons precious. Once believing he actually had control of his life and an expectation for each day proved his folly. His arrogance for planning, looking to the future, and striving for his goals all seemed meaningless to him now. He wanted so much from life and sacrificed time to get it. As he gazed into the night, he learned time was not a lesson of sacrifice, but one of balance.

* * * * * * *

"What is it about two huge boulders teetering on the edge of a cliff that interests you so much?" Wil asked. He looked up at the unique Wichita Mountains Wildlife Refuge rock formation.

"It's not just the boulders. It's what they represent," Ayita replied.

"Okay, I give up." Wil blocked the sun with his hand and continued looking up. "What do two huge boulders teetering on the edge of a cliff represent?"

Ayita pushed Wil on his shoulder. "They represent us, you goof!"

Wil shook his head and looked at Ayita. "We're rocks?"

"Oh, come on!" Ayita grabbed his hand and pulled him to the base of the granite bluff. Up close, the twin boulders appeared to be the size of small cars positioned an arm's width apart. "From here, they really do look like a crab's eyes peering over the ledge. I've always thought that whoever gave this the name of Crab Eyes must have had a vivid imagination. Look at how they balance so perfectly on the edge. They look like the slightest wind could send them crashing down. But there they are, together, standing on the edge facing the world. Just the two of them," Ayita stated.

"Honey," Wil gestured. "You never cease to amaze me at how you can turn something as simple as Crab Eyes into a metaphor. Why did I have to fall in love with a writer?"

"Those boulders are us." She leaned in and kissed him. "Standing together, high above all that surrounds us and keeping each other from falling. These rocks are special. It's our little place on the earth that neither the elements nor time can alter."

"You never told me this before. I thought this was just your happy place on the refuge?" Wil asked.

"It will always be my happy place. It's where I knew we were meant to be together," Ayita smiled. "Remember how you swooned me with your flute?"

"Swooned you? I think you mean I romanced you."

"You never play your flute anymore. I wish you would. You are so good at it."

Will held her hands. "I knew I loved you the moment I saw you."

"Telling me you loved me after eleven days of meeting me was quite the mystery, I must say. I thought you were nuts." Ayita grinned.

"Hey! When you know you're in love, you know. And I knew. Going on that hike with you here only confirmed it. It's the only thing I've ever known so well in my life." Wil held her close. "You're the love of my life. And when you told me your name, that sealed it for me."

"What is it with you and my name?"

"It's what your name means that's so interesting. It fits you perfectly. Ayita, first to dance." Wil cast a desirous grin.

"And why do you like my name so much?"

"You know why, I've told you a thousand times," Wil answered.

Ayita leaned closer. "Tell me a thousand and one."

Wil tightened his embrace. "Because you are so full of life. Your smile, your personality, how you peek to the side under your hair with that flirty look. You make me feel alive. I can be me when I am around you. It feels so easy."

"I'm swooning again," Ayita teased.

"Except for your laugh," Wil countered. "You laugh like a donkey."

"What? I do not!"

"Aww…eee…aww…eee!" Wil imitated.

"Okay," Ayita tried to push away. "Someday, our daughter will grow up and be just like me. Then we will see who is laughing."

Wil rolled his eyes. "If Laura is anything like you, I'll chain her inside and not let her date till she's forty."

They stared into each other's eyes and met with a longing kiss. So often, they debated the terminology of soul mates. But they did not care about the outcome. They knew their love was lasting and rare. Only the determination of time would limit their loving bond. They placed their hands on the sheer granite wall and spoke their love for each other. Taking a final look at the boulders above, they made their way down the winding trail to the valley below. A seasonal stream cut across the valley floor marking the lowest point of the terrain. The twin boulders towered in the distance, a testament to their unfailing love for each other.

"Do you think love can transcend time?" Ayita asked.

"Where do you come up with these questions?"

"Well, do you? Do you think love can last beyond our time here on earth?"

"I guess so. I think it depends on if we're both together in the next life or if one is left behind. There's only one way to find out that question, and I don't want an answer for a long time." He kissed her hand and continued walking along the stream.

"I think love can last forever. Beyond anything that life is and everything after it. I believe that is what true love can do." Ayita stopped to face Wil. "If I depart before you, I want you to know that is how I love you, beyond time."

Wil stood in awe at the poetic gesture from his wife. Searching for the words to compliment his bride, he said what came to mind without regard. "I never want to know life without you, no matter the time. Like I said, you are the love of my life." He paused to allow his words to resonate and then motioned for her to continue walking. "Why are we talking about this? I don't really care for this topic."

"I just want you to know. I want you to be happy and with no limitations. To live life like an endless hike in the Wichita Mountains. The place we love."

"I couldn't imagine living life without you," Wil said. "I love you."

Ayita became withdrawn. "And I love you, very much. And you will live life. You will live it for our daughter." Ayita began to walk back toward Crab Eyes.

"Honey, wait. Wait! Please don't go."

Ayita faced Wil. "You are always my love." She smiled with soothing assurance and continued toward the twin rocks.

Wil watched her walk away. Anguish overwhelmed him as he yelled for her to come back.

"Daddy!"

Wil shuddered as everything around him turned black.

"Daddy!"

Wil felt the calling behind him. He struggled to see Ayita, desperate to not let her go. The voice behind him called again. Wil reluctantly turned around to see Ayita standing behind him.

"Go, my love."

"No!" Wil reached for Ayita and fell to the ground.

"Daddy, where are you?"

"Ayita!" Wil felt the hard granite against his face and stammered to his feet. His mind raced with frantic despair to gain orientation. All around him was darkness. His eyes adjusted as the awareness of his surroundings became true. He looked up to see stars glistening across the cosmos. The moon cast a dim paleness over the land. His senses shocked him into consciousness and the realization that he was standing on the mount of Little Baldy. He hurried down the side of the granite slope, rubbing his eyes and feeling with his hands to negotiate the terrain. He slid down the remainder of the hill and reached the stability of level ground. Wil raced through the woods toward the campsite.

"Please help me."

Wil stopped and turned toward a large oak tree. The sound of crying drifted through the air. He moved in the direction of the noise, trying to focus through the darkness. A movement in the leaves revealed two bare feet tucked against the tree trunk. "Who's there?"

"Daddy, is that you?"

"Laura!" Wil rushed to his daughter's side. "What are you doing out here? Why don't you have your shoes on? Where is your mother?"

Laura kept her head bowed on her knees with her back against the large oak. She slowly raised her head, revealing streaks of wiped tears across her cheeks. "I came looking for you. I didn't know where you were."

Wil became uneasy. "Sweetie, where is mommy?"

Laura peered into his eyes and started crying. "Mommy went to sleep."

* * * * * *

The Thursday afternoon sun cast its rays across the cloudless sky. The late November climate kept the high temperature steady at forty-six degrees. The crisp air and slight wind made the perfect combination for hiking the Wichita Mountains Wildlife Refuge. The weekday on the refuge meant fewer locals and visitors on the trails and better opportunities for solitude and quiet. An old white Chevy pickup pulled in to the wooded picnic area and parked. Wil and Laura looked through the windshield at the majestic view before them, Elk Mountain towering in the distance. Its many rugged cliffs and jagged contours appeared as scratches cut in the rocky slopes. The mountain portrayed steep, granite walls along its western face. Its flat top rose in to the blue sky and dominated the area.

Wil opened his door and reached for his pack. He checked it thoroughly, ensuring the center pouch was securely fastened. Laura shoved her water bottle into her backpack and slid off of the front seat. They met at the tailgate for a final gear check. Wil adjusted his straps and stared ahead at the trail leading to the Charon's Garden Wilderness Area. He exhaled with a mix of dread and resolve. Focused on their journey, he faced Laura and extended his hand. She observed her father with a solemn tone as he rubbed her cheek. Anticipating the moment, they started toward the trail without words.

Eager to make time, they followed the trail, contrary to the family rule. They thrived at hiking off-trail and enjoyed the thrill of exploring. The opportunity to walk up on deer, longhorn, or the rare occurrence of an elk made taking the road less traveled more alluring. The quest of every hike was to see a bison. The most prized of their wild animal encounters, they loved viewing the bison in their native habitat. They watched the Great Plains beasts lumber across the terrain for hours. The existence of the bison reflected their ancestral presence in the region with a mutual belonging. They respected the animal and treasured every sighting as a successful variable to the day.

Wil led the hike with rare determination. Laura struggled to keep pace with her father's wide stride. She enjoyed the scenic surroundings that Wil passed by, paying them little regard. They navigated the rolling hills and washes to an open field that they referred to as the bison roaming grounds. Bison often grazed the grassy, remote field in large numbers. Laura frowned at the empty pasture, hoping to see her favorite animal. Wil surveyed the mountainous panoramic and allowed Laura a quick rest.

"There they are," Wil pointed ahead. "Not much further."

Laura followed her father through the field. Piles of dark bison dung littered the area. Large wallows dotted the pasture, appearing as circular islands of dust in the brush. She searched the field and adjacent trees for signs of the bison but came up empty-handed. Together, Wil and Laura trekked through a wallow near the edge of the field. Laura kicked the dust into a brown cloud that stirred in the breeze. Wil scowled at her and coughed. She avoided her father's glare to see several sets of bison prints. The prints appeared as two large orange slices completing an oval. The relative size hinted at a smaller bison roaming with its mother. Laura's curiosity peaked as they started down a slope.

They navigated the valley and crossed the dry stream bed. Laura noticed her father's pace begin to slow. She moved along side of him and saw his quivering lip. Tears streamed along his cheeks as she reached for his hand. "Daddy, what's wrong?"

"It's okay. We're almost there. We'll stop at the bottom of that cliff."

Laura saw two enormous boulders balanced on the edge of the cliff. "That's Crab Eyes," she exclaimed.

"Yes, it sure is."

They traversed the winding trail to the base of the cliff. Laura dropped her pack and sat on a rock. Wil removed his pack and handed Laura a water and a small package of M&Ms.

"Here. These were your mother's favorite. No matter how long the hike, she would crunch on these the whole way," Wil stated.

They enjoyed their snacks and talked of memorable stories about Ayita. Laura finished her water and observed the boulders. "Those sure are big."

Wil stood by the base of the granite cliff. "Your mother and I have been at the top where those two boulders are. She wanted to jump between them, but I wouldn't let her. She was always so daring."

"She could have fallen," Laura said.

"No, not your mother. She was quite the hiker and climber." Wil turned toward the valley and the expansive view. "This was your mother's favorite place in the mountains. We came here on our first hike together. She was so fascinated with these rocks and how they looked like they could fall off at any moment."

"I like it here too. I wish I could stand between them." Laura shielded her eyes from the sun.

Wil smiled at his daughter and wiped his eyes. "This place is very special. I asked mommy to marry me right here. I was so excited. We went on a hike and she wanted to go over to the Valley of the Boulders, but I kept insisting we come here. She knew I was up to something, but she played along. It was right here that I surprised her and asked her to marry me. It was a wonderful day for us."

"Did you kiss her?" Laura asked.

"Yes." Wil beamed. "She said those two boulders were her and me. That just like the boulders, we were standing together to keep each other from…"

"Daddy," Laura hurried over to Wil. He knelt and pulled her in to a longing embrace. They cried together, releasing the weeklong strain of emotion on their shoulders. The pain of losing Ayita bonded them as father and daughter more closely than ever before. Wil cleared his throat and consoled Laura.

"Come here. It's time." Wil opened his pack and carefully pulled a cloth-wrapped object from the pouch. He opened the cloth and held up a small urn. They stood together and faced the scenic view. Wil looked at Laura, comforted by her soothing expression and the appearance of Ayita in her eyes. "This is what mommy wanted. Take hold of it with me."

"Like this?" Laura asked.

"That's perfect," Wil replied. A gust of wind rushed through the valley. "Let's say it together. Ready?" The wind passed around them with angelic timing. Wil opened the urn and lifted it with Laura.

"We love you, mommy!" The wind carried their testimony high in to the air and continued westward toward the setting sun.

The breeze calmed as they lowered the urn. Laura wrapped it in the cloth and placed it back in Wil's pack. She wiped her eyes and turned suddenly, hearing a sound coming from Wil standing behind her. Facing the western horizon, Wil began emanating soft tones from a wooden flute. His fingers danced along the perforations of the stained wood with sequenced precision. The melody flowed with an ancestral presence that echoed across the valley. Nature seemed to pause in homage of the solemn event. Wil carried the song with tribute and love in each breath. Laura witnessed her father in a new perspective. She heard her father practice a few times before and enjoyed his meager attempts. The perfection in Wil's tune and the peace of each note calmed her sadness. Wil finished his song and lowered the flute. She watched him whisper in to the air with the flute across his heart.

"That was beautiful." Laura hugged him.

Wil held her face in his hands. "I want you to always know that I love you."

"I love you, too, daddy."

They embraced a final time and gathered their things. Laura jumped on top of a small boulder to watch a red-tailed hawk soar by. "Daddy, look! Over there, by those trees." A herd of thirty bison grazed along the far side of the valley.

"Yeah, I see them. But, not this time." Wil glanced at the sun. "We need to head back."

"Can we take the long way? I don't want to follow that boring trail again. Let's go our own way."

Wil watched Laura's hair blow in the wind. Everything about her reminded him of Ayita. "You sound like your mother." He fastened his gear and stepped next to Laura. "Okay, let's go check them out. But I better not see you dragging behind me complaining about your feet hurting."

Laura slowly moved away from Wil. "Beat'cha to the stream!" She bounded off of the rock and raced toward the valley.

Wil watched her run with joy. He looked up at the twin rocks and whispered a final time, "I love you." He jumped across the rocks in quick pursuit of his fleeing daughter. His boulder hopping cut the distance to Laura by half.

"Not fair! You're cheating." Laura ran faster, giggling at Wil's pursuit.

They reached the stream bed and navigated toward the bison herd. The land rolled with rocky hills and ridgelines. Forests of scrub oaks intertwined with thick undergrowth altered their route several times. Washouts led to ravines that carved through the ground in deep cuts. Cedar groves appeared as dark green barriers scattered across the terrain. Their visual attempt to hike a straight-line direction proved pointless. The many twists and turns of the terrain were camouflaged from their starting point at Crab Eyes. Laura's eagerness to see the bison kept them moving forward. Wil appeased his daughter and negotiated the obstacles to provide her some emotional relief from the day's sadness. They angled up a slope and peeked over the tall grass.

"They should be here," Wil stated.

"There they are." Laura pointed toward a distance field.

"Hmm. They migrated pretty fast. I've never seen a herd move that fast before, unless they were spooked." Wil noticed the sun sinking along the horizon. "Let's cut across the field and make some time. Our hike took longer than I thought."

"But they will see us," Laura said.

"I know. We'll come up behind them for a better view. Try to stay quiet." They rushed through the tall grasses and circled around the main body of the herd. Wil waved at Laura to follow and crawled alongside a large oak tree near a pile of boulders. They climbed the rocks and peeked over the top.

"Wow!" Laura exclaimed.

"Shh, stay low."

The bison herd spread across the field, creating a symbolic scene of the refuge. The majestic animals ripped up the prairie grasses in large mouthfuls. Every bison sniffed the ground for remnants of green vegetation. Laura laughed at the symphony of grunting and chewing from each creature. Several younger bison toyed at their mothers for attention. A showdown between two smaller bison mimicked a duel normally performed by the older bulls. Laura watched as two calves butted heads and then backed away with offended looks.

"Daddy, look at that one!"

A male bison strolled out of the woods. The massive animal towered above the others, with its thick fur highlighting a muscular frame covered in shades of tan and dark brown. Its blunt, black horns revealed several scars and scrapes. Its battle-tested stance proved its earned position in the herd with a large hump on its back, accentuating its powerful posture. The bison portrayed a leader role and cast an intimidating presence to any challenger. It moved slowly through the herd and stopped by a grazing female. The two bison calves continued frolicking near the leader while its large, dark eyes remained focused across the field.

"That big one looks like it's staring right at us," Wil said. "It's almost like it sees us."

Errr.

Wil froze at the peculiar sound of a low-toned growl behind them. Laura turned around and pointed at the tree. "Daddy..."

Wil saw Laura's face paralyzed in fear. He slowly shifted his stance for a better view behind them. "What is it?" Laura began to breathe heavily. "Honey, what is it? I don't see anything."

Laura's arm began to shake. "In the tree!"

Wil observed a large limb at the base of a nearby oak. He squinted his eyes to see the returning stare of a crouching mountain lion. Wil inhaled a massive gulp of air and grabbed Laura by her arm.

"Run!" Terrified by her father's rare display, Laura tripped across the boulder in front of Wil. "Laura!" Wil's foot snagged against Laura's back. He struggled for balance and plummeted headfirst in to the rocks below.

"Daddy!" Laura scurried to her feet and slid down the boulders. Wil moaned against the ground and rolled to his side. Blood oozed from his forehead. Laura reached for her father and began to cry.

"I'm okay." He rubbed his head and prepared to stand. His left knee buckled, sending him back on to the ground in pain. "Is it still in the tree? Do you see it?"

Laura wiped her eyes. "No. It's gone."

"Get against the rock. Keep the rock at your back." Wil crawled next to her and leaned against a boulder. He pressed his hand against his forehead and felt a deep gash. Blood pooled in his hand as he struggled to focus. "What's that sound?"

Laura crawled up the boulder. "All of the bison are running away."

"Laura, reach in my pack and get the first aid kit. Hurry." Laura became worried for her father. His face streaked with blood and dripped on his shirt. She helped with the bandages and contained most of the bleeding. Her silence of the moment displayed her childlike innocence and concern for her father's declining condition. Wil noticed her distress. "I'll be okay, but I think I broke my nose, too. I just need to get cleaned up and stop this bleeding." He felt his dizziness intensify. "Do you see anything?"

Laura checked again. "No. It's getting too dark to see." She thought for a moment. "Do mountain lions hunt at night?"

Wil held his wrist toward Laura. "What time does my watch say? It's hard for me to see it."

She rubbed smeared blood off of his watch. "Um, twenty minutes after six, I think."

Wil rubbed his head, feeling anxiety creep over him. "Well, that isn't good. Can you tell where we're at? My head is pounding." He searched his backpack and opened the side pouch. Frustrated, he hit the pack and threw it against the ground.

"It's getting hard to see. I can't tell where we're at. The valley is down there through those trees," Laura pointed.

"Honey, is there any chance you have a flashlight in your pack?"

"No. Don't you have one?"

Wil rolled his eyes. "No, I didn't think we would be out here this long. Daddy's mistake. Seems I'm making many mistakes today."

"What are we going to do?" Laura asked.

"Okay, let's head for the valley and follow the stream west. It will be easier walking. Maybe we can get to the highway and follow it to the truck. I need you to pay attention. Tell me if you hear anything."

Wil took her hand and hiked toward the stream. The thought of encountering a mountain lion terrified him more than any other animal on the refuge. He knew it was extremely rare to see one in the open. He recalled the dangers that the big cats were capable of as opportunistic hunters. He surmised that the mountain lion was spying on the bison calves. Their small size made them easy targets for the predator. He tightened his grip on Laura's hand, suddenly realizing her vulnerability. He shuddered to think that of all the moments to witness such a unique event, it had to be at dusk with his daughter in a remote area of the Wichita Mountains.

His concern for Laura's safety became paramount as they stumbled through the darkening valley. His injuries became more convincing for the dreaded decision he knew he would have to make. A coyote howled in the distance. The lingering cry echoed down the valley penetrating Wil's desperation and dashing his failing hope. He wiped his eyes to no avail and dropped to a knee. He felt Laura grab his arm.

"Daddy, it's getting really dark. I can't see where we're going. What are we going to do? Did you hear that wolf? It sounded really close."

"That was a coyote." Wil dabbed his forehead and nose. Fresh blood covered his fingers. Feeling his head begin to spin and hearing the fear in Laura's voice, he surrendered to the moment. "We're going to do something that we have never done before. We are going to backcountry camp tonight. What do you think of that?"

"Um, okay." Laura hesitated in her response. "But we don't have a tent."

"I know. That's why they call it backcountry camping. You camp with what's on your back! It will be fun." Wil did his best to raise her spirit and hide his concern, knowing he did not have a clue what real backcountry camping involved. He walked into a clearing and checked the area. A large shadow protruded from a rise on the other side of the stream bed. "Over there. I think that is a group of boulders on that ridge. We will stay there for the night. It will keep us out of the wind and cold."

They climbed to the other side, with Laura supporting Wil. The boulder pile formed an inlet between the rocks allowing enough room for them to fit. Wil crawled in to the confining space and struck a match from his pack. The dirt floor and rock walls appeared perfect for their situation, with only one way in for security. They entered the confinement and emptied their packs. Laura bundled up with everything she had.

"I'm cold," she said and rubbed her sides. The small rock room became silent. "Daddy?" She leaned over, feeling for her father in the darkness. "Daddy, what's wrong?" She felt his leg and reached for his head. Wil sat motionless with his back against the boulder. "Dad!" She shook him by his shoulders and heard a slight moan. He raised his head and touched her hand. Without words, he slowly slid along the rock wall and passed out on his pack.

Chapter 2

The night sky glistened with a collection of stars. The late November darkness settled with a hard cold that beckoned the first frost. The waning crescent moon cast a dim hint of light upon the ground. The air stiffened from the rare vacancy of an Oklahoma wind and magnified every sound. A lone coyote howled its distant presence across the terrain. A daring critter rustled through the dry leaves digging for a meal. Its movement resembled footsteps creeping through the dark forest below. The nocturnal inhabitants woke from their refuge slumber and lurked through another night in the Wichita Mountains.

The coyote howled again. Laura hid in the shadowed entrance of the small rock enclosure and peeked around a boulder. The nighttime blackness shrouded everything and the moonlight tricked her eyes. She struggled to focus on nearby objects that appeared to move in the pale hue. Fear taunted her as the coyote's baying seemed to get closer. The sounds of leaves crunching and sticks snapping echoed from the valley below. Shivering from the cold, she retreated inside the boulder cave and cried in her sleeve.

Laura cupped her hands over her mouth to warm her frozen fingers. She wiped her eyes and watched the stars wink at her through the opening. A moment of silence soothed her ten-year-old mind. She remembered her father talking about backcountry camping. His many lessons of the outdoors and hiking began to penetrate her suffocating dread. She felt for her father's backpack and searched through the limited items. A last pack of M&Ms fell on the ground. She felt the canteen and wrestled with the cap. She drank the remaining water with satisfaction. Wil moaned and rolled on to his side. His hand rested in Laura's lap. She cuddled next to him and wrapped his arm around her. She placed her hand in his and felt a small box of matches tucked in his sleeve.

Laura shook the box and heard several matches rattle inside. She crawled to the rock room opening and used the dim light to open the box. Remembering how her father showed her, she grasped a match in her shaking hand and struck it against the box. The match broke in half and fell to the ground. Laura grunted and tried another match. The fragile stick cracked against her frantic strike. The third attempt snapped with the same result. "Ah!" she yelled and threw the box against the boulder wall. Her frustration calmed as she thought through the moment. Pressing the box against the ground, she warmed her hand and struck another match.

The tiny stick ignited in a startling display. She panicked and released the frightful flare. "No!" She watched it land perfectly in to the open box. The matches erupted in a hissing fireball that illuminated the entire enclosure. Laura glimpsed at several small piles of leaves and sticks gathered along the edges of the rock room. She hurried to gather the dry items and placed them carefully over the burning matchbox. The sound of crackling leaves led to eager flames that lifted in brilliant orange and red colors. The fire began to strengthen as she snapped sticks and spread them gently across the burning leaves.

Minutes passed, with the fire intensifying. The welcomed flames cast their light and filled the enclosure with ample heat. Laura grinned at her success and hurried to gather more wood. A fallen oak tree rested near the opening of the enclosure. The fire highlighted several broken branches scattered around the decaying trunk. The amount of wood appeared sufficient for the night. The coyote's distant howl chilled her confidence as she leaned near the opening and watched for any signs of movement. She thought of the earlier encounter with the mountain lion and hesitated. Her mounting fear lengthened the distance to the wood with haunting reservation.

Dispelling caution for survival, Laura bolted through the opening and gathered as many branches as she could carry. She dragged the wood to the enclosure and placed some larger pieces over the coals. The fire engaged the dry oak and consumed it with fury. It roared against the cold and turned the granite enclosure into a cozy outdoor oven. Assured that the fire was stable, she piled the remaining wood near the opening. Laura sat near the fire and tore open the last bag of M&Ms. She relished the billowing warmth and crunched with joyous achievement.

The vibrant glow of the fire allowed Laura to change her father's bandages. She cleaned his face and tried to nudge him awake. The extent of his injuries left him unconscious and in developing need of medical attention. She rested next to Wil and watched the fire. The experience of her ten-year-old mind had finally reached its limit. The darkness outside remained a fearful barrier for any thought of crossing the terrain for help. Hope for the coming morning became her only resolve. She emptied the bag of M&Ms and tossed the wrapper on the flames. The only way out of the enclosure was now blocked by the established fire. The comforting heat calmed her as her eyes surrendered to fatigue.

* * * * * * *

Laura shivered and nestled closer to Wil. She turned on each side, finding no relief from the cold. She opened her eyes to see a dim, orange light against a grainy rock wall. She sat up abruptly as her memory rushed through her waking confusion. Glowing, hot coals simmered in a pile at the opening of the granite enclosure. Her deep sleep faded the recollection of her circumstance. The surrounding walls and frigid night air reminded her of their predicament. She tossed the remaining wood on the coals and backed away. The dry lumber caught fire instantly, lighting the small room and restoring the needed heat supply. The fire burned higher than before from the thick bed of coals underneath.

She checked Wil's head and bandages. The bleeding subsided, leaving him in a therapeutic sleep. The darkness remained at the entrance of the enclosure. She returned to Wil's side as the flames engulfed the wood. Her confidence returned with the warmth. She thought about the mountain lion and listened for the coyote. The endurance of the night felt as though she had been there for a week. The fire blocked the entrance and provided protection against any predator's attempt to enter. The pace of the night seemed to drag in the cold. She checked her father's wristwatch certain that morning was upon them. Cleaning off the grime, she stared in disbelief. "Twelve-thirty?"

She thought about their eventful day and how they would endure the next one. She feared for her father's health and wondered what to do. Unable to fall back asleep, she thought about her mother. Her passing left a hole in her existence that hurt her soul. She lay next to Wil, watching the flames flicker across the rock ceiling. The concentration upon her feelings made for an eventful day of sadness, joy, anxiety, and fear. Each emotion charged her soul in various ways. The development of her feelings became strong from her recent experiences and the depth of her mother's passing. She recognized her feelings as a reluctant part of growing up. Her feelings also developed instinct. Lying next to her father, her instinct led her to a peculiar feeling…the feeling of being watched.

She angled her head toward the opening of the enclosure. The fire crackled and popped with a voracious appetite consuming the wood with ferocity. She raised slightly for a better view. The thought of the mountain lion crouched at the opening and ready to pounce crept into her mind. She listened for the coyote's howl and expected it to be closer. Summoning her remaining courage, she exhaled and squinted through the fire. A human face stared back at her from the other side of the flames.

"Ah!" Laura screamed. The flames highlighted the person's face with a hellish use of orange and red. The rising heat distorted the person's expression against the darkness. The person leaned toward the fire, becoming fully visible. Laura gasped at the recognition of a man crouching near the entrance of the enclosure.

"Laura…"

"Daddy!" Laura lunged at Wil.

"Is someone there?" Wil struggled to focus and rubbed his eyes.

They both watched the man enter around the fire and continue to stare at them. Laura looked into his eyes. The fear of the moment left her wondering what to do about the strange man. She stared in awe at what her mind could not comprehend but questioned what she recognized in front of her.

Wil sat up and pressed his hand against his head bandage. "Who is that?"

Before Laura could answer, the man turned toward the opening. He became uneasy and shifted his stance. He faced Laura a second time without any expression. Wil steadied himself for a full view of the man. A loud voice sounded in the distance. The man crouched and stepped between the fire and the opening of the enclosure. He motioned with his hand and looked at them with continued curiosity. Appearing as mystified as Wil and Laura, he grabbed a large stick and stabbed at the coals. Sparks flew in the air. Wil and Laura shielded their eyes from the burning specks. They looked back to see darkness on the other side of the fire. They watched the entrance and searched their thoughts for an explanation.

"What is going on?" Wil asked and rubbed his head. "Who was that?"

"I don't know. But he looked like…" Laura paused and turned toward the opening. The sound of footsteps stomping rapidly over rough terrain grew louder. Laura moved near Wil. "I think he is coming back."

"Get behind me," Wil said. They watched as another face leaned into the opening. "Get out of here!" Wil yelled and threw Laura's backpack. The pack landed in the fire scattering more sparks and ash throughout the rock room.

A blinding flashlight filled the small enclosure. A large man entered and pulled the backpack out of the flames.

"Whoa there! You might need that." The flames reflected off of a shiny piece of metal on the large man's coat. Laura recognized the design. "You two campers wouldn't happen to be the Brooks family, would you?" He smiled as if he already knew the answer.

"Yes, we are," Wil replied.

The large man unhooked a radio from his belt and leaned out of the enclosure. "Search Team Leader, this is Six. I found them. They appear to be okay, but the father has a head injury. Send up the medic and some blankets. I'm on the ridge west of the valley in area three. Look for my team." The large man looked back at Wil and Laura. "It's a good thing you had this fire going. We've been searching for you two for hours. I'm Officer Ken Stockton, Cache Police Department. The refuge called everybody in for you. We've got search teams all over the place. You should be thankful you have such caring neighbors. Otherwise, your little get-away could have gotten much worse."

"I don't know how much worse it could have gotten, Officer," Wil replied.

Officer Stockton laughed. "There's a snowstorm arriving in five hours, and the temperature has been falling all night. You would need to burn half of the valley to survive it."

Laura crawled out of the rock room. "Hello, little lady. Your name is Laura, is that right?"

"Yes, and that's my, uh, Wil." Laura became nervous standing next to the intimidating policeman.

"What's that? Did you say Old Wil?" Laura became confused at his misunderstanding. "Okay, Old Wil it is. Do you need any help getting out of there, Old Wil?" Officer Stockton asked.

Wil shoved all of their belongings out of the enclosure. He shook hands with the officer and stumbled in to him. "Thank you, Sir. I can't thank you enough."

Officer Stockton helped Wil to the ground. "You can thank me by sitting still." He shined his flashlight across Wil's face. "Looks like you've seen some action. You stay put. I don't need you passing out and making matters worse. Sit next to the fire, both of you, until my team arrives. We'll get you cozy here shortly." Officer Stockton grabbed his radio and watched several flashlights navigate the valley below.

Wil and Laura warmed by the fire. Wil pulled Laura close and whispered. "I'm so proud of you!" He kissed her on the cheek. "You're my brave girl. Your mother would be so proud of you, too. You saved us, sweetheart." He hugged her again.

Laura beamed with pride. "I was scared. When you fell asleep, I didn't know what to do."

"You did everything you could do," Wil replied.

Laura glanced at the officer waving at the approaching team with his flashlight. "Daddy, who was that other man, the man that looked at us?"

Wil stared into the fire, fighting to stay conscious. "I don't know. I didn't see him very well, and maybe you didn't either, okay? My head was hurting, and it was very dark. It could have been anything. I really don't remember."

Laura faced Wil. "But he was right in front of us."

Wil became apprehensive. He turned to locate Officer Stockton and continued to whisper. "Honey, I don't know what you saw. But sometimes, we have to pretend we didn't see things so that people will not bother us. When something cannot be explained, it is best to just leave it alone. Don't talk about it to anyone. It will just make trouble for us. Besides, I don't think anyone would believe you or me. Do you?"

"I guess not."

Wil noticed her disappointment. "Once we get out of here, some people may ask you lots of questions. You say what is on your heart. If you are not sure of what to say, just say you don't know. We just came out here to say goodbye to mommy and watch the bison. That way, all of this will end, and we can go home."

Laura leaned against Wil's chest and watched the beams of ten flashlights bounce toward them. "Okay, Daddy."

* * * * * * *

Laura opened the recovery room curtain and stood on a chair. Giant snowflakes whizzed by the window. Heavy gray clouds filled the air with a white spectacle that covered everything below. The prediction of moderate precipitation proved to be an expected gamble against the challenging Oklahoma weather. The wind slashed the freezing temperature in half with a threatening chill. The early arrival of winter on the plains brought wonder and gratitude to the fatigued observers.

"The flakes are so big!" Laura exclaimed. "Can we go outside?"

Wil sat on the edge of the hospital bed, examining his head bandages. "We will when we get home…if we get home." He watched the blizzard worsen. "Did you sleep well?"

"Yes," Laura replied with her eyes fixated on the window.

"I'm glad they let you stay with me."

"Can we go now?" Laura begged.

"Good morning!" A voice from the door announced. "Who's hungry in here?" A nurse entered the room with two trays piled high from the breakfast menu. She arranged the room and situated her patients. Wil and Laura complied willingly, anxious to sample the culinary delights. "I was told you two would make short order of this, so dig in." She checked Wil's condition and departed the room. Wil and Laura expressed appreciation by waving as their mouths were already full.

"What's for breakfast?" Wil and Laura saw two uniformed officers standing in the doorway. "It must be good! I don't hear any jibber-jabber in here." Officer Ken Stockton entered and shook Wil's hand. "Good to see you, Old Wil. Looks like you're getting your strength back. This is the refuge manager, Russell Riley. He led the effort to find you. And how is the little lady doing?" Officer Stockton addressed Laura. "I'd reach for a piece of that bacon, but I'm afraid I'd lose a finger!" Laura snickered and sat next to Wil.

"Thank you, gentlemen, for finding us. I am truly grateful," Wil stated.

"You're welcome, Mr. Brooks," Officer Riley replied. "I'm glad we got you out before that storm hit."

Wil nodded. He observed Officer Riley's appearance, curious of any American Indian descent. "Yes, I'm glad Officer Stockton found us."

"It was your fire that led me to you. I hear your daughter did that all on her own?" Officer Stockton asked.

"Yes, she was very brave," Wil replied.

"Mr. Brooks, you know you have to register with us for any overnight camping on the refuge. If it were not for your neighbors calling us, we would not have known you were out there," Officer Riley stated.

"Yes sir, I was wrong. We were paying our respects to my late wife near the Crab Eyes rock formation, and our return got a little sidetracked. I'll make sure it never happens again."

"Crab Eyes?" Officer Riley asked. "That's quite a sidetrack. You were nowhere near there when we found you. And I heard you encountered a mountain lion?"

"Yes sir, a big one. Scared me silly," Wil responded.

"Did you see anything else?" Officer Stockton asked. The room became silent. "Any chance there was anyone else out there with you?" Officer Stockton sensed their uneasiness. "What about you, little lady?"

Laura looked up at Wil. He glanced at her with an uncomfortable smile and spoke for her. "Those coyotes and their howling kept her pretty close to me. It made for a long night, almost. It's a lot to expect from a ten-year-old in a situation like that, especially with her mother being gone and all."

"Well, I'm sure that was quite an adventure. I'm glad it ended safely." Officer Stockton approached the door to leave.

"Mr. Brooks, Laura, you both get better, and please make sure we don't have to meet like this again, okay?" Officer Riley shook their hands and departed with Officer Stockton. The two officers walked the hallway toward the exit and fastened their overcoats. "Well, what do you think, Ken. Did they sound convincing enough?"

Officer Stockton tightened his gloves. "I think they rehearsed their story well. That little girl was petrified."

"Yeah, Old Wil wouldn't win any awards for acting. He was working hard on that sympathy vote for his daughter. Something had them spooked out there other than their situation. And it didn't seem to be that mountain lion, either. They didn't mention anything about your part. Are you sure you don't want to put that in the statement?"

"Yes, I'm sure. I don't know what reason they would have to hide anything," Officer Stockton replied. "And no one else has turned up missing."

"It was a crazy night. Don't beat yourself up over it."

"I won't. But I'll tell ya, Russ, I saw a third person standing in front of that fire just like I am seeing you now," Officer Stockton said.

"I believe you. But you said it yourself. It was too dark for a description."

Officer Stockton watched the snow accumulate on the window. "Crazy is a good word for it. Whoever that was just up and disappeared right in front of that fire. I searched all around those boulders and found nothing."

"Search? It was you alone with a flashlight and enough light distortion from that bonfire to blind an owl. We got them out alive. That's what matters." Officer Riley extended his hand. "Thanks for your help, Ken. Sorry I had to trouble you and your guys."

"Glad to do it. It was good to see one of these rescues end on a good note."

"Hey, I hear I might be looking at the new Sheriff of Cache?" Officer Riley asked. "Let me know when you're confirmed."

"Confirmed to what? The job or the nut house?" Both men laughed and departed through the snowstorm toward their vehicles.

* * * * * * *

Wil parked his truck on the driveway of their home and watched the snow accumulate on the windshield. The lifeless dwelling appeared cold and dark against the wintry onslaught. The absence of Ayita took any warmth from the home that used to stand up against any ordeal. Wil wanted to share their harrowing adventure with her. Only Ayita would understand the adventure and foolishness of their previous plight. What anyone else would have questioned for sanity, Ayita would have inquired for intrigue. He reflected on her spirit and thought of their past.

Laura flung the passenger door open and prepared to leap in to the winter wonderland. "Honey, wait a minute." Wil pulled her by the hood of her coat and closed the door.

"But dad, look at all of that snow!"

"I know; I'll let you go play in just a minute." Wil paused to frame his statement to her understanding. "Remember back there at the hospital when I asked you not to say anything about what we saw at the refuge?" Laura stared at him without regard. "You know, that man we saw by the fire?"

"Oh, yes daddy."

"Look, I don't want you to lie. I just didn't want those police officers asking a lot of questions. Okay?"

"I know dad, you already told me that. Can we go outside now?" Laura turned toward the window.

Wil became confused with his intent. "Laura, it's not that I want to hide anything from you. I just want to make sure you are safe. Can you understand that?"

Laura faced her father. "Are you saying that you know who that man was by the fire?"

Wil turned toward his window. "Well, no. I mean, I…" He looked in to this daughter's eyes. "One last time, do you remember where we were when all of that happened? Did you see any familiar rock formations or mountains or anything?"

"No, dad. It was too dark. Why do you keep asking me that?"

"It's kind of important. A long time ago, your mother and I thought we saw someone that looked just like that man you and I saw last night. We couldn't remember where that was at either. I'm just wondering, that's all." Wil stopped his inquiry.

"Maybe you should ask the police? I bet they would know where we were. After all, they found us." Laura reached for the door handle.

Wil grinned at his anxious daughter. "No, I can't ask the police. But then again, you are right. They are the only ones that would know. I'll think about it."

"Can we go outside now?" Laura asked.

"Sure, go have fun." Wil pulled her hood over her head. Laura bounded out of the truck and ran through a snowbank. "Don't get too wet. And come in when your fingers and toes get cold."

"Yes, dad. Are you going to play with me?"

"No, not yet. I need to go inside and warm up the house." Wil entered their home and left his shoes by the door. He turned up the heat and walked down the hallway to his bedroom. He pulled a locked metal box from underneath the bed and placed it on the mattress. He reached behind the headboard and pulled a key off of a small hook. Unlocking the box, he took a journal from the contents. Wil gently ran his hand over the leather cover in an act of homage. He grabbed the upper corner of the book and opened it. He turned several pages, admiring each one as he skimmed the writing.

Minutes became an hour as he searched the manuscript. Writings on a page produced tears while he read multiple excerpts written by Ayita. He continued thumbing through the journal and stopped midway through the pages. He sat up on the bed and focused on the wording dated many years earlier. *"Had a strange encounter on our hike in the refuge today. The sun went down before we could get out of the mountains. No moon that night. Followed a stream bed, hoping it would lead away from Crab Eyes and back to the main trail. We got lost. We built a fire to keep warm and hoped to be seen by refuge rangers or other hikers. We fell asleep and woke to see a strange man staring at us from the other side of the fire. Could not make out who he was. Wil stood to confront him, but the man did not say anything and walked away. We both got scared. We did not want to wait for daylight anymore, and we made our way out of there. It took hours. Finally found the road and followed it to the picnic area early morning. Never saw the man again, but from what I could tell by his clothing, he looked strikingly like…"*

"Dad." Wil jumped at Laura's unexpected presence in the bedroom and slammed the journal shut.

"You scared me. I thought you were playing?"

"Are you coming out or not?" Laura asked.

Wil placed the book back in the box. "Yes. I just wanted to check on something. Is it still snowing?" Laura remained quiet and stared at him. "What's the matter?"

"Is that mom's book?"

Wil was astonished. "How did you know that?"

Laura walked to the edge of the bed and picked up her mother's journal. "Mommy showed me one time. She even read some stuff to me. I like all of her hiking stories. She said when I got older that we would go hiking together, and she would write stories about us." Laura held the book tightly in her hands. "I guess that will never happen now."

Wil took the journal from her and placed it back in the box. "I tell you what, someday, when you are older, I'll let you read your mother's journal all by yourself." Laura nodded her head. "In fact, why don't we get you your own journal, and you can start writing about your own adventures?"

"Dad," Laura paused. "Mommy already got me a journal a long time ago. I've been writing to her in it."

Wil fought back tears. "Good, sweetheart. That's good."

"When can I read her journal?" Laura asked.

Wil began to cry. He wiped a tear and turned away from Laura. "Not today." He closed the box and slid it back under the bed.

Laura watched with a solemn appearance. "Why?"

"Because I said so!"

Laura backed away from his sudden outburst. Wil observed her stunned expression and reached for her. "I'm sorry, Laura. I didn't mean to yell at you. Daddy's got a lot on his mind, that's all. When I read mommy's journal, it makes me sad." Wil knelt in front of her. "Now is not a good time to read mommy's journal. There are things in it that you will better understand someday when you are older."

"Okay, daddy. I didn't mean to make you mad."

"You didn't. That journal is as much yours as it is mine. I know mommy would want you to have it when you are ready. When you get older, I'll let you read it."

"Do you promise?" Laura asked.

"I promise. Can your daddy have a hug?"

Laura stretched her arms wide, and they embraced with a tight squeeze. "Since you are feeling sad, we can just stay inside," Laura stated.

"I have a better idea. Let's go outside, and then you can write in your journal about our huge snowball fight!"

Laura smiled and ran for the front door. The cold wind scattered snow through the door and across the living room carpet. Wil grabbed his coat and hurried after Laura. A distinct giggle echoed through the stiff breeze behind him as a hastily packed snowball hit his back. The joy of his ten-year-old daughter calmed him. He scooped some snow and threw it toward her. Satisfied with evading the concerns of the journal, Wil embraced the moment. He formed another snowball and watched Laura run behind a tree. The giant flakes filled the sky, adding several inches of winter bliss across the front yard. Wil laughed without regard and ran in pursuit of his little girl.

Chapter 3

Wil parked his truck in the driveway and fumbled for his keys to the front door. He entered his home and flipped on the lights. The quiet and darkness intermingled with his solitude. He kicked off his dirty hiking boots and tossed his backpack on the recliner. Wiping the sweat from his forehead, he hurried toward his bedroom. He reached behind the headboard for a small key. Moving several items from underneath his bed, he pulled out a small metal box. He placed it on the mattress and held the key near the lock.

Wil paused and observed the box. His hands shook as he unlocked the lid. He lifted his wife's journal out of the container and placed it on his lap. He exhaled with a sense of urgency as he ran his hand over the cover. The moment triggered his recollection as he surmised the number of years since he last held the treasured book. He recalled his outburst toward Laura and his refusal of her request to read it. But most importantly, he remembered his promise, a promise that he made to her ten years ago.

Now, at the age of twenty, he knew Laura would approach him again about Ayita's journal. Her subtle hint at breakfast earlier in the week let him know the moment he avoided for a decade was at hand.

His mind raced with frantic options, none of which brought resolve to his situation. He looked at a picture of Ayita hanging on his bedroom wall. Panicked, he stood from the bed and stopped in front of her portrait. "Forgive me."

Wil grabbed his backpack and ran out the back door. He checked the driveway and continued through the yard, stopping in front of a circular stone fire pit. Placing the journal on the edge, he gathered small pieces of dried kindling and charred remains from a previous fire and heaped the wood in the center of the pit. He grabbed the journal and opened it to several pages. The remaining pages flipped quickly in the steady breeze. His desire beckoned him to read the words of his late wife as he looked toward the sky. Unwilling to observe his own action, he took hold of a selection of pages and tore them from the journal. He placed the journal on the edge of the firepit and reached in to his pack. He flicked a lighter and ignited the torn pages. The aged paper erupted in flames. Wil shoved the pages under the wood heap to keep them from blowing away and watched it burn.

"Dad, what are you doing back here?"

Wil swung around as the wind flared in a violent gust. "Laura! I, I didn't think you would be home so soon. I've been out to the mountains and thought it was time to come home. With all of this wind, I thought there might be a storm on the way."

"So, you come to the back yard and start a fire? What's going on with you? And last I checked, you've been gone for three days. Have you been in the Wichitas all this time?" Laura asked and approached the firepit.

"I felt the need to get away for a while, that's all. I just wanted to build a little fire and get rid of some paperwork," Wil responded.

Laura snickered and pointed at the firepit. "I wouldn't call that a little fire, dad. What are you burning in there, a book?"

Confused, Wil turned around to see the journal consumed in flames. "No!" He reached for the journal cover that was spread open across the burning heap. As he lifted the cover, the sudden blast of air fed the flames with a vigorous rush that engulfed the book. The fiery pages burned Wil's hand. He dropped the book back on top of the heap and hurried to find a metal poke.

Laura stood in disbelief. "That looks like mom's journal!" She grabbed a longer stick from the woodpile and shoved it under the cover. She lifted the stick with both hands and flung the flaming cover away from the firepit. She ran to the cover and stomped on it. The flames challenged her desperate fight and finally surrendered in a smoky defeat. Laura reached down and held up the charred remains. Every page was gone.

"Oh no! This can't be happening." Wil grabbed the journal and held the blackened cover. "The wind must have blown it off of the edge. How could I be so stupid!"

"What were you doing with mom's journal?" Laura asked. She stared at the destroyed book in his hands. Shock and anger began to rage within her. "What were you thinking?"

"I obviously wasn't thinking at all!" Wil threw the cover back into the fire pit and stormed away toward the house. Laura watched the flames reignite the cover. Tears streamed down her cheeks as the journal incinerated before her.

* * * * * * *

Jennifer Tanner stood on a boulder pile deep in the Charon's Garden Wilderness Area of the Wichita Mountains. She stared in amazement at the canyon before her. The steep walls and jagged granite tops lined the slopes of each mountain, coming together to form the valley. The rolling layers of red and gray granite colorized the canyon in the midday March sun. The canyon channeled the wind in a southerly direction. The chilled remnants of winter blew past her face in a gentle breeze. The view stretched from the surrounding mountains of the wilderness area through the valley and across the neighboring plains. The farmlands appeared as a patchwork that continued toward the horizon into Texas. Her elevation provided sights of Granite and Twin Rocks Mountains behind her. Her first time in the pristine area proved to be everything she had hoped the off-trail experience would be.

Satisfied with her hike, she bid the view a final glance and climbed off of the boulders. Pushing through some cedars, she stopped in the clearing and found the skeletal remains of an elk that lay scattered over the ground. The chalky white bones were picked clean of any flesh. The grisly scene appeared unseemly against the landscape. She kicked a few bones aside and witnessed the terrain before her. Boulders, gorges, ridges, and tree lines dominated the imposing trek. Jennifer visually mapped her return route through the wilderness area and started across the obstacles.

Avoiding the rocks, she journeyed through a grassy pasture. Mounds of broken quartz and granite were dispersed along the small field. Several pits, most full of water, were next to the rock mounds. Jennifer studied the holes, noticing each one was dug by hand. Some of the pits were angled deep into the ground. She dropped some rocks in the water and observed the bubbles continue for many seconds.

Other pits ended abruptly from the daunting challenge of digging through solid granite. Blocks of white quartz lay separate from the mounds as discoveries from previous explorers that left them behind.

She continued to Styx Canyon and navigated to the bottom. Failing to find an easy way out, she chose the most approachable canyon wall and began her climb. The damp, cool air of the canyon made the handholds and footing unstable. Clumps of moss and loose rocks broke away from the wall. She changed her freestyle course several times to minimize the danger. She swung her leg over the edge and sat at the top. Out of breath, she rested in appreciation of the easier trail hikes she was used to. She hiked for the scenery and uniqueness of the Wichita Mountains and preferred the horizontal path compared to anything of a vertical direction.

She continued her chosen route to her vehicle and kept the refuge boundary fence within sight. Her off-trail adventure led her to boulder hopping and navigating the granite terrain for the most expeditious means out of the mountains. The ground was strewn with various sized boulders and rocks all intermingled with the terrain itself. Jennifer considered her Wichita Mountains adventure as an opportunity to hike an area altered only by the passage of time.

Boulders and rolling terrain transitioned to cedar trees and grassy pastures. Jennifer turned east for the washouts and the neighboring parking area. Movement to the left caught her attention. She looked to see a small man walking thirty yards away. She stopped in surprise, making a quick assumption that she was being tracked. She observed the man walking with a slight bend to his upper back, causing him to lean forward. He wore a faded orange cap with an unusually long, black bill. The cap appeared as a woolen material with the bill shading his face. He wore a weathered black and red checkered heavy wool coat with tattered brown, corduroy pants. Unable to see his shoes, she watched the man approach a granite rock shelf. He crouched for a moment and jumped from the small ledge behind a cedar grove.

Curious of the moment and confident his appearance was not threatening, she walked toward the man and pushed through the thick cedar limbs to the other side. A small, horseshoe-shaped clearing opened with the granite shelf to her left. Scattered scrub oaks filled the opposite side in a sage grass field. The granite shelf appeared about five feet high. She looked around the granite and checked the cedars for the lone man. The oaks were young and only eight inches around. The random spots of sage grass provided no place to hide. She walked to the opening of the small enclosure and stared across a larger field toward the washouts. Two longhorns and a bison grazed in the distance. *Where could he have gone?*

Her curiosity began to change. Her control of the moment transitioned to confusion. Her thoughts and reasoning became altered. Finding no sensibility to the situation, she placed her hands on her hips and surrendered to question. *Where did that guy go?* She watched the bison continue to graze as an odd feeling crept up her spine. A cold vacancy entered her chest. Her breathing paused. Her arms and neck became covered in goosebumps as a sensation occurred within her.

An overwhelming urge to run infiltrated her thoughts. *Run now!* Jennifer took off through the grass. Fear consumed her and she sprinted across the field. *Run to something alive,* she thought—her capacity to reason diminished as she ran toward the bison. *Alive, run to something alive,* her mind demanded in repetition. She jumped a small stream and splashed her boots. She continued toward the bison and began to notice her rapid breathing. She turned and looked back at the enclosure.

Seeing nothing there, she kept running forward. The bison raised its head from the grass. "What am I doing?" Jennifer yelled. She stopped twenty yards in front of the animal. The massive beast ignored her approach and enjoyed the patch of greenery along the curving stream. With her mind re-engaged, she realized she was running toward a temperamental two-thousand-pound bison bull. Her reasoning resumed with the dissipation of any previous fear. She looked back again. The open terrain and wooded backdrop were all that she could see. The fear subsided, but her memory engaged. Unsure of what was to be remembered, she routed around the bison and hurried to the parking area.

Jennifer threw her hiking gear in the front passenger seat and closed her driver's side door. She sat for several minutes staring through the windshield with her hands grasping the steering wheel. *What just happened?* she thought. *Who was that?* Her mind searched for reason without any resolve. She watched the nearby cedar trees with anticipation of a pursuer. The odd desire to see someone step from the branches and explain her experience was her desperate hope. She yearned to see the man hike across the distant field or walk out from the woods. Jennifer wanted anything to justify her experience as a simple oversight. The scenic view before her remained undisturbed, with the passing wind creating the only movement.

Without provocation, her mind unwillingly strayed toward a possibility that she never would have imagined in her structured life. Perhaps it was not *who* that was hiking near her, but *what* that was. Jennifer gasped at the sudden realization that slithered through her veins with a sinister presence. She quickly tried to deny the absurd thought as her mind began to piece together the strangeness of her experience. No other option seemed to prove otherwise. Her mind began to make sense of her experience as the goosebumps slowly returned. She jammed the key into the ignition and started her car. Shaking with denial, she backed sharply on to the road and sped toward the refuge exit.

Jennifer thought of the perplexing encounter during her drive home. With the location safely behind her, she began to consider the haunting possibility. She thought of the man's vivid description and how he looked like a normal person. She could not help but wonder if the man saw her run away. And why did she feel the way she did standing in the opening by the cedars? Her overwhelming urge to run to something alive scared her. The thought that she could not control herself and her emotions was something she had never experienced before. Struggling to control her fear, she focused on her curiosity and the pursuit of explanation.

She arrived at her apartment and rushed up the stairs to her computer. She began typing in various links and websites to start her initial research. Emotion drove her determination. She searched several Wichita Mountains websites looking for anything that could substantiate her experience and theory. Frustrated, she sat back in her chair and surrendered to reason. She remembered the many hand-dug mines and mounds of quartz scattered throughout the wilderness area. Trying to make her investigation less surreal, she searched several links that led her to historical sites about mining, gold, the Meers mining town and early settlements of the Wichita Mountains.

The more legitimate her search became, the more she began to make sense of her encounter. The Charon's Garden Wilderness Area proved to be inaccessible, as mentioned in many of her readings and references. Jennifer began to understand the slight possibility of what could have happened to her during her hike. Hours passed without her awareness as she continued her analysis. She became fascinated with her newly found understanding of the Wichita Mountains and its history until she discovered a particular website that sparked her interest. She accessed the website and began reading. Her hunger pains subsided as the fear she experienced earlier returned. Jennifer's eyes widened halfway through the article. She sat back in her chair, stunned by the information before her. The hint of goosebumps teased her neck. "Unbelievable!" she yelled and grabbed her phone.

* * * * * * *

The phone rang, posing an interference to the long-awaited night and the welcomed end to a miserable workday. Donna grabbed the remote and muted her favorite television drama. Anyone that knew her or referred to her as a friend also knew not to call during the cherished hour. Frustrated, she grabbed her phone and recognized the name. Puzzled by the call, she answered and hoped for a commercial.

"You of anybody should know not to call me now! You'd better be dying or have just met the hottest guy on earth."

"Hello to you, too," Jennifer replied.

"Where have you been? Are you watching this? The investigator knows! I can't believe her cousin confessed. How are they going to get out now?" The phone remained quiet. "Are you there?" Donna asked.

Finding Sunset Peak

"Yeah, I'm here." Jennifer paused. "Remember when you told me about that rocking chair, the one you keep in the basement of those living quarters there with you?"

"Yeah. The old hospital. Why on earth are you talking about that now? We only have five minutes left on the show! Do any of your clocks work over there?"

Jennifer surrendered. "Okay, fine. I'll talk to you later."

"Hold on. Is something wrong?" Donna detected a difference in her friend's voice.

"No…" Jennifer replied.

"You would never call during our show. What's the matter?"

"It's kind of hard to explain."

Donna became frustrated. "It can't be any harder than you deciding to call me during our show. Come on, what is it."

"I went hiking today and, well, I've been doing some research and…" Jennifer paused again, unsure of how to proceed.

"Did something happen?"

"Yes. I think I had an encounter. Like the one you had in your quarters. Only I, I think I actually felt something. I'm not sure."

Donna turned away from her television show. "You felt something? As in you touched something?"

"No. It was like a feeling, an emotion. It's kind of hard to explain," Jennifer stated.

"Well, try. What did it feel like?"

Jennifer became frustrated. "I don't know. Fear, I guess. But more like a provoking. Like someone telling you to do something, and you don't know why."

"Where were you at?" Donna asked.

"I went hiking in the Charon's Garden Wilderness Area. It's a remote area of the Wichita Mountains on the refuge."

"I know where it's at, Jen. I've been there before."

"Well, you never asked me to go with you! I've never been there. I was on my way back from my hike, and I saw this guy."

"Were you hiking by yourself again? I told you not to do that!" Donna warned. "What about this guy? Oh my gosh, did something happen?"

Jennifer told Donna her experience with vivid details. Donna listened with an unconvinced assessment but definite curiosity. The enthusiasm and description of Jennifer's story curated empathy from Donna. The conversation continued with Donna harboring more doubt than she was willing to express. Questions abounded from Donna with no satisfactory answers from Jennifer. Frustration was kept at bay due to the strength of their long-time friendship.

"Are you sure the guy didn't just turn around and go the other way? And what do you mean going after some guy following you on the backside of nowhere? You know better than that, Jen. He could have been some looney," Donna said.

"I told you it wasn't just what I saw, but what I felt," Jennifer replied.

"Forget your feelings! Maybe you need to do more thinking instead. What's the matter with you?"

Jennifer ignored her harassment. "Also, I've been doing some research. That whole wilderness area is covered with old mines. I read that mining was really big in the Wichita Mountains back in the early 1900s. I saw a lot of mines while I was out there. So, I thought about it, and after I did some research…" Jennifer hesitated.

"What?" Donna became impatient.

"I'm just guessing, but I think I saw the ghost of a miner." The phone became silent as Jennifer continued. "As scary as it sounds, it all kind of makes sense."

"You mean to say as *stupid* as it sounds!" Donna could no longer hold her frustration. "It sounds like you have taken a hike to insanity, lady."

Jennifer kept explaining. "And listen to this, because this is why I had to call you right away."

"Oh, this should be good. Smearing the icing on the cake."

"Will you just listen, please? I could really use your support on this. I didn't ask for this today, okay? And, I would appreciate it if you would just hear me out. I don't know what else to do. It really scared me, Donna. Nothing like this has ever happened to me before."

Donna realized she pushed her friend too far. Feeling some slight remorse, she encouraged Jennifer to continue. "Okay, go ahead. What made you want to call me right in the middle of our all-time favorite show?"

"I was curious what the name Charon's Gardens means. When I looked it up, some website said it was from Greek mythology. I kept reading, and do you know what that name means?" Jennifer waited as Donna remained silent. "Charon is the mythical name of a ferryman that carries the deceased to the land of the dead. Can you believe that? Isn't that crazy? I mean, that can't be just coincidence, can it?"

"How befitting," Donna replied. "You searched pretty hard for that one, didn't you? I'm sure they named that place precisely for that reason."

"What does it matter? The fact is I saw something I can't explain. There was no way that guy could have hid anywhere." Jennifer became defensive. "I really thought you would have more understanding than this, Donna. Why can't you just give me a moment here and accept the fact that just maybe I saw something out there that I cannot explain? You know, the classic phrase of 'what if'?"

Donna noted the tone in Jennifer's voice. Watching her show end and having pushed the record button minutes earlier, she decided to give her friend the benefit of the doubt. "This adventure of yours today is really bothering you, isn't it?"

Jennifer recalled the moment and focused her reply. "It's not just what I saw, Donna. I've never felt anything like that before. It's like something passed through me, telling me to run. And the oddest thing, I remember the distinct feeling, almost like an urge, to run to something alive."

"Okay, now you're freaking me out. Running toward a giant buffalo is not normal."

"I know. That's why I called you. I remember you told me about that sensation you felt when you first entered the basement of those quarters and how you couldn't think straight," Jennifer stated. "You said you felt sick."

"Yeah, but I didn't go looking for it and possibly putting my life in danger." Donna changed the subject. "Look, regardless of all that has happened to you with miners and ferrymen and all that stuff, I want you to promise me that you will not go back out there. Do you hear me?"

Jennifer contemplated her friend's demand. "But Donna, just think, if what I saw and felt was actually real? What if I made contact with something?"

"Or what if something made contact with you!" Donna said. "This whole thing isn't guaranteed to be a positive experience, you know?"

"True, but what if it is real?"

Donna replied without hesitation. "Then you should never go out there again."

The two friends continued their conversation, switching to the dramatic ending of their television show. They debated next week's episode with the clear understanding that neither would call unless it was a commercial break. Jennifer expressed her unhappiness with her friend's departure several months ago. She was proud of Donna receiving a promotion but was remiss her closest friend had to move so far away. Their promise to stay in touch remained strong. They exchanged pleasantries and prepared to part for the night.

"Thanks for talking. Sorry I interrupted our show. I couldn't wait. Once I found that Greek meaning to Charon's Gardens, I had to call," Jennifer said.

"It's okay. Actually, you helped me make up my mind about something at work today that may be as crazy as your hiking adventure. I've got some guy over here bugging me about an interview that he wants with me. Long story, but I think I'll give it a shot," Donna replied. "It might get us some free advertising."

"Or maybe he's looking for more than an interview!" Jennifer laughed.

"Yeah, right. That's the last thing I need right now. All work and no romance. Get some sleep, lady. Talk soon." Donna hung up and fluffed her pillow. Jennifer's story weighed on her mind. Her friend's experience in the Wichita Mountains and subsequent phone call added to the oddities of her day. Donna rolled over to the edge of her bed and reached for her notepad. She re-read the yellow stickie from her secretary and snickered at the perplexing request. *This has definitely been a weird day,* she thought and clicked off the light on her nightstand.

Chapter 4

"Wow, have you ever seen a sky like that before?" a young man asked.

He watched the sun slip behind the distant Huachuca Mountains displaying a canvas of color over the southwestern sky. High level cirrus clouds cast a fiery collection of reds that wisped across the darkening horizon. Simple shades of orange and blue blended into a desert palette of scarlet, turquoise, and indigo. The artistic scene complemented the arid climate with a rich flare that would inspire the eye of any painter. The magnificence of the fading celestial event posed a perfect ending to the day.

"I've seen 'em all my life," a white-bearded old man responded. "Gives reason for the good Lord's gift of sight."

"It's amazing how a sunset can be so different from place to place. I've been to many places, but I've never seen one look the way they do out here," the young man continued.

He looked down the desolate dirt road watching the breeze attempt to form a small dust devil. The collection of air swirled along the median. The wooden stores, saloons, and walkways lined the street on either side, facing each other in a standoff with history. Old hotels and converted restaurants supplemented the timeless town.

The rugged scene appeared the same way it did since its early founding in 1877. He remained captivated by the moment as the desert air drifted by Allen Street, ushering another night in Tombstone, Arizona.

"Are you all from around here?" the old man asked.

"Yep, some of us are from Tucson and some from Sierra Vista. We're scattered all over."

"I see. I would think that locals would know better. I thought only those Hollywood folks did this kind of stuff?" the old man challenged.

"It's all in the name of science," the young man chuckled and extended his hand. "I'm Jeff Finbow. I'm the lead historian on the team tonight. They're not getting started without me. Thanks for letting me in."

"Yeah, Finbow. Your buddies in there said you'd be late. I'm Ed Silver." Ed began sizing Jeff up as a self-indulged college student.

"Late? I'm never late, Ed. They got here too early!" Jeff nudged Ed on the shoulder.

"I see," Ed smirked. "Since when is looking for ghosts a science? You kids watch too many of those TV shows. The last bunch we had in here did the same thing. Big, fancy equipment and scatter-brained ideas. All of you are just chasin' your tails if you ask me."

Jeff leaned against the center double doors of the Bird Cage Theater, ready to stoke the enticing debate. "It's simple. All you really have to ask yourself is 'what if'? If you chase that, you get answers."

"Heh!" Ed huffed. "You're always looking for answers. You kids might find out someday that there aren't answers to everything. It's just life. Sometimes, sittin' back and watchin' a sunset is all you need."

Jeff patted Ed on his back. "I've got a lot of life left, and I'm chasing that 'what if' just as far as I can. Answers are everything! That's my motto. I'm not headed for the rocking chair any time soon. So, you just leave the heavy lifting to me, my friend."

Ed snickered and ushered Jeff in to the building. "You go get 'em, tiger."

"You bet I will, old-timer! Don't worry, I've got this. Life is good!" Jeff paused before entering and observed the structure. "I've been in here many times, but never at night. Can we expect a good show?"

Ed looked at the building with reverence. "It's quiet now, but there was a time when this old theatre was the place to be for a good show."

Both men watched the evening light fade against the arched triple entryways of the historic landmark. The nostalgia of the old nightspot could be imagined as they stared up at the 1881 painted on the wall. The relic preserved the lore of the old west within its confined walls and represented the timelessness of the treasured town. Each man appreciated the converted tourist attraction as a staple of the Arizona landscape.

Jeff carried his belongings inside as Ed locked the door behind him. Jeff clapped once and pointed at Ed with an arrogant grin. "You sleep good now." He began to walk away and heard a tapping on the glass door pane. He looked back to see Ed still standing outside, pointing his finger at him.

"Life is always good when the answers go your way. But I wouldn't want to be there when you find the answers that don't."

"That's when I'll call you," Jeff replied. "We'll see you at breakfast, old man. I like my pancakes thick and light on the syrup." Jeff expressed a taunting laugh. Ed walked away, shaking his head with an agitated mumble.

Jeff strolled into the center of the theater to see a young blonde woman calibrating a camera and tripod. He dropped his pack against the wall and held his hand over the lens. "Hey, beautiful. Is this place romantic or what?"

Karen Farris kept her attention upon the eyepiece. "Move your hand and step away from the expensive equipment, moron."

"Ooh. Hostility and name-calling, all in the same night. If you're finished flirting, what do you say we rekindle the old times when the lights go out? A little kiss in the Cage, perhaps?"

Karen adjusted the lens without looking at him. "Elise is looking for you. She was by the piano next to the stage. And on your way over, drop dead."

"And I thought being friends was going to be difficult." Jeff grinned at Karen and approached the foot of the stage. Several tables with computers, monitors, handheld radios, microphones, laboratory equipment, and cameras lined the sidewall. Two men worked plugging in wires and setting specialized cameras at various angles throughout the room. Jeff grabbed a radio and turned up the external volume. "Attention everyone. Area 51 called. Will the Blackburn brothers please report to the mothership?"

"Let me guess who that is! We were wondering about you," Mike Blackburn said, looking over a monitor.

"Howdy stranger. How's the famous historian?" Tommy Blackburn turned around and extended his hand. "It's been a while."

"Yes, it has. How are the computer geniuses doing? You guys still chasing warps and portals?" Jeff shook their hands.

"Gosh, man. How long has it been?" Mike asked.

"Over a year at least. Last time I scouted with you all was Montana," Jeff replied.

"Yeah, Custer's Last Stand. Now that was a Kodak moment! What have you been up to?" Tommy asked.

Jeff stepped over a bundle of wires. "Touring, mostly. I've got a pretty good gig with the university running around telling stories and instructing. The pay keeps me from starving, and I finished my second book. It should be out in a few months."

"Sounds like graduate school is the good life," Mike replied.

"It is when someone else is paying for it," Jeff stated.

"Glad you could make it!" a voice from the stage yelled.

Jeff looked up to see Gene Saige standing near the edge. "I wouldn't miss it." Jeff jumped on a chair and reached to shake hands. "How's the manager of space and time?"

"Oh, doing the deed and wondering how to pay the bills. Good to see you, Jeff. I read about your last event in the paper. You're really making a name for yourself."

Jeff rolled his eyes. "I'll do anything to keep from getting a real job, you know that. Looks like you landed another big one getting the Bird Cage, not bad."

Gene observed the historic hall. "Yeah, we've waited years to get in here. Hopefully it will pay off. This place is a target opportunity. Elise has been really excited about it."

"I'll bet." Jeff looked around the stage area. "Where is the illustrious team leader at, anyway."

"She's downstairs trying to focus on tonight. It's our last chance, and then they're kicking us out. We've been here for three days. I tried for more time, but funds are tight and, well, you know how it goes with getting any results. We pulled an all-nighter last night.

She didn't sleep much today." Gene pointed toward the stairs. "We're starting in a few. Tell her to hurry up."

"Hey, Gene, do you have any idea why she called me? I was kinda surprised to hear from her. I haven't heard her that excited since that night at the Little Bighorn."

Gene had a devious expression. "Yeah, I do."

Jeff glared at Gene and went down the creaking steps. An assortment of displays unique to the building filled the room. He noticed a woman standing near a poker table exhibit reading a flyer. "You can toss that tourist guide out the window, lady. I can tell you anything you want to know about this place."

Leonora Elise Saige turned and grinned. She stepped toward Jeff and opened her arms for a welcoming embrace. "I know you can, Mr. Finbow. Why do you think I called you?" They hugged and held each other for a moment. "It's so good to see you. The team's missed you not being around. It's been too quiet without you. No one can replace that ruckus humor of yours."

"Hi Elise. You're pouring it on a little strong, aren't you? I think Karen wishes I was one of the casualties at the OK Corral, but it was good to see everyone else."

Elise snickered. "Well, what do you expect when you date as long as you two did and then hit on her best friend behind her back? I think I would take a shot at you, too."

"Ah, it was a harmless flirt. Just me being me," Jeff replied. "It's not like I wanted to marry her friend or anything."

"Still as humble as ever I see," Elise teased and hugged him again. "Yes, you had better avoid Karen while you're with us, or you might become a permanent resident at Boot Hill."

Jeff leaned against the railing and admired the poker table display. "Can you imagine a thousand dollar buy-in to a poker game back in those days? And the game lasted over eight years. That's a lot of rich folks for that time."

"There is a lot of history here, for sure," Elise stated. "That's what we are counting on tonight."

"I'd give a thousand dollars to know why you would pay to have me come all the way over here to see it. I sure do recall a certain someone that looked just like you telling me to pack my gear and step in front of a moving truck."

"The moving truck was Karen's idea." Elise leaned closer to Jeff and observed the poker table. "I needed you to be here tonight, for all of us. Let's put the past behind us. There are more important topics to address."

"Such as?" Jeff waited for her response. Elise kept silent with a ponderous expression. Jeff's eyes widen with sudden realization. "Oh no. Not again. You had a dream, didn't you?" Elise remained quiet. "Great, I'm going to die, aren't I? Please tell me you didn't have a dream with me in it! I'm young, I'm in love, I'm not ready to die!"

Elise took Jeff by the shoulders. "Are you finished? The only thing you've ever been in love with is your mirror. Yes, I had a dream, and you were in it."

"But?" Jeff asked.

"You were with someone. Someone from here, in this theater, tonight." Elise became serious in her tone.

"Please tell me she is tall, brunette, and gorgeous," Jeff joked with sternness. "I'm waiting, Elise."

"I couldn't see the face, but I know it was a man. Which is why I called you. I kept seeing your face with the man. I can only guess, but I think it may have to do with your study of the area when you were with us last. I'm not sure."

"You've never been wrong before, and that's what scares me. When did you have this dream?" Jeff asked.

Elise became reserved. "Last year."

"And you're telling me now? Come on, Elise! I know we had our differences with the team last time, but I thought we were better friends than this?"

"Calm down! It has been reoccurring. I thought there would be something again last night, but nothing happened," Elise replied.

"Again?" Jeff asked.

Elise let the moment build with anticipation. "Your guy showed up."

"Guy?" Jeff paused and read Elise's expression as realization overcame him. "Poker Face! You saw Poker Face?"

Elise calmed his exhilaration. "Well, yes, our first night, but I'm not entirely sure. He was hard to make out, and the window closed before we could capture a good sighting."

"He's always hard to make out! Man, that guy is everywhere. How many sightings does this make, three? Did you get photos?"

"Yes, but they aren't that good, not for solid recognition. Even our identity software had trouble with the proofs."

"Elise, you could have just sent me the photos. You know I could have recognized him in an instant," Jeff said.

Elise hesitated and turned away from him. "I know. But this time, it was different, almost as though he was trying to do something. It wasn't like my dreams."

Jeff became frustrated. "Oh, I see. You flew me down here to provoke one of your dreams. You want to call him out. Come on,

Elise. You know how I hate being the bait! It never worked before. You remember that little outing down at Bisbee. We nearly burned the place down with your last stunt. And don't get me started about our little venture just down the road here at the Oriental. I'm surprised anyone in the City of Tombstone let you all back in town after that episode."

"Okay, maybe I have some hidden intentions," Elise countered. "I flew you here to interpret. I need your skills on this one. This is history at its best. We just might have a window of opportunity here. And as much as your ego doesn't need to hear this, you are the best at what you do."

"I know that." Jeff jeered. "Look, a folklore historian is not exactly a physicist like you and that hubby of yours. I think you might be a bit off course on this one. You were right the last time we spoke. This is science, not science fiction. Besides, I've given up research on all of this. Poker Face is a dead end. I spent over a year trying to find any historical reference on that guy. Nothing. I tracked his paper trail all over this area. It was looking really good, and then it was like he just disappeared, along with my study about him. No historical records or anything."

"Do you still have it?"

"Have what?" Jeff stared at her with a devious smile.

Elise shoved him on the shoulder. "You know, the map?"

Jeff laughed. "Ah! You mean the illustrious treasure map to nowhere? All that work and research for a map that someone thought someone else had that no one knew anything about when the hard questions were asked."

"Yes. Do you have it or not? That map was a vindication of our work."

"That map nearly got us killed. I thought for sure that guy was going to shoot us."

"He never pulled his pistol. It was public property. We had every right to be there. This is the last time I'm going to ask you," Elise stated.

"Yes, I still have it. I keep it as a steady reminder of what can happen when you chase hope instead of reality. I knew I should not have trusted that girl that worked at the historical society. She never did prove where she got that from. She probably drew it up herself. I should have dumped her after the first date."

"Hey, she said that map is real. I trust her reputation. It is proof that our science, combined with your historical knowledge, can work."

Jeff became frustrated. "That map and anything to do with whomever Poker Face may be is just history, nothing more. And all of that is questionable, in my opinion."

Elise motioned toward the stairs. "Which is exactly why I need you and your historical knowledge here to keep us on track. If it happens tonight, I wanted you to be here. And after what I think I saw on our first night, I know you wouldn't want to miss this opportunity either. No one knows Poker Face better than you do."

Jeff smirked at his former boss. "Elise, with proper motivation, I think you could sell life insurance in a graveyard."

"Good thing for you, we don't deal with the dead." Elise looked Jeff in the eyes. "Can I count on you tonight? This time could be the one we've all been searching for. A real window. It could really work out well for us. It's all about the science, remember?"

Jeff turned toward the stairs with her. "I'm sure it could work out well, unless you're the bait."

Jeff and Elise returned to the theater. "Lights out in three minutes," Gene announced. "Jeff, I've got your position over here, right where it used to be, front and center. If anything happens, you can jump in the middle of it."

Jeff stopped next to a high-backed bar stool. "Ah, you still have my perch! Man, I miss this old butt rest. I'm glad you kept it."

"Nothing else fits between the equipment," Gene replied. "Everything is set and ready. The trigger is on the right, and zoom is on the left."

"Just a walk in the park," Jeff stated. He sat on the barstool and grabbed the handhelds. Two high-powered digital television cameras were mounted on each side of his stool. He put on the headset and powered each device. The motorized action of the cameras moved in conjunction with Jeff's head movements. "You've updated the drive system. These really move."

"Yes, they turn with the same speed and direction as you do. What you look at, they look at," Gene responded.

"And the digital capability? Did you finally get high definition?"

"It was costly, but yes. And the adjustment speed is even faster," Gene replied. "We use hydraulic lines instead of the old mechanical gearing. It turns and stops in the blink of an eye. And if one drive system should go out or stall, the other one initiates on its own. There are five batteries now. So, back up should no longer be a problem with the electronics and the new LED lighting. It works great with the sensory array, too."

"Sensory array?" Jeff asked.

Gene smirked and adjusted a camera. "It's all about the science."

Jeff positioned himself in the chair and lowered the monocle across his left eye. "After all of that, I think we need to test this baby out!" He turned his head and looked across the room at a bare wall. "Clear in front, shooting!" He pulled the trigger. The entire system flashed with multiple strobes and high-density lighting that lit the entire theater. "Boy! If that doesn't capture the window, nothing will. I can't wait to see how the actual photos look. Nice, Gene. I could see everything. The infrared is balanced perfectly. I could switch between views with just a click."

"I figured you would like that," Gene answered. "And the Blackburns synched the cameras to the triggers. So, whenever you shoot, it snaps still-shots and instantly sends them to their servers in the back. We can analyze and process in seconds compared to before."

"What's that contraption on the floor? I don't remember that. Wait, let me guess. It's either some high-tech gadget born from your brain, or this is where you tell me it's all about the science?" Jeff asked.

Gene crossed his arms and thought for a moment. The rest of the team stopped what they were doing and listened intently for his response. "Let's just say…"

"It's all about the science," Elise interrupted. "And explaining it is way above your GPA. So, enough with the one-liners and let's get ready."

Gene leaned toward Jeff and whispered behind Elise. "It's a new vertical imaging lens I've been working on that takes digital HD shots from the ground up in synch with the sensory array to create a 3D view of the window when it opens. The problem is getting the window to open directly over the…"

"Gene, Elise is right," Jeff interjected. "You have a double doctorate in applied sciences, and I spell physics with an F. I'm happy with keeping it about the science. Let's hit the lights and start shopping!"

"Here's your audio feed," Karen stated and threw some wiring at Jeff, hitting him in the head.

Jeff grabbed the audio jack and plugged it in. "There. All set. I like it a little romantic at night, so if you can find me a soft rock station on this thing, I'd really appreciate it. You know, for old times' sake?" He winked at Karen.

"Jerk." Karen walked back to her station and turned her main monitor away from him.

"Alright, everyone. Take your stations. Lights are going out," Elise said. "You know what to do and what to look for. It's our last night in here, so make it count." Elise looked at each member of her team. Her eyes expressed what her emotion could not put in to words. "Okay, let's open a window! Mike, Tommy, it's in your hands in five, four, three…"

Mike adjusted his headset and lowered his hand as Tommy pressed a remote. The dim theater lights shut off. The main hall of the Bird Cage became engulfed in darkness. Each team member sat motionless with their night-vision focused on their instruments. Karen monitored the sound equipment and listened to every creak of the old building. Mike and Tommy checked their communications and ran system checks with routine precision. Gene observed his monitors and focused every camera in the hall at various angles for coverage. Each team member texted across their screens that they were good to go.

Jeff grinned at the nostalgia of the adrenaline rush he had forgotten as he caressed the equipment triggers. His infrared and night vision monocles allowed him to see the entire hall. He looked to his left and saw Elise walking slowly in the darkness, stopping at random intervals throughout the theater. She stared at the floor, unable to see in the darkness, and appeared to stroll in slow motion. Everyone in the room panned from Elise to their equipment, watching with trained expectation. Elise paced the theater several times and then sat alone near the stage.

Time passed slowly in the darkness. Karen listened for distinct sounds and marked the recordings of those she could not identify. The desert wind interfered with her observations by whistling through the cracks of the drafty dwelling. Each team member texted their hourly reports to Gene. Midnight came and went for the group beckoning an occasional yawn and quiet nibble of a sugar-filled snack. Gene whispered an occasional encouragement over the headset to keep everyone focused.

Pop! Tommy Blackburn checked his monitor. "Sorry," he whispered over the headset realizing the volume on his monitor was too high. He adjusted the tone and ignored the scolding look from his brother.

Jeff looked at Elise, still leaning against the stage with her head down. He knew her tendencies and watched her more than his equipment to determine if anything was going to happen. He loosened his watchband and exhaled at the time. "Two seventeen," he mumbled. He switched his monocle from infrared to night vision and observed the theater's ceiling. He fumbled with his watchband while trying to recognize the array of bullet holes and count each one. He followed the ceiling to the stage and noticed Elise turning toward the stairs. The shadow of a human figure walked past Elise and stood behind Gene's station.

"Gene, it's behind you," Karen whispered over the headset. She had a clear view from the other side of the room. "I'm rolling. All sensors are reading."

Gene didn't answer. Jeff watched him move his hand slowly over an arming mechanism.

"Not yet, Gene," Mike warned over the headset. "I'm not getting any change in room atmospherics."

"You will," Gene whispered back. "Look behind you."

Mike held his breath and peered at his brother. Tommy's eyes were frozen in a trance with his mouth wide open. Mike leaned further to see three shadowed images pass between them. His readings illuminated with multiple responses. "Gene, I think this is it." Tommy's eyes followed the silhouettes with his mouth still open.

"There, along the wall. Jeff, get ready. A window is opening right in front of you!" Gene said. He reached for the arming mechanism and initiated it. A low hum began to resonate throughout the theater. A tingling of static electricity danced across Jeff's arms as he felt the floor begin to vibrate. "I'm engaging the array," Gene stated. "Stand by. Engaging in three, two, one, now!" A loud tone resembling a subwoofer echoed throughout the building. The large drives of the camera lens began to power up in preparation for a high-tech photograph. Each team member covered their ears. A brilliant white light flickered near the wall. The striking light appeared in the shape of a cat's pupil. The unexpected intensity caused everyone to shield their vision.

Jeff looked to see Elise grab his arm. "Pull the triggers! The window is opening right on top of the array."

Caught off guard, Jeff released the safeties and stared at the light. "Shooting!" He pulled the triggers and focused forward.

Nothing happened. "Shooting again." He engaged the triggers a second time and heard pressure building in the hydraulic lines. "I think it's jammed!"

"Keep trying!" Gene yelled. "Hurry!"

He pulled the triggers multiple times. "It's not responding!" Furious, Jeff stood and checked the lines. The light began to intensify, revealing one of the hydraulic lines pinched between a hinge in the support structure. Desperate, he reached across his chair to pull on the hinge. His arm slipped, cutting his wrist against the railing and hitting his watchband. "Enough of this!" he yelled and pulled on the stuck hydraulic line with both hands. The line ruptured, releasing highly pressurized fluid that exploded across his arms and face. The torn line ripped in half, flinging violently into his arm. His wristwatch flew off of his arm as he fell against his equipment, narrowly missing Elise's head. "Watch out," he yelled and reached for Elise. The intense light flashed and disappeared. "Are you okay? Guys, turn on some low lighting. Elise may be injured."

"No, I'm fine." She turned and hugged Jeff with a wide smile. "I'm beyond fine. We did it! Guys, Karen, please tell me you got that!"

"We got that and more," Mike replied. "Washing it through the system now."

"Karen, what about you?" Elise asked. Karen did not respond. Elise turned toward her station to see her hands pressed against her headphones. Karen looked at the far wall in a panic.

"Shh!" Karen exclaimed over the headset. "I hear piano music, and it isn't coming from a radio. It's still happening!"

Jeff and Elise watched the wall. "I don't hear or see anything," Jeff said, holding his injured wrist.

"Mike, Tommy, are you still rolling video?" Gene asked. The two brothers remained motionless behind their monitors. "Guys, talk to me."

"Look for it," Mike responded. "Look along the wall."

Everyone trained their attention on the wall and saw a man and a woman walking gingerly in front of them. The man was well dressed in black pants and a coat with a large, black brimmed hat. The woman walked with her arm around his and wore a white dress carrying a parasol. She laughed as the man whispered in her ear. The team watched the cheerful couple acknowledge a gentleman waiting to depart with them. They walked toward the front of the theater and faded away as the window closed in the darkness.

The team remained motionless. Each one of them stared at the wall in awe, hoping for an encore. No one spoke as their equipment continued to operate. Jeff moved to the center of the room and observed the entire hall. Everything appeared exactly as it was when they started. He looked at each team member and focused upon Elise. She stared at her husband, Gene, while he stared back with glaring satisfaction. Eventually, all eyes centered upon Jeff still standing in the middle of the room.

"Wow!" Jeff bellowed as everyone cheered. They quizzed each other for details and shut down their equipment. Elation filled the room as they gathered in the center to express their version of the experience.

Gene calmed his excited team. "Alright, it's safe to say that was the best one, ever. Look, I know we're all eager to compare stories, but let's shut the rest of the equipment down, pack up and get out of here so we can process our readings. If we can get going now, maybe we can catch a few hours of sleep before we begin analysis."

"Sleep?" Tommy asked. "I won't be sleeping for the rest of the week!"

"I know," Gene replied through everyone's laughter. "Come on, get everything broken down and packed up. The sooner we get the hard stuff done, the sooner we can get back to the hotel and start processing." The team returned to their stations, still discussing the event. Gene approached Elise and Jeff and interrupted their recollection of the incident. "What happened with the equipment?"

"One of the hydraulic lines got stuck in this elbow joint of the support structure. I couldn't engage the triggers or turn. I tried several times to activate it, but it wouldn't budge. I heard the pressure building in the line, so I tried to pull it free," Jeff answered. "I guess that wasn't a good idea. It blew up all over me."

"That's a nasty cut." Elise pointed at Jeff's wrist. "There's a first aid kit in the truck."

"I'm just glad you are okay. It looks like you were still able to initiate most of the shooting and the array engaged. I guess I still have some work to do on the support structure. If there is anything to the science, we'll see if we get any evidence from what you were able to shoot. It's all hypothetical at this point. Unfortunately, we really don't know if this will work or not."

"Tell me, Gene," Jeff inquired. "How is anything we just witnessed hypothetical?"

Gene and Elise laughed and began gathering their items. The team worked with fevered spirit to disassemble and pack their gear. The two hours of work required to tear down their equipment took longer due to the barrage of eyewitness accounts. Time passed without regard to sleep deprivation or hunger as adrenaline fueled the team. Each member was anxious to view their readings. They packed the gear and toted each case to the back of the building. Tommy opened the door to see the sun well above the horizon.

"Daylight already?" Mike asked. "I'm starved. Where's a good breakfast around here?"

"It's almost nine o'clock. If we're going to eat, we'd better get going," Karen stated. "Gene was right; I'll probably crash for a few hours before I start processing. The audio alone will take hours to clean up."

"Come on, I know a place here in town," Tommy replied. "Hey Gene, you're buying breakfast, right?"

"No, not today he's not," Elise replied. She lowered her phone and faced her husband with a wide smile.

Gene looked at her in confusion. "Honey, I always buy the team breakfast. You know that. Besides, we need to celebrate this one."

"Celebrate at dinner tonight." Elise waved her phone in his face with joy. "Fort Huachuca just called. They agreed to meet with us in two hours!"

Gene's eyes widened. "Uh, breakfast is on your own. I'll pick up dinner. And no whining, Mike!"

Elise approached Jeff. "I want you to come with us."

"No thanks, the only place I am going is to bed. That event last night will be difficult to beat, so count me out," Jeff said while bandaging his wrist. "Has anyone seen my watch?"

"Forget about your watch. Fort Huachuca called; they're meeting us in two hours," Elise stated.

Jeff noticed her seriousness. Realizing the opportunity, he leaned toward Elise. "I'll sleep when I'm dead." He grabbed the keys and hurried toward the truck. "Come on, I'm driving!"

* * * * * * *

Jeff parked the truck in front of the Fort Huachuca Housing Office. Gene and Elise walked in front of the vehicle admiring the surroundings. The Huachuca Mountains surrounded the old fort, casting a rugged, high plains desert setting. The nostalgia of the military outpost and elevated view of the southwestern terrain complimented the scene. The installation flourished with its modern-day mission of intelligence and technology. They stood together, relishing in the long-awaited moment.

"You can almost feel the history in this place," Gene said.

"Almost?" Jeff asked. "This place is history. The Apaches, Geronimo, Arizona Territory, the Buffalo Soldiers, it doesn't get any more southwestern than this. To be stationed here back in the day, you had to be one tough son of a gun."

"It's beautiful. And here we are," Elise stated.

"And just how did you pull this off?" Jeff asked. "You've waited years for this opportunity. First the Bird Cage Theater and now Fort Huachuca? You're doing pretty good these days."

"Yes, windows of opportunity," Elise smiled. "Come on, let's go see what awaits."

The team entered the main office and stopped at the secretary's desk. She signed them in and escorted them to the director's office. A young woman ended her phone conversation and rose from her chair. The secretary introduced the team and seated them around a large conference table.

"Thank you so much for meeting with us, Mrs. Bradford. We really appreciate your time," Elise said.

"It's Miss Bradford, but you can call me Donna."

"Indeed, we shall," Jeff answered. "Certainly, a pleasure, Donna." He smiled with deliberate purpose and admired her long, brunette hair.

"Easy, cowboy," Gene whispered.

"Yes, thank you. My secretary said you have been quite tenacious with arranging a meeting. Sorry I haven't been more available. I'm still getting somewhat settled here," Donna responded. "She mentioned something about an interview?"

"It's more like a field study," Elise replied. "We partner with various educational organizations that explore unique studies of physics and applied sciences in a field environment. We pursue various locations with certain historical significance, and Fort Huachuca has been on our list for a long time."

"Well, that certainly is a mouthful. But, I'm still not sure what exactly it is that you want to do here," Donna stated. "I've never heard of history and physics as a study?"

"The unique studies my wife referred to involve the exploration of energy, time, and matter and how they can produce various outcomes in a special environment of, let's say questionable or even peculiar circumstances," Gene said.

Donna sat with a blank stare. "Peculiar circumstances? Doctor Saige, why don't you just say what's on your mind?"

"We explore areas of significant historical value that have unexplained phenomena," Jeff replied. "There, that wasn't so hard now, was it?"

The room remained quiet for several seconds as Donna became uncomfortable. "I'm assuming from your very calculated responses that you are ghost hunters?"

"No. We explore areas that may have ghostly encounters to determine the scientific evidence of them," Jeff responded.

"And, what exactly do you do, Mr. Finbow?"

"I'm currently working on my doctorate in history, but I moonlight with the Saiges to provide counsel on various, unexpected historical occurrences during our research. It's quite involved, but I'd be happy to break it down in layman's terms. Perhaps, over dinner tonight? You and I could…"

"What our immodest friend is trying to say is that we incorporate science into areas that possess a high energy level or capacity for unexplained occurrences, such as ghost sightings," Gene explained.

"That certainly is original," Donna said. "I can't say that I have ever been asked about anything like that before. And I've never been asked out to dinner like that before, either." She glared at Jeff as he nodded in hopeful acknowledgment. "As exceptionally peculiar as this is, I don't think we can assist with anything like that here. Portraying ghosts on our installation is not something we want to express to our service members and their families."

"It would not be about ghosts, Donna. We focus on the energy and the event itself. We try to determine how something like that *can* exist." Elise sat up in her chair. "Look at it like this. When we die, our souls or spirits transition. But our bodies stay behind. So, we ask questions such as how can there be clothes or recognition of people that have passed on, if clothes cannot die and the body is left behind. We believe there may be a science there that can lead to some fascinating studies."

Donna brushed some lint from her pants. "Again, as intriguing as all of this is, I am just not sure how we can help you. With respect, this is a military installation, not a graveyard."

"If you have a location of unusual, high-density activity, we would like to bring in our crew and set up our equipment. It would be for one or two nights, depending on any potential. And nothing would be made public, I promise. We like to keep our studies scientific, professional, and private," Elise added. "We are not a television show."

Donna thought for a moment. "Even if I had something remotely close to what you are asking, I doubt I could have it available for a few days or even a week."

"Anything is fine. Just being on Fort Huachuca is all the potential we need," Gene replied.

"And I'd be happy to answer any questions you have and even take you on a tour of what we do, Donna," Jeff said. He stared at her with a continuous smile.

"Yes, I'm sure you would," Donna replied. "Okay, let me think this over and discuss it with my supervisor. If you could give me a few days, I'll let you know."

"Certainly," Elise replied. "Thank you for your time, and we hope to hear from you soon. Please call if you have any questions."

The group provided their pleasantries and departed the room. They passed the secretary's desk and stopped by the main entrance. "Well, that bombed," Gene stated.

"I don't know, I think I got her attention. She was curious about dinner. Do you two know of any romantic joints around town?" Jeff asked.

"You're hopeless," Elise replied. "Come on, let's get back to the team and get some rest. They will need help with the processing. At least we have last night's event to look forward to."

"Excuse me, Elise…" The group turned around to see Donna standing behind them.

"You see! Ask a woman out to dinner, and it's game on! Quick, where's a happenin' spot that's enticing, but with prices on the menu?" Jeff whispered to Gene.

"Yes ma'am," Elise answered.

"I may not have much here that suits what you have described, but I do have a friend that experienced something recently that just might be exactly what you are looking for," Donna stated.

"We are always looking for what we call opportunities," Elise replied. "What exactly did your friend experience?"

"Oh, she would have to tell you herself. I must say, when she told me, it was quite fascinating, to say the least. I almost wonder if she fell and hit her head or something. But I think it might get your attention and maybe even determine if she is crazy or not. No offense."

"That's okay, none taken. We understand. Is there somewhere we could meet her and talk? I'd rather not do something like this over the phone," Elise asked.

"Yes, but it might involve some travel on your part."

"That's not a problem, we go anywhere," Jeff said. "And if she is as attractive as her friend here, it would be worth the journey."

"How flattering, Mr. Finbow. I'll be sure to warn her about you. She should have plenty of time to get ready for your arrival," Donna replied and winked at Elise.

"That's good," Jeff stated. "And where exactly is this friend of yours located?"

Donna leaned toward Jeff with a smirk. "Oklahoma."

Chapter 5

The wind blew through the golden sagebrush, creating the appearance of waves across the terrain. The rugged ground proved difficult to traverse. Elise struggled to maintain her footing against the various sized rocks and tall grass. As she continued up the unforgiving slope, her breathing became burdensome. She yelled in frustration as the ground's angle steepened. With several lunges, she reached the top of the ridge. A dense fog obscured her elevated view. She adjusted her stance and watched the fog clear for a moment. A towering column of rock became visible in the distance. The break in the fog revealed a unique formation before it vanished in a thick cloud. Her footing became unstable, sending her cascading through the fog down to the dark valley below.

"No!" Elise grabbed the door and reached toward the dashboard.

"Easy, honey. Count to ten. You're awake. Let go of the door handle." Gene rubbed his wife's shoulder while he focused his attention on the road. "You must have been running, falling, or escaping one heck of a situation. You've been sleeping for about four hours now."

"Where are we?" Elise asked. She looked through the passenger window, still in a daze.

"We're about five miles from the exit. We've made good time. Jeff is still passed out on the back seat."

Elise stared at Gene. "It seemed so real. But, no matter how hard I tried, I could not stay on top of that ridge."

"Which dream this time? The one with the fog?" Gene asked.

"Yeah. But this time, it cleared for a moment. I actually saw something. It looked like a rock column. I only saw it for a few seconds," Elise responded.

"Interesting. Maybe you're right. Maybe this place has something to do with your dreams."

"I don't know. I struggled so much to climb that ridge. I know there is something there for me to see, but it faded away. It's like it is teasing me."

"Or, you just aren't meant to climb that ridge," Gene replied. "But, one thing's for sure, you haven't spoken this clearly about a new dream before."

"It does seem sudden, doesn't it?" Elise looked out of her window. "You said I was asleep for four hours. How long have we been in Oklahoma?"

"About two hours."

Elise contemplated his response. "I've had association dreams with locations before, but never this fast. It's almost like…"

"A connection?" Gene answered.

"Yes. Or maybe a vision."

"A vision? Now that would certainly make things interesting."

Elise thought about his response and stared at the passing scene. The rolling hills and grass-covered land followed the interstate into the horizon. The vastness of the view accentuated the depths of confusion with her dream. Since childhood, she realized her dreams were unique. The idea of her possessing a gift never amounted to much until she lived a series of moments that she had dreamed about many months before. The thought of her having a gift to see things before they would happen led to intrigue. With age and maturity, the intrigue led to a pursuit of knowledge. A quick study in Psychology ended with an awe-struck encounter involving a physics major and a vivid imagination. Meeting Gene led her to focus on the practical and scientific possibilities of her gift. Instead of wondering 'why me,' Gene motivated her to ask 'what if.' The loving couple finished their doctorate degrees together and married with the pretense to explore life's more curious aspirations.

The balance of Gene's scientific wizardry and Elise's appeal to idealism united with passionate intent when the two shared an experience they could not explain. Watching the contoured plains pass by, Elise recalled the moment from long ago. "I don't know why I'm thinking about it, but do you remember our first encounter together?"

Gene looked at her briefly and then returned his attention upon the road. "What kind of question is that? Of course, I do. What made you think that?"

"I don't know. Do you still think it wasn't a coincidence?" Elise asked.

Gene grinned at his wife with seasoned understanding. "Let's get this straight. You and I are teetering on the edge of disaster with our car engine going out, the radiator has a gash in it wide enough for me to squeeze my hand through, we are twelve hours from home with no one around that we know. It's getting late, I have a few bucks to my name, we're stranded, I'm scared half-to-death wondering how I am going to take care of you, and we've got two days to get back before the semester starts. All of a sudden, this young man walks up, smiles at us and without even looking under the hood or asking us any questions, tells us what is wrong with the car, gives us directions to a service station, and lets us know that a man will be waiting for us when we get there. I thank him, we follow his directions, and just as the car is about to die, there sits a man leaning back in a chair against the service station waiting for us. Now, I ask you, nothing about that situation seemed odd to you?"

Elise shrugged her shoulders. "Just coincidental?"

"Whatever. You know what I think he was."

"Yes, but how do you prove it?" Elise asked.

"That's just it. I can't. But there is no earthly way anyone could have done that and have been that accurate."

Elise laughed. "Okay, but that still doesn't prove…"

"For crying out loud, people! What the heck was he?" Jeff shouted from the backseat.

Gene and Elise shuddered as Gene yelled at Jeff. "I thought you were sleeping! You scared the air out of me."

"I'm waiting. Having just endured that miserably boring story, I deserve an answer," Jeff demanded.

Elise turned around. "An angel. Gene thinks he encountered an angel."

"Uh huh. And what do you think," Jeff continued.

"I don't know. But it made me feel the same way I do now. It's like there is something elsewhere, elusive."

"Man, if I didn't know you two, I'd swear you both were unhinged and leaking freaky all over the floor," Jeff replied.

"It wasn't just that," Gene stated and looked at Elise. "Go on, tell him."

"Yes?" Jeff asked.

Elise turned around toward the windshield. "I dreamed about him the night before. He smiled at me, the same way he smiled at me when he finished talking to Gene. And then he walked away."

Jeff raised his eyebrows. "Okay, I got a few goosebumps going on here. I'll give you that one. Still a bit shallow, but interesting."

Elise faced the door window. "I watched him disappear when Gene wasn't looking."

"Huh?" Jeff asked with his mouth open.

"Yeah, smart guy. Who's feeling unhinged now?" Gene asked.

Jeff remained silent as Elise interrupted. "Maybe that's it. Maybe being here is provoking something. Maybe something is trying to reach out. Ever since Donna back at Fort Huachuca mentioned Oklahoma, it's like something awakened. It's almost like something is trying to communicate with me or let me know it's here. The closer we have gotten to Oklahoma, the more vivid my dreams are becoming."

Gene held her hand. "All in time, sweetheart. Don't overthink it."

Careful to avoid desperation, she surrendered to her more basic needs. "I'm starving. Where are we meeting this woman? I feel like we've been in this car for a week. I didn't think Arizona to Oklahoma took this long."

"If we had flown here like I suggested before I was abruptly overruled, it wouldn't have taken this long," Jeff stated.

"Shut up, Jeff." Gene glared at him in the rearview mirror and answered Elise. "We are meeting her right up there." Gene pointed ahead at a small town as he exited the interstate through a toll station.

Elise noticed a concrete water tower with giant red letters across its white top. "Elgin? I thought she was at Fort Sill?"

"That is where she works. She wanted to meet us in Elgin," Gene replied. "Besides, it's a Saturday. Now help me look for that restaurant."

They drove along the two-lane road, observing the local shops and small businesses gathered along either side. A towering, metal silo dominated the quaint skyline. It served as a tribute to the area's farmers and ranchers. An adjacent railroad stretched toward the horizon as a staple and history of the Great Plains town. The bustle of the two gas stations was matched only by the subtle convenience stores, car wash and hometown grocery store. Gene continued through the downtown with its corner bank and distinct city hall. The rural post office flew Old Glory across from the town's educational campus.

Elise noticed the sign as they passed by. "The Elgin Owls. I love little towns like this. You can go from Kindergarten to your senior year all in one place."

"I think I took a wrong turn," Gene stated. He stopped the car and checked the map. "Yep, I should have stayed on Highway 277." He turned around and drove toward the only intersection stoplight in the town. "There it is. She was right. You can't miss a name like that." Gene stopped the car in the parking lot of a restaurant.

"Boompa's Burgers," Jeff read out loud. "That sounds about as local as you can get." The group stretched from the long leg of their drive and entered the building. "Now, this is a burger joint," Jeff commented as he observed the décor. Football jerseys, helmets, and banners displaying Oklahoma University and Oklahoma State adorned the interior. Large television screens covered nearly every wall telecasting any sport available. Shades of crimson and orange highlighted the room with the enticing aroma of grilled beef.

"Welcome to Boompa's!" a lady greeted them from behind the cash register. "Sit wherever you'd like." The threesome found an open table in the center of the room. A server distributed the menus and took their drink orders.

Gene looked around the restaurant. "I don't see anyone that seems to be looking for us. Maybe she's late."

"Who cares. I'm ordering," Jeff exclaimed.

"How are you folks doing?" a husky voice asked from behind them. They turned to see a jolly man wearing a Boompa's t-shirt holding a menu. "Need any help with your orders?"

"What's the best burger you've got?" Jeff asked.

"All of them," the man replied.

Jeff laughed. "Fair enough. What do you recommend?"

The man presented a devious smile. "Anything on the front page."

"How about the mushroom swiss burger?" Gene asked. He watched Jeff position himself for another antagonizing question.

"An excellent choice, one of our best-sellers," the man answered.

"That sounds good. I'll take that also," Elise said.

"Okay, make it three," Jeff stated.

"Three it is," the man replied. "Good thing you have friends to help you out, huh?"

"Maybe if they pay my bill!" Jeff laughed at his own joke. "And while you're at it, what exactly is a Boompa?" Jeff asked.

The man pressed his thumb in his chest. "That's me. Fries all around, and I'll get these on the grill. Let us know if you need anything else." The man took their menus and walked into the kitchen.

Jeff gulped his soda and sat back in his chair. "Wow. The owner takes your order, goes to cook it, and even has a sense of humor. Heck, I might have to move here."

Gene began to chastise Jeff as Elise reached for her phone. "Shh! It's Karen. Gene, did you bring the laptop?" Gene opened the case next to his chair and placed the small computer on the table. "Okay, it's coming up. I'm going to put you on speaker so they can hear. Go ahead."

"Hi Gene," Karen greeted, deliberately ignoring Jeff. "Mike and Tommy are here too. We finished analyzing all the data. We broke it out by frames and isolated the initial and background noises and lighting, and then ran it through again. Compared to other samples, this event is most definitely a window, the best we've ever seen." Gene, Elise, and Jeff eagerly continued listening. "We can't send it all to you right now, but we wanted Jeff to see these two particular frames and confirm for us what we think we are seeing. You should be receiving it on your laptop now. Let me know when you get it."

Gene, Elise, and Jeff leaned toward the laptop and opened the file. "We got it, Karen. It's opening now," Gene said.

"The first one is a close-up on the man walking with the woman. We slowed it down so you can see by frame. Watch for frame seven; he turns slightly to the right when he greets the second man that approaches them. Wait for him to raise his head. It is hard to see him because of his hat."

The group watched the slow-motion play and leaned closer to the laptop as the frames played through. Jeff reached and hit the space bar, pausing on frame seven. "Oh my gosh. It can't be."

Elise squinted at the screen. "What? Who is it?"

Jeff played the frames forward and backward, stopping on frame seven each time. "Wow! This is unbelievable."

"What?" Gene asked.

"Come on, Jeff," Mike spoke over the phone. "Confirm it for us!"

Jeff shook his head and sat back in his chair. "That's Wyatt Earp!"

Mike, Tommy, and Karen started laughing over the phone while Tommy spoke with added excitement. "And look at the guy approaching them. Jeff, you tell me right now if that isn't Doc Holliday! Look at his silhouette."

Jeff examined the frame again and rubbed his hand over his chin in contemplation. "It could be. It very well could be. This is remarkable."

"But that's just the half of it," Karen stated. "Look at frame sixty-six. We had to magnify it because of the lighting, but look at the figure sitting at the table on the left by himself." The group anxiously leaned toward the laptop.

"Three mushroom swiss burgers with fries." All three of them jumped at the presence of the server. "Anyone need any refills?"

"No, Ma'am," they answered in unison. "Thank you."

"You're eating at a time like this?" Tommy asked over the phone.

"Bad timing, never mind." Jeff pressed the space bar on the laptop for the next frame. The group watched the figure stare toward them and then look at the floor. Jeff stared at the frame in confusion. "Poker Face."

"Yes, we thought so too," Mike said. "As usual, his face is hard to make out, but we thought that was him. He actually turns to a full-frontal view before he bends over toward the floor. He looks like he is reaching for something."

Jeff looked puzzled. "Poker Face was at the Bird Cage Theater in Tombstone. Imagine that." He looked at Elise. "It looks like your dream was accurate. Poker Face and I were at the Bird Cage Theater." Elise nodded without reply.

"It's too coincidental to me. I don't think it's him," Karen said.

"If it is, he sure does get around," Gene stated. "The question is, why was he there?" Jeff remained quiet.

"Good work, everyone," Elise said. "We will call you when we get settled and review the rest. Any word on Fort Huachuca approving our request?"

"No, not yet," Karen replied. "I'll call you as soon as I find out."

"Make it quick," Gene added. "I want you all to pack the gear and fly out here to Oklahoma as soon as possible. I'll book the flights. The whole team needs to be here in case we get an opportunity. I don't want to miss anything. That sensory array worked well. Hopefully we can try it again if I can get a good power source to wherever we are going."

"Hey, Tommy, Mike," Jeff interrupted. "Do me a favor and show this footage to the city historian there in Tombstone before you leave. I met him at a conference once. He might remember me. Mention my name and see if he will give us a second opinion on all of this. I'd like to know before we start convincing ourselves too prematurely."

"Do you think that's wise? Sharing our evidence to the public before we finish analysis?" Elise asked. "We don't need any attention on this until we are sure. And I don't want anyone taking our credit or exploiting our work."

"And that's exactly what I am hoping to do, Elise. I want to be sure. Just show him the footage of the figures and see what he thinks," Jeff stated.

"What about Poker Face?" Mike asked.

Jeff thought for a moment. "Yeah, you can show the historian that frame too. Maybe he can make something of it. I don't know. Just don't reveal our history with Poker Face. I'm still not sure what to make of Elise's dream or why he was there in Tombstone."

The group started their burgers and sat in silence. The magnitude of the footage swirled in their minds. Gene and Elise played the scenes again for anything that could have been overlooked. Jeff ate his burger with a peculiar stare. Elise noticed his expression appearing as though he was in deep thought. Jeff finished his burger and watched them review the scenes and continue their discussion.

"How were the burgers?" Boompa asked.

Jeff looked up at him. "Mine was outstanding. The best I've ever eaten. Heck, forget Arizona, I'm staying."

"Are you all from Arizona?" Boompa inquired. The group nodded. He turned around and summoned a young, blond woman standing by the cash register. "Then maybe you are the people Jennifer is looking for." He moved aside as the woman approached the table.

"Hi, I'm Jennifer Tanner, Donna Bradford's friend."

Jeff pushed his chair back and stood. "Hello indeed. I'm Jeff Finbow. Please, have a seat." Jeff grabbed a chair from an empty table. The group exchanged introductions and how they came to know Donna at Fort Huachuca.

"I've got to admit I was surprised when Donna called me and said you were interested in my experience. I was concerned that people would think I'm nuts." Jennifer explained her encounter to the group and included every detail. Elise listened and asked questions while Gene recorded the discussion and took notes. Jeff observed her long blond hair and striking blue eyes, hoping for an opportunity to change the conversation with her. An hour passed as the group became more intrigued with Jennifer's story.

"Do you think there was any chance the person you saw hid from you or ran away before you could go over to see him?" Elise asked.

"I've wondered that too—many times. I think about it over and over in my head, but each time I remember how I searched the area. I would even say that could be a possibility if it weren't for..." Jennifer became reluctant. She observed everyone's faces and stared at the table.

"You felt something, didn't you?" Elise watched Jennifer raise her head with an expression of relief.

"Yes. I did. I tried to explain it to Donna, but she didn't understand. I had never felt anything like that before. It's almost as if..."

"Something had passed right through you?" Jeff asked.

"How did you know that?" Jennifer asked.

Jeff looked at Elise and Gene for visual acknowledgment. "Montana. The Little Bighorn. Trust me, some things are hard to explain. But, let's just say I realized you can feel things deep inside of you whether you can understand it or not."

Jennifer felt comfortable enough to finally open up. "It was like something overwhelmed me and gave me this urge to run. To run to something alive. I got chills. I got scared. I couldn't even think straight. I just took off running toward a bison I saw in the distance. I realized what I was doing and stopped. I looked back and didn't see anything. I can't explain it. I also told another friend of mine. She is

Kiowa and has heard of this type of thing. I told her what happened, and she told me to never look back. She said that if it is a spirit, it will twist your face or make you feel paralyzed."

Jeff sat closer to Jennifer. "You did a pretty good job of explaining it just then. I can relate. It sure sounds to me like…"

"Jeff," Elise interrupted. "Jennifer, we are not here to diagnose your experience. We are interested in the scientific aspects of experiences like yours and then determine anything from there." She gave Jeff a sharp glance.

"Donna made it sound like you were ghost hunters or something," Jennifer stated.

"No. We don't get involved with anything like that," Elise replied.

"What makes you think you saw a miner?" Gene asked.

"I researched the area and during my hike, I saw several pits that looked like mine shafts. I don't know, it just seemed coincidental. And the way he was dressed seemed to match the situation too," Jennifer responded. "One reference I found referred to the Charon's Garden Wilderness Area as the land of the dead." Jennifer adjusted in her seat and focused on the group. "Look, I know you said you aren't here to diagnose anything, and you are scientists, but please tell me. Did I see a ghost or what? I really would like to know."

"Something like what you experienced can be kind of tricky," Elise said. "We try to explain it in this perspective. When you die, everything that was your body stays behind. Your clothes don't die, so how could a so-called ghost have clothes on? It's this type of question that is where we focus our science and try to determine what you saw."

"Do you think you could show us where you had your experience?" Gene asked.

"No, not today. I told Donna to tell you. I have to go out of town for a few days. But, I'm happy to show you on a map I've got. I hope you all like hiking."

"Perhaps you could be our guide when you return?" Jeff asked.

"Sure. I'd like that," Jennifer answered. "Are you an avid hiker?"

Jeff avoided eye contact with Gene and Elise. "The best. I love it." Jeff handed her his card and circled his contact information before asking for her number.

"Also, if you stop by the visitor center at the Wichita Mountains Wildlife Refuge, they have staff out there that can show you on one of their refuge maps where to go," Jennifer stated.

The server returned with the bills and handed them out. "I'll take that," Jeff said and took Jennifer's bill. "Hopefully, it's the first of many we can share together." Gene and Elise shook their heads.

"What are you going to do when you get out there?" Jennifer asked. "How do you know you will even see anything?"

"It's hard to say right now. It depends on what exactly is out there," Gene replied. "We will check it out and go from there."

"And you still won't say if I saw a ghost?" Jennifer asked.

Elise withheld her irritation with Jennifer's prodding. "We entertain the quest for proof and truth through science. We research a hypothesis, not a mystery."

"It's all about the science!" Jeff yelled.

"Shut up, Jeff," Gene mumbled as Jeff hurried to escort Jennifer out of the restaurant.

* * * * * *

An old Chevy truck rumbled over the embedded cattle guard. The tires created the sound of several drums beating at once that echoed throughout the cab. The unmistakable noise summoned a greeting through the entryway. Laura Brooks drove her father's truck along the winding blacktop road and passed the welcome sign to the Wichita Mountains Wildlife Refuge. The road provided a direct route from her hometown of Cache to the refuge visitor center. She slowed her vehicle and focused upon clearing her mind and leaving her worldly inhibitions back at the cattle guard.

She felt a gradual calmness upon entering the mountains. Thick oak forests and tall sage grass lined the road. Granite boulders and rock ridges bordered the outer edges of the valley. The higher hills and mountains of the range stretched in every direction. The rising terrain formed a natural barricade protecting the wild beauty within from its tamed surroundings. The road appeared as a black scar cutting through the pristine sanctuary. She drove from anguish and toward hopeful tranquility. The peace of the mountains was her refuge from the past. Her eyes welled with tears as she watched a bison roam in the distance.

Her strength waned the further she went. The many times before along this same route brought her solace. But today, it was different. What was once a vibrant tribute was now a struggle for memories. The span of a decade had taken its toll upon her. Time and the many realities of life had finally darkened her mind. She cried with anguish and slowed her vehicle. The pain of the day did not seem as painful. The time her father said would come had arrived. On the day of her mother's passing ten years ago, Laura felt peace.

The years of anguish, reasoning, and questioning seemed to compound each year after. The loss of her mother never subsided.

Laura grew to embrace that loss, expecting it with each passing season. She never believed that the pain would ever go away. She refused the guidance of her father and family counselor and despised the generic phrase of, 'time heals all wounds.' She wiped her eyes with humble acceptance. On her yearly memorial trek for her mother, it was now easier to say good-bye. Disappointed by the unwelcomed feeling, she noticed the green metal roof of the refuge visitor center.

She thought of the yearly ritual of her mother's death. She drove to Doris Campground and walked by the campsite where her mother died. With the same silent words of regret, she then journeyed to the Sunset Picnic Area and hiked to the Crab Eyes rock formation. There, she said a prayer and spoke out loud to her mother. Laura felt that her mother's spirit roamed the Wichita Mountains and was happy to hear Laura come talk to her on the day of her passing. She went alone to feel the presence of her mother all to herself.

"Not today, Mom. I'm not going to let you go." Laura wiped her eyes and turned toward the visitor center. She thought of other topics to ease her mind and avoid confronting her unwanted feeling. She parked near the entrance and hurried to the front glass doors. She entered the building and felt relief. She approached the huge bison display and artistic panoramic. The rustic scene always made her smile. The design of the building entrance invited tourists and visitors with a museum semblance of the refuge. The recording of the refuge history played non-stop in the theater. She could recite the looped narrative entirely and allowed the soundtrack to replace her thoughts with the place she loved.

"Hey there, young lady!"

Laura turned around at the familiar voice. "Sue!" Laura embraced her friend with relieved joy. Unable to control her emotion, she released from their hug and looked away.

"Uh oh. What is it?" Sue asked and held her close. Laura released her tears and buried her face against Sue's shoulder. "Come with me." Sue waited for the last person to leave and escorted her into the theater. "What's got you so upset?" Sue pushed Laura's long, brunette hair out of her eyes.

"Everything."

"Okay, then let's take them one at a time."

Laura sniffed and wiped her eyes. "Today is Mom's…" Laura stared in to Sue's eyes, unable to continue.

"Oh, I forgot. It's today, isn't it? I'm sorry, dear. I knew it was coming up," Sue stated and held her again.

"It's not just that," Laura said. "I'm starting to forget her! It's like I don't feel the same anymore. I feel as though something changed in me. I don't understand it."

"It's been what, ten years now? Honey, it is simply your way of coping with such a tremendous loss. It takes time. And it has taken a lot of time for you. Precious time to heal." Sue caressed Laura's hair. "Did you hike out to Crab Eyes yet?"

"I was on my way out there, but I couldn't do it. It felt so different this time. It was like I was going out there to say goodbye forever."

"A loss like yours is different for everyone. You aren't forgetting her; you are making her part of your life. You are learning to carry her with you every day, no matter how you feel. It takes maturity and time. And you have developed both." Sue wiped a tear from Laura's cheek. Laura clung to her as more than a friend. The endurance of ten years and Sue's closeness to the family provided a motherly influence and support. Experiencing life at twenty years old, Laura depended upon Sue for understanding and guidance. But most of all, Sue filled the void of a mother's love.

"Now, that's better. What else is bothering you?" Sue asked.

"I'm sorry for bothering you like this. You've got a store to manage. I'm sure you've got customers waiting."

"Don't you be concerned about that. The staff will cover for me. How is Wil doing?"

"Dad's fine. He keeps busy. He started painting. I think it takes his mind off of mom," Laura replied. "The other thing is that I've been waiting to see if I've been accepted to Oklahoma University. I thought I would have heard something from them by now."

"That's right. You submitted your application several weeks ago, didn't you?"

"Yes. It's also the financial aid packet. Without the funding, none of it matters." Laura began to regain her composure. "I wish they would hurry up. I can't stand waiting like this. It's taking forever."

Sue walked her out of the theater toward the store. "It will make you stronger. Think of all the things you could finish while you wait for this. And, keep in mind, when you get accepted, your life is going to change again. Use this time to prepare and be ready. Your poor ole father's life is going to change, too. Spend as much time with him as you can while you are here. You don't want any regret holding you down."

Sue kissed her on the forehead as they walked in to the Friends of the Wichitas Nature Store. Sue showed her the new merchandise, and they shopped the latest selection of refuge tee-shirts. Several books, hats, and souvenirs accentuated the store with an inviting, local flare. Laura enjoyed the store and appreciated it as her first job in high school. Working in the nature store provided a refuge for her from the hot summers. Sue returned to her register as Laura listened to a recording of American Indian flute music. The tranquil tones penetrated her pain with a soothing, ancestral harmony. The music reminded her of the rare moments when her father played his flute. The soft melody he made floated through the night-time air of their backyard as they sat together under the stars.

"Laura, come here. I have some folks I'd like for you to meet," Sue said. Three people stood near the counter as Sue directed them toward Laura. "Laura, this is Gene and Elise Saige and their friend, Jeff Finbow. We were talking before you came in, and I think you would be the perfect person to help them out." Everyone shook hands and greeted each other. Jeff stood in silence, staring at Laura. Gene nudged him on his arm.

"Hi, I'm Jeff."

Gene and Elise stared in amazement. "Jeff, are you okay?" Elise asked.

Jeff continued staring at Laura. "You have the most beautiful eyes I have ever seen."

Laura grinned. "Thank you."

"Are you American Indian?" Jeff asked.

"Yeah," Laura snickered.

"Me too, to some extent. I have some great-grand somebodies in my DNA, or so I'm told. Are you from Oklahoma?"

"Born and raised." Laura and Jeff watched each other with envious smiles as the introduction faded.

Sue beamed at the moment. "Laura, these folks are visiting all the way from Arizona. A friend of theirs here locally told them about a place in the Wichitas to go hiking. Do you think you could find it for them on the refuge map?"

The group observed a map on the countertop. "Our friend said this is a great place to check out." Gene pointed at the corner of the map. "She said it was along this ridge and not far from the boundary fence. Kind of in this area. She said it might be a bit rugged in some spots. All we have to go on is a map from a brochure she had."

Laura studied the location. "That's Charon's Garden Wilderness Area. A bit rugged is an understatement. She told you to go hiking there?"

"Yes. She is really familiar with that area. We like to take pictures and will be bringing some equipment with us. Is there any part of it that isn't too rugged?" Gene asked.

"Yeah, the highway." Laura chuckled. "Your friend certainly picked a challenging hike for you. Have you ever hiked out there before?"

"No, this is our first time in Oklahoma," Gene replied. "But we like a good challenge, you might say."

"You're going to get one out there, for sure. Charon's Garden is the toughest terrain in the public use area of the refuge. I'm guessing you prefer to hike off-trail?"

The group stared at each other as Elise stepped forward. "We were told this is a great area to explore. Regardless of any trail, we just want to see it with the little time we have here. We are working on a project for a university study, and we would really appreciate any directions on the best way to get there." Elise crossed her arms, attempting to hide her impatience.

Sue watched the dialogue begin to stall between them. "You know, Laura, instead of just pointing at it on a map, why don't you go and show them where it's at, in person. Nobody knows these mountains better than you. Besides, we don't want our visitors from Arizona getting lost their first time out in the Wichita Mountains."

Laura glared at Sue, watching her portray an innocent expression. "Well, I did hope to finish my plans for today." Laura frowned at Sue as Sue stepped from behind the counter.

"Oh, I'm sure you can squeeze them in. Besides, it would be good for you to make some new friends." Sue pinched Laura on her side.

"We would be most grateful to you if you could," Gene stated.

"I know I would be grateful too," Jeff said. "I hear you have buffalo and wild cows roaming around on the range, or something like that."

"They're called bison and longhorn cattle," Laura replied.

"Ah! There, you see? Already you have saved me from insulting the local habitat, and we haven't even left the building. Imagine if I were to hand my constituents a bag of carrots and then send them off to feed those very same bison. Would that spell disaster or what?" Jeff asked.

Laura grinned at Jeff. "That would probably get them a one-way trip in an ambulance." Everyone laughed as Laura surrendered to their prodding. "Okay. I'll take you out there. I had planned to go near that area anyway." Laura sneered at Sue while Sue pinched her again. "Let's go back out on highway sixty-two and enter through the Indiahoma gate. The place you want to go to is right there. You'll see a small parking area as you come in on the left. Just follow me."

"We will be right behind you," Gene replied. "Thank you so much, Laura."

"Do you mind if I tag along with you?" Jeff asked Laura. "Perhaps we could discuss the proper techniques for feeding bison and avoiding hospitalization?"

Laura giggled. "I don't associate with people that have a death wish. Never feed the wildlife around here, Arizona."

"Fair enough," Jeff replied. "Then would you mind if I could simply keep you company on the ride out there?"

"She wouldn't mind at all." Sue shoved Laura away from the counter and toward the exit. "Enjoy your hike, everyone. It was nice meeting you!" Everyone said goodbye as Laura scowled at Sue, waving at her with a wide smile.

Chapter 6

Laura drove along the highway with Jeff staring at her from the passenger side. Gene and Elise followed from behind, hoping to preserve as much daylight as possible. Jeff enjoyed the opportune moment alone with Laura and remained awestruck by her natural beauty. Laura pretended to be upset with Sue but was inwardly excited at the rapid pace of meeting the handsome Jeff. Dating was never a priority in her high school days, and trying to meet the right guy proved to be more sophisticated than expected. Guessing Jeff was a few years older, she felt flattered by his obvious attention.

"You are a Wichita Indian? I'd say you are the first I've ever met. I don't know if we have many Wichitas in Arizona. Is that who they named these mountains after?" Jeff asked.

"That's what my dad says. The Wichitas have a lot of history here. My dad is quite proud of our lineage," Laura replied. "He really gets in to history and family heritage and all that stuff."

"He sounds like my kind of people. What about you?"

"It's not that I don't. My dad enjoys it enough for both of us. He thinks people should appreciate where they come from."

"If you can track your history, sure, he's right. History is proof of who we are. There is nothing better, at least not to me."

"What are you, some kind of history buff?" Laura asked.

"You could say that. I work for a university back home, teaching and speaking for various historical societies and seminars. I write and publish historical works on various places and events in history. I'll do it until something else comes along." Jeff observed Laura, still struck by her beauty. "What about you? Got any big plans? What do you do besides hike the Wichita Mountains?"

"I'm trying to get into Oklahoma University," Laura replied.

"Cool." Jeff became more subtle. "What about a boyfriend? A girl as pretty as you must be in someone's heart."

Laura blushed. "No, no boyfriend. Too much going on for that."

"Wow. You must have a lot going on to not have anyone in your life. I find that interesting. In fact, that's almost hard to believe." Jeff stretched his arm across the bench seat near Laura.

"Maybe. But what I find interesting is you and your friends driving all the way from Arizona to explore one of the most remote areas of the Wichita Mountains, and all you can say is you want to take pictures? Now that is almost hard to believe." Laura glimpsed at Jeff with a devious smile.

Jeff slowly moved his arm back to his side. "Okay, so you're no pushover."

"And you're no hiker." Laura watched him fidget while taking great pleasure in exuding her confidence against his arrogance. "That I could see as soon as I met you and your friends. Why don't you tell me what you are really here for? Your friend mentioned something about a university project? Talk about hard to believe."

Jeff looked out of his window. He contemplated his words and addressed Laura. "You don't miss much, do you?" Laura grinned at him without a response. "Elise would hand me my head for this, but what the heck, you seem like you will find out sooner or later. And besides, somehow, I think you deserve to know."

Laura waited for his response. "Well?"

"About a year ago, we took an opportunity at the Little Bighorn in Montana. We call it an opportunity when we find a place that has potential for what we do. We finally got permission to conduct a study there. It wasn't where Custer fell, but close to one of the larger skirmishes. It was our very first night on the grounds. Just before dark, we got set up and ready to roll when I saw this guy riding a horse up the hill toward us. I could tell something wasn't right because the horse ran with this odd kind of stride, almost like it was in slow motion. I alerted the team, and everyone saw him. He was riding toward one of our team members stationed outside of our main group. I yelled at the rider to stop. He must have heard me because he stopped the horse and looked at me. We stared at each other for what seemed like minutes, but it wasn't. He turned the horse, pulled out his revolver, and galloped straight toward me. I reached for anything I could find to defend myself. I braced for the worst when I watched him grab his side and fall hard on to the ground. The horse ran right by me."

Laura listened intently. "What happened?"

"One of our team members managed to activate the video cameras. When we played back the footage, it showed the horse disappear right in front of me. It was there for a moment and then gone. Almost like it went behind a curtain or something. It just vanished."

"What about the man?" Laura asked.

Jeff paused and stared across the dashboard into the distance. Laura noticed the concentration on his face. "His body just laid there, not moving. A few of us ran toward him. But before I could get to him, this figure appeared next to him and walked toward me. It walked right through me."

"It walked through you?" Laura asked in a searching tone of intrigue.

"I saw it coming. It passed right through me. I remember feeling cold, with something like goosebumps or when your hair stands on end. But this felt odd, confusing. I couldn't think straight. I just stood there. Elise ran up and shook me, or so I'm told. I remember I came to and saw her shining a flashlight in my face. I couldn't remember how she got there, but she said I was just standing there staring out across the valley, like a statue."

"What was it, a ghost?" Laura asked.

"I don't know. But the next day, we played back the video footage entirely."

"And?"

"The guy on the horse was dressed like an old cavalry soldier. Uniform and all," Jeff replied. Laura focused upon the highway without response. "His body just disappeared, in an instant. Almost like turning off a television. We couldn't even get close enough to see if he was dead or alive."

"Everybody saw this?" Laura asked.

Jeff nodded his head. "We told the park rangers what we encountered, and they were, of course, skeptical. We took them to the site and showed them where the soldier fell. They marked it just to appease us, and we left the next day. About a month later, we got a call from some guy they hired to search the site with a metal detector.

He found a corroded belt buckle, old ammunition, some buttons, and a spur. He even found a horseshoe nearby."

"That certainly seems ironic," Laura stated.

Jeff looked in to her eyes. "And then he sent us a picture of a rusted revolver near the same spot."

"Oh," Laura replied with a wide-eyed expression. "Are you serious?"

"We heard they did some research to determine if a soldier fell there, but it was inconclusive," Jeff said.

"What about your ghost?" Laura asked. "The one that walked through you?"

"I don't know. I really can't remember it all, and the cameras didn't pick up anything, for some reason. But I do remember that as it approached, I actually got scared. I could see what looked like a body and even some features like arms and legs, but I could not see a face."

"Did you blackout?" Laura asked.

"No, it was like I was paralyzed. It's hard to explain."

Laura turned through a gate and pointed at a parking area. "We're here. That is some story you've got. I don't know what to think of it."

Jeff leaned next to her as she stopped the truck. "And that is what my friends and I are really here for."

"Wait, what?" Laura looked at Jeff as he smiled and hurried out of his door. Gene and Elise parked next to them and opened their trunk. They each pulled a pair of hiking boots and snake guards from the compartment and changed. Laura watched as they strapped different colored reflective belts across their chests. Gene retrieved a large camera and handed Elise a small carrying case. Jeff shoved several small devices into a backpack and slung it over his shoulders. The team gathered their belongings and joined Laura at the front of the vehicles.

"We've got an extra water if you need one, Laura," Gene said.

"I'll be fine. We aren't going very far. The area you want is by that first ridge before the mountains. If you're ready, follow me." Jeff strolled next to Laura and put on a camouflaged boonie hat. "Nice hat," Laura stated. "I guess I was wrong about you all. You did come prepared to hike."

"We can hold our own," Jeff replied.

"What's with the reflective belts? We aren't going to be out here after dark," Laura asked.

"The belts are so we can identify each other from a distance. They are helpful in case things get a little tricky."

"Or spooky." Laura laughed at Jeff. "You should be safe from the cavalry out here!"

Elise pulled Jeff by his arm and walked next to him. "What did she mean by that?"

Jeff glanced at Elise and adjusted his shoulder straps. "Nothing, Elise. She was just kidding."

"Did you tell her about us?"

"Look, she asked, alright? I told her about The Little Bighorn, that's all. She has more questions than answers."

Elise stopped him as Laura and Gene continued walking ahead. "We don't need any added attention. You know how important this is to us. If you are going to flirt with every girl you come across, do it without discussing our business, okay?"

"That's not very fair," Jeff countered. "I'm just as interested in this as you are. We were just talking. I didn't tell her anything specific about what we do."

Elise glared at him. "If you told her about the cavalryman, she probably thinks you're nuts anyway. Come on, let's catch up to them."

The group hiked near the west boundary fence toward the Charon's Garden Wilderness Area. Rising granite columns and rock formations dominated the area. Sheer granite walls towered above the network of valleys and washouts, forming layered mountains of rock and boulders. Wild grass fields and dry stream beds weaved between cedar groves. The rocky terrain rolled into foothills of more granite. Shades of tan, peach, and rust highlighted the scenic view against the blue sky. Oak forests thinned as they increased in elevation.

"I've seen rugged terrain before, but nothing like this," Gene stated. "Jennifer wasn't kidding when she said this was going to be some rough hiking."

"How in the world could miners get in here? They must have hand-carried everything," Jeff asked.

"I guess they did," Laura responded. "Where exactly did your friend say the location was? If we go any further, we will be heading in to the mountains."

Gene and Jeff looked at the map and debated their position. Jeff reviewed his notes and showed Laura the map. They determined their location as Gene noticed Elise standing near a ridge. He watched as she leaned over and fell to one knee. "Elise!" Gene motioned toward Jeff. "Grab a camera. Aim at Elise and take pictures at every angle around her. Come on!"

"You want me to snap photos while I'm running?" Jeff asked.

"Just do it!"

The group ran toward Elise and helped her to her feet. Elise pushed Gene away and stumbled toward a granite slab protruding above the ground. She grabbed her stomach and moved closer toward the drop-off.

"Honey, watch your step. That's quite a drop!" Gene yelled and reached for her. Elise heaved twice and vomited across the ground. She stumbled forward and fell short of the small cliff. Gene grabbed her arm and knelt beside her. Elise passed in and out of consciousness. Her body became limp as Gene struggled to hold her upright. She grabbed his arm and turned away, throwing up a second time. "Jeff, help me get her to her feet. We're getting out of here."

"Should I be recording this or taking any readings?" Jeff asked.

"Forget about that. Help me get her moving. This may be more serious than I know."

Laura gathered their belongings and guided them off of the ridge. Elise moaned and resisted each step. They hurried through the woods to an open field. They carried Elise across an embankment and saw the vehicles in the distance. Both men carried Elise up the slope and slipped in the loose footing. They tumbled down the embankment and landed in the soft earth of the stream bed. Gene and Jeff scrambled toward Elise.

"Wait, I'm okay," Elise stated and sat up. She wiped her mouth. "I'm feeling better. Just let me sit a minute."

"What happened to you?" Jeff asked.

Elise stared at the embankment and caught her breath. "I don't know. I was walking up that hill and then got nauseated. There was a dull pain in my stomach. I couldn't focus. Even after I threw up, it didn't help. I couldn't think straight." Elise made eye contact with

Gene and Jeff. "Not until you got me out of there. Then it stopped." She continued to catch her breath.

"Did you feel something?" Laura asked.

The two men looked briefly at Laura and then returned their attention upon Elise. Elise focused upon Laura as if in contemplation of her reply. "I felt sick."

Gene and Jeff helped Elise to her feet and escorted her to the vehicle. "That's not what I meant," Laura mumbled. She looked across the field toward the distant ridge. The beauty of the wilderness area stretched into the distance. She thought of her mother and the memory of the day. A gradual regret filled her heart. She knew Sue was trying to help by taking her mind off of the day, but it was not enough. Laura yearned for her mother. She turned away from the view and walked toward her truck. Elise rested in the passenger seat and waved at Laura. Laura approached the door while Gene and Jeff stowed their gear in the trunk. "Are you feeling any better?" Laura asked.

"Yes, I'm fine." Elise sat up. She observed Laura, watching her expression and tone. She searched her eyes for a glimmer of genuineness and spoke with spared reservation. "What did you mean when you asked me if I felt something?"

Laura was surprised by her question. Hesitant to respond truthfully for fear of perception, she evaded her intended answer. "Uh, I guess I thought you might have had an allergic reaction or something."

Elise shook her head. "No, you didn't. You were asking if I felt a presence, didn't you?"

Laura was astonished. "I guess you could say that."

"Why would you ask me something like that? Is it because of what you and Jeff talked about on the way out here?"

Laura was perplexed that Elise knew about their conversation. "Well, yes. Maybe. It's just that you got sick so suddenly, and I figured there was something else. You all seem like you are looking for something, but you won't say what it is. It's becoming rather obvious."

Elise smiled at her response. "How much do you know about these mountains?"

"It depends on what you are asking," Laura replied.

"Have you ever had any experiences out here that you cannot explain?" Elise asked. "And please, don't act surprised. I could tell by your face when you asked me earlier that you knew what you were asking me."

"We're all packed," Gene interrupted. "Come on, Elise. Let's get you to the hotel."

"Just a minute," Elise continued with Laura. "I'd like to try and continue our conversation, if you don't mind. Would you like to join us for dinner tonight? I would really appreciate it."

"Sure. Is it okay if I bring my father?"

"Of course. Bring your whole family if you like."

"No, I have no other family. It's just me and my dad." Laura watched Elise stare at her as though she was thinking very deeply. "Are you okay?"

Elise came back to the moment. "Your father…yes, please invite him to come. I'd like to meet him."

"So would I," Jeff stated and walked up behind them. "If you like, I could pick you up?"

"Jeff, can you give us a minute, please?" Elise spoke without looking at Jeff and focused her attention on Laura. "We passed a restaurant on the other side of that lake just off of the highway. Jeff, what was the name of that place Jennifer recommended for dinner?"

"Ann's Country Kitchen, I think."

"How about meeting us there, say, seven o'clock?" Elise asked.

"We will be there." Laura smiled as Jeff winked at her from the back seat.

Elise watched Laura depart and stared through her windshield. The thick cedars tossed in the passing breeze. The woods leading to the washouts cast a gray, lifeless appearance. Elise placed her hand over her stomach and began to breathe erratically. She shook her head and blinked her eyes in an attempt to focus. She began to see a vision of a mountain and pictured the face of a man more clearly than before as he faded from her mind's view.

"Elise, are you okay?" Gene asked from the driver's seat. He started the car and leaned toward her. "Is it happening again?"

"I think it's this place. Parts of my dreams are becoming clearer, but it's still hard to make them out. Let's go. I'm feeling nauseated again."

"Do you think you are being provoked? I didn't want to say anything in front of Laura," Gene asked.

Elise bent over in pain. "I don't know. But I want to talk to her again. There is something about Laura. It's as if she knows something but is uncertain. Or she is hiding it."

Gene backed the car away from the parking area and sped toward the highway. The wind whispered through the branches as a shadowed figure watched them depart from the cedars.

* * * * * * *

Wil and Laura drove to the gravel parking lot of Ann's Country Kitchen restaurant. Wil hurried inside to savor the aroma of their chicken-fried steak. They walked through the entrance and stood by the glass door dessert refrigerators. Homemade pies and cakes lined the shelves tempting their arrival. The walls of the dining room illustrated the nearby Wichita Mountains with a colorfully painted mural. Laura watched a server pass by with a fry bread Indian taco.

"Laura, over here."

Laura saw Jeff waving from the back corner. A large table with two empty chairs awaited them. Laura escorted Wil to the back of the restaurant. "Sorry we're late. One of us decided to be more ornery than usual." She glanced at Wil.

"You're fine. It gave us time to polish off some appetizers. The fried okra is practically its own food group." Jeff extended his hand toward Wil. "Welcome, Mr. Brooks. I'm Jeff Finbow. I'm sure your lovely daughter has told you all about me."

"No, she hasn't."

"Allow me to bail you out, again." Gene reached across the table. "Hello, Sir. I'm Gene Saige, and this is my wife, Elise."

Wil shook hands and saw Elise standing at the end of the table. Her eyes widened with revelation. She approached Wil and extended her hand. Wil noticed her reaction as they held their grasp.

"Young lady, you act as though you have seen me before?" Wil asked.

"Perhaps I have," Elise replied and let go of his hand.

"In person or elsewhere?" Perplexed, Elise stared at him without response.

"I think what he is trying to ask is does he look familiar to you, Elise." Laura gave Wil a stern look. "Why don't we order, dad?"

The group placed their orders and continued with their formalities. Questions abounded with general, anticipated inquiries about the local area, brief individual histories, and occasional laughs orchestrated by Jeff's unrelenting humor. The intrigue of meeting each other settled with their meals. Each person found their comfort zone and pursued more in-depth topics with slight reservation. The conversations morphed with several tangents to various stories, each trying to relate to the other for interaction and understanding. As the evening progressed, everyone began to notice the eye contact between Wil and Elise that became more obvious with each passing moment.

A brief lull occurred among the group. Wil stared at Elise and spoke without any introduction to the topic. "Laura told me you got sick during your hike today. Are you feeling better?"

Elise kept her focus upon Wil and answered without expression. "Yes. Thank you."

"Does that often happen with you?" Wil asked.

"I'm not sure I understand your question, Mr. Brooks?"

Laura became nervous. "What my dad is trying to ask is…"

"What I am asking, without the need of an interpreter, is do you get sick like that in your line of work?"

"My line of work?" Elise asked. Wil remained silent.

Laura glared at Wil and addressed Elise. "I told my dad some of what Jeff said to me on our way out to Charon's Garden Wilderness Area. It was the only way to get him to come to dinner."

All eyes turned toward Jeff. "Whoa! Now wait a minute. All I mentioned was our Montana trip and some highlights. Nothing out of the ordinary."

"Nothing out of the ordinary?" Laura asked condescendingly. "Someone passing right through you is nothing out of the ordinary? Okay, if that's the case, then how would you explain Gene telling you to take pictures of Elise while she was throwing up? What would you call that? A documentary?"

Everyone at the table became quiet. Jeff looked for a server as everyone else thought of a proper response. Gene expressed a slight smile toward Laura and surrendered to the moment. "What I asked Jeff to do is a procedure we call capturing. We take several photos of the surrounding area while our attention is on the central event, which, in this case, was Elise. We do it to capture any possible happenings that may occur on the exterior or around the event taking place."

Another pause engulfed the group before Wil interjected. "You all hunt spirits, don't you?"

Gene laughed at his statement. "Well, not really, Mr. Brooks. I guess if I had to answer bluntly, you could say we hunt the past."

"Taking pictures of a current event does not capture the past," Wil stated.

"Well, yes, I guess you could say that," Gene replied.

Wil leaned toward Gene. "It is a desperate attempt to capture spirits, Mr. Saige. And from what my daughter tells me, you seem to have had one capture your wife."

"You talk as though you have some knowledge on this topic, Mr. Brooks," Elise added. "Is there anything you care to share with us? We would appreciate any insight."

Wil became reserved and sat back in his chair. "All I know is that some things in this life are not to be shared. They should be left alone."

Elise became intrigued. Watching Wil retreat from the conversation, she yearned to provoke him. Curious to discover more about him, she continued the discussion with the hope of making a connection. "I find it interesting that you use the term spirits. We don't explore anything involving the dead, but in our experience, we believe we have most likely encountered ghosts, or spirits in this case, before. We aren't experts by any means, but nothing else could explain what we have experienced in some of our encounters. What I find interesting is how one would define a spirit or a ghost. I've never been able to get my head around how, when we die, some claim to see ghosts wearing clothes or possessing physical items. How can a person die and then be seen as a ghost wearing, let's say, a flannel shirt, blue jeans with a pair of boots, and a cowboy hat? What do you think?"

Wil observed everyone in the group before responding. "I think people like you should leave this alone and find something else to do with your time."

"And that is exactly what we do, Mr. Brooks," Gene said. "We pursue time. We hunt the past." Wil stared at Gene. Gene continued, noticing Elise's interest in the old man's words. "What we aspire to do is attempt to explain, scientifically, if certain sightings are images of ghosts, which we do not deal with, or if those sightings are actually something else. Something we call rips in time. An actual episode, or what we like to call a *window* of the past. Just as my wife mentioned, we don't believe that the clothes a person dies with goes with them. Clothes don't have a spirit; only the person has a spirit. What we are studying is, when we see an image of a person that is not with us in the present state or time, is that image a moment or window from another time. A window to the past that allows us to see that moment back in time."

"Is that what you think you saw in Montana?" Laura asked.

"Yes!" Gene answered. "And we had a very similar occurrence recently in Tombstone, Arizona, which was quite fascinating, I must say. Our experience there had every indication of actually witnessing a moment from the past. We saw people interacting as though they were alive, not dead. We saw light, heard noises, and even heard music playing from the same piano in the room with us. Only it wasn't playing in our time; it was making music from the other side of the window. We believe it was being played by someone from another time in history. And judging from the type of piano music we heard, we researched it and found the music to most likely be from the late 1800s."

Wil listened with mesmerized interest. His fascination with Gene's explanation was evident with his enthralled attention. His expression beckoned for more from Gene as he waited patiently for added discussion from the intriguing trio. His apprehension to join Laura and meet them for dinner was gone. The dialogue occurring between them was more than he expected, and he wanted more.

"How do you know where to find these windows in time?" Laura asked.

"That's where I come in," Jeff replied. "We believe that some locations possess certain qualities or events that carry a kind of historical significance that creates an energy or residue from that moment in time. Most of the time, it involves events surrounding war or death, but other times it can be a place of historical value with a large presence of people."

"And how does that involve you?" Laura added.

"I'm a historian. An interpreter of the past, you might say. These scientific master-minds need me to determine any historical significance of a location or any sightings of people. It's not near as challenging as trying to explain all of this on a resume. Talk about a great way to be thanked for your time and then shown the door barely halfway through the interview. For me, it's not something I can talk about much."

"So, let me get this straight. You all go around the country to historical places looking for these windows to see if you can prove that what you see in them is from a moment back in time?" Laura interjected some slight skepticism.

Jeff and Gene looked at each other and then turned their attention toward Elise. Anticipating Laura's eventual question, Gene addressed the maturing topic. "Well, that part you asked regarding going around the country is rather difficult to explain. You see, we have this variable that…"

"I have a gift," Elise interrupted. She sat with her elbows on the table with her fingers intertwined in front of her. She waited to see how Laura and Wil would respond to the revelation explained to them by Gene and Jeff.

"A gift?" Laura asked.

"Yes," Elise replied. "I have an ability to…"

"See moments in your dreams?" Wil asked. Everyone turned toward Wil in disbelief. Seconds passed as the stunned group waited for someone to speak.

"How did you know that?" Jeff asked with a rare expression of bewilderment.

Wil stared at Elise with a strange grin on his face and answered with his attention upon her. "Science cannot explain what is not science."

Elise began to smile at Wil. A warm feeling of trust consumed her. Elated at Wil's response, she felt any reluctance to talk freely with Wil vanish. "Yes, Mr. Brooks. You are correct. And I can feel when people or the images of people are near."

"Like you did at Charon's Garden," Laura implied. "That's why you got sick. But, was that from one of your windows or something else?"

"That's what we have to figure out," Elise replied. "I've felt things before, but never in the few times when we have encountered a window. It's only when it's been something else." Elise looked at Wil in reverence. "When it's been a spirit. It's when I can feel them."

"And they can feel you," Wil replied.

Elise yearned to further connect with Wil. His distinct charm and bold candor appealed to her inner sense. His portrayal of knowledge about her intrigued her. Curious to know more about him, she sought to pursue his wisdom. Relieved with not having to hide the details of her gift, she enjoyed the rarity of Wil's intuition and spoke openly to further develop trust with him.

"Your insight serves you well, Mr. Brooks. Perhaps you could further impress us by providing your assistance with an image I've been dreaming about since my arrival to Oklahoma. I think it is a mountain. It has been hard for me to make out, but it seems to become slightly clearer when I focus on it. Do you mind?"

Gene handed Elise a pen. She grabbed a napkin from the dispenser and flattened it on the table. She stared ahead in deep concentration. Blinking her eyes several times, she began to sketch on the napkin. She drew gently across the paper, careful not to rip it with the pen. She turned the napkin about and sketched several lines across its length. Satisfied with her crude attempt, she handed the napkin to Laura.

Laura set the napkin between her and Wil. They stretched it across the table and observed the simple portrayal. Elise watched as Laura's eyes widen with revelation. Laura faced Wil. Wil remained unmoved. He observed the drawing for a few seconds and held it in the air. After closer review, he set the napkin back on the table and slid it toward Elise. Laura watched as her father stretched his arm behind her and sat up in his chair.

"I can't say that I recognize that at all," Wil said. He glanced at Laura and turned toward the restaurant windows. Laura faced Elise without saying anything.

"Are you sure, Mr. Brooks?" Elise asked.

Wil remained hesitant and finally responded. "It is hard to say. That could be anywhere."

Elise reached for the napkin. "Okay, then. Thanks for looking."

Wil leaned over toward Laura and whispered. Laura exhaled and whispered back before facing the group. "I guess it's time for us to call it a night. I need to get my dad home."

"Do you want any dessert? It's on me," Jeff asked and stood with Laura.

"No, but thank you. It was nice talking with you today. I really enjoyed your story," Laura said. She stood next to Jeff and stared into his eyes.

"I really enjoyed meeting you. How would you like to finish that hike we attempted? And then maybe afterward we could have dinner, just you and me?"

"Okay, I'd like that. Where do you want to go?"

"Anywhere. You pick. But we need to make it soon. Unfortunately, I think we are going back to Arizona in a few days." Jeff handed her his card with his number on the back. Laura exchanged her number with him, and Jeff held her hand for a brief moment. "I'm looking forward to seeing you again, Laura."

"Me too."

Everyone exchanged farewells and departed for the parking lot. Wil hurried to his truck and waited on Laura. Elise approached Laura and Jeff and extended her hand. "Laura, I hope I didn't say anything to upset your father. I thought we were connecting there for a while."

"You're fine, Elise. He is just ornery tonight. Ever since I told him about you all and a little about what you do, he became different. Almost irritable. I've learned to deal with him. He will come out of it later on," Laura replied.

"By the way, if you don't mind me asking, where do you and Wil live?" Jeff asked.

"We live in Cache. It's on the other side of the refuge from here. Are you all staying in Lawton?"

"No, we got a cabin in Medicine Park. Our friend recommended it to us," Elise stated.

"I was wondering how you found this restaurant. Not many out of towners venture out here. Is your cabin near Medicine creek?" Laura asked.

"We got a large one right before you enter town, near a chalet-looking home. You and your father are welcome to come by if you like." Elise said.

Laura looked at her father waiting in the truck. "I would love to, but I'd better get him home. I think he has had enough." She thanked Elise and turned toward Jeff.

"Would tomorrow afternoon be a good time to meet? I don't want to risk missing out on our hike and dinner," Jeff insisted.

"Sure, call around one o'clock. That should give us enough time to get in a good hike and talk some more about your ghost stories."

"They are adventures! It sounds more intriguing that way," Jeff responded.

"I think you are way beyond that," Laura laughed. They waved as Jeff watched her drive away.

Elise stood next to Jeff. "One of these days, all of these girls you flirt with are going to catch on to you and really mess you up."

"Nah. They all want the dream."

"And what exactly is that?"

Jeff flashed a cocky smile at Elise. "Some romance here, a kiss there, and a memory made for a lifetime."

Elise shook her head. "What did you think of her father?"

"Not sure yet," Jeff replied. "But say what you want; they both recognized your drawing on that napkin and played dumb."

"Yeah. Gene said the same thing. Wil disengaged when he saw it. It's obvious to me, they are hiding something."

"Intrigue. I love a mystery!"

Elise laughed. "Only if it is blonde or brunette."

"Hey, that's not fair. I've dated a few red-heads on occasion. They're just a bit feistier." Jeff wrapped his arm around her.

"You are impossible. Come on, Gene's waiting. Let's go see what Medicine Park lodging has to offer."

"Yeah, I need to send those pictures I took of you throwing up today to the team in Arizona. I know Gene will start asking about them," Jeff stated.

"What? You better not have any of me getting sick. I will review those pictures myself, you got me?"

"If anything was there, you probably scared it away with your barfing."

Elise pinched him on his arm. "You keep it up, and you will be walking to Medicine Park!"

"Gene," Jeff yelled. "Quick, grab the camera. Looks like another eruption from Mount Saint Elise could occur at any time!" Elise ran after him as they both entered the vehicle. They continued their conversation and drove toward the scenic mountain town watching the late first quarter moon rise in the evening sky.

Chapter 7

Elise snapped awake and sat up in her bed. She glimpsed at the clock on the nightstand. Seconds passed as she waited, staring at the door of her darkened lodge room.

Tap, tap, tap.

Locating the distinct noise, she quietly got out of bed and reached for her robe. Gene remained asleep as she put on her slippers and tip-toed toward the front door. Jeff's bedroom door remained closed. The one nightlight in the main room cast enough illumination for Elise to peer out of the side window. The silhouette of a person stood on the porch. Checking that the safety chain was in place, Elise carefully opened the front door as far as the chain would allow. A brief silence passed before Elise peeked through the two-inch opening.

"Who is it?" Elise asked.

"Elise? It's Laura Brooks. From the restaurant last night."

"Laura?" Elise removed the chain and opened the door. "Is everything okay?" She stepped on the front porch.

"Yes, everything is fine. I'm sorry to wake you. I couldn't sleep, and after all that happened at the restaurant last night with my dad, I couldn't wait any longer. I had to come see you."

"No, that's okay. It's five o'clock in the morning. How did you find our lodge in the dark?" Elise asked.

"It wasn't hard to find, plus I wrote down your car tag number at the restaurant."

"Smart girl. Do you want to come in?"

"No. Actually, I was hoping you could come with me. I have something to show you. I'd like to get out there before the day gets started."

"Can I ask where we're going?"

Laura paused. "The Wichita Mountains. We're going out on the refuge. And just in case, can you wear your hiking gear? I have some food and drinks in the truck. We can eat on the way."

"Um, okay. Let me get ready. I need to leave a note for Gene unless you want him and Jeff to come along too?"

"No, I'd feel better if it is you and me."

"That's fine. Give me a minute." Elise hurried back to her bedroom and gathered her things. She scribbled a note for Gene and taped it to the bathroom mirror. Laura waited in her truck as Elise climbed in to the passenger seat. She set her gear in the middle of them and arranged some belongings in her pack.

"What's that?" Laura asked.

Elise held an object from the seat. "It's a long-range radio. I found out the hard way how valuable it is to have one, especially when we are in the field. These other items are for anything off agenda."

"Off agenda? I like that," Laura stated.

"Experience, my dear. That and simply being prepared. And from that look in your eyes, I think I had better be fully prepared for this. Am I right?"

Laura smiled at Elise and headed toward the refuge. "Yes ma'am."

They drove through the cobblestone town of Medicine Park to the main highway leading to the Wichita Mountains Wildlife Refuge. The sky remained darkened by the night. Stars glistened across the horizon as they rumbled across the cattle guard and on to the refuge. The stillness of Lake Lawtonka appeared as a mirror reflecting the heavens. Laura turned on the truck's high beams as they passed the wooded base of Mount Scott.

"Why the bright lights all of a sudden?" Elise asked.

"We're on the refuge now. And at night, everything that calls this place home comes out of hiding. We don't want to hit a longhorn or a bison crossing the road. Not to mention everything else that is out here roaming around at night."

"From the looks of it, I think we are the only ones roaming around out here. So, what has you so troubled that you would come out here before sunrise and roam around with the critters?" Elise asked.

Laura stared through the windshield as the expression on her face changed to apparent frustration. "My father."

"Are you sure there was nothing I said that upset him last night?"

"I'm sure. In fact, I was hoping it wasn't the other way around. I thought he may have upset you."

"No, he seems like a very nice man. But I did notice how he went silent when I showed him my sketch on the napkin. I still have it in my pocket." Elise unfolded the napkin and placed it on the dashboard.

"My father lied to you. I guess we both did. We recognized your sketch. My father did not want to tell you. He is curious, but he does not trust any of you. He has never been one to get involved with anything or gain attention. And not only that, I also think he is hiding something from me. That's why I didn't say anything when you showed us your sketch. I've been waiting to see if he is going to talk to me. He has some explaining to do."

"Why would he do that?" Elise asked.

"I think it stems from my childhood. We were hiking one evening, and the sun went down before we could get off of the refuge. We were stuck there overnight. We found shelter in a small rock cave. It was freezing, and the only thing I knew to do was to build a fire."

"Most kids would burn the house down," Elise stated.

"I remember waking up and seeing someone standing in front of the fire. My dad woke up too. We didn't know who it was. For some reason, my father never talked about it. He wouldn't even tell the police when we got rescued. He told me not to say anything so no one would ask questions."

"Sounds like he was trying to protect you. But from what?"

"Exactly. Or he was hiding something from me!" Laura yelled. "My mother died when I was ten. She kept a journal and loved to write. She used to read to me. My dad promised me he would let me read it when I was older. The other day I found my father with my mother's journal by our fire pit in the backyard. He burned it. He said it was an accident, but none of it made any sense."

"Why did he have her journal by a fire pit?" Elise asked.

"I don't know. But he broke his promise. That was my mother's journal, not his." Laura began to cry. "He is hiding something. I don't know what it is. But it may have something to do with the sketch on your napkin." Laura faced Elise. "And I think it may have something to do with you, too."

"Interesting," Elise replied. "I'd be happy to talk to him again if he wants to."

Laura wiped her eyes. "I don't know, he might."

"So, is this a mountain that I sketched on the napkin?"

"I'm not positive, but watching my father's reaction when you drew it makes me think it is. If your sketch is the mountain that I am thinking of, it is located on the west side of the refuge. Since you can picture it in your mind, I'm guessing you might recognize it if you see it."

"Does it take very long to get there?" Elise asked.

"No. We are going there now."

Elise stared out of her window. She expected to have a revelation or some feeling about the mountain, but nothing happened. She envisioned the mountain from her dreams. Unable to fully focus on its appearance, she surrendered her effort and noticed the sun beginning to brighten the landscape. The higher clouds transitioned from peach to pink, while the darker clouds changed from lavender to violet. The terrain became visible with its rugged rocks, boulders, and rolling plains. Grassy fields lined the paved road that curved through the valley. Herds of longhorn and bison were scattered across the land. The crisp morning air alluded to a warm spring day that brought the slumbered wildlife in search of a meal. She watched a large bison stand by a stream, enjoying a cool drink as they drove by.

They passed the refuge headquarters area and a side road leading to the Elk Mountain picnic area and trailhead. Elise admired the rising granite mountain accentuated with scrub oaks and cedars. The sun pierced the morning sky casting orange rays that highlighted the many natural features. Elise viewed the cliffs and contours of Elk

Mountain and then looked across the expansive valley toward the south.

"What are those two big rocks out there?" Elise pointed toward Laura's side window.

"Those are the Crab Eyes. They are two boulders balanced on the top of a high ledge. They are very special to my dad and me. And to my mom." Laura glanced at the rock formation. She remembered that she still had not completed her yearly venture to the site. She felt regret for not yet giving her annual respect. But by not doing so, she avoided any potential for closure. In her mind, avoiding closure kept her mother's memory alive.

"Would you like a moment?" Elise asked. She noticed Laura's solemn appearance.

Laura returned her focus upon the road. "No. I'm okay. But thank you." She reduced her speed and pointed ahead. "This is what I want you to see."

They continued along the angled rise of a grassy ridge and slowly reached the top. A westward panoramic expanded before them. Elise admired a gathering of deer in a field and then turned forward. She inhaled deeply at the unexpected view.

"Stop!"

Laura steered off of the road and pressed the brakes. Elise sat for a moment and opened her door. She stepped from the truck and walked toward the front. She stood unmoving. Laura checked for traffic and hurried next to Elise. Overwhelmed by the sight before her, Elise stared ahead without words. A magnitude of emotion filled her eyes with joyous tears. The revelation overcame her as she dropped to a knee. Laura grabbed her arm and helped her up. Observing her intensity, Laura allowed Elise her moment and held the napkin in front of them. Elise wiped her eyes and observed her sketch. "That's it."

Laura whispered, "That's Sunset Peak."

Elise compared her sketch to the actual view in front of her. The granite chimney peak rose above the wooded foothills. From their vantage point, three large contours sloped together to form the mountain. The eastern side of the mountain appeared with a larger, rounded, granite top. Several ridges accentuated the mountain with rugged terrain and boulder-covered features. The actual sighting complimented her mental picture of the mountain. Elise cherished the sight and celebrated it as another mysterious dream brought to a curious reality.

Elise exhaled and hugged Laura. "I tried to envision this mountain so many times. It was always dark and difficult to see. It's almost as if it has something to hide but wants to be known. Now it is right in front of me. It is so beautiful." She contemplated the view. "Why am I dreaming about this mountain? What does this mean?" Elise continued concentrating on the scene, searching her thoughts for reason. She yearned to provoke her dreams for answers, knowing she was never able to accomplish that before. Feeling the moment create more questions than answers, her happiness quickly dwindled to a focused resolve. "Laura, what do you say we stretch our legs and go for a morning hike?"

"I figured you were going to say that. But, can you do me one big favor? Can you please try not to get sick this time? I could really do without that."

"That makes two of us," Elise observed the mountain one more time. "I've waited for this moment, not even knowing what I was waiting for. We aren't taking on this opportunity empty-handed. Where's my radio?"

* * * * * * *

Jeff sat at the kitchen table, waiting for Gene. The unbearable delay taunted his waning patience. Feeling his attention span plummet, he reached for his laptop and plugged in a camera. He unlocked the software and downloaded several pictures from Elise's mysterious sickness at Charon's Garden. He scrolled through the list of photos waiting for the image enhancement to finalize. The computer signaled its completion and opened the recognition program. Each photo displayed individually on the screen. Jeff began his analysis and studied every frame.

He observed the pictures with subtle motivation. His mind swirled with various topics that crowded his concentration. The encounter at Tombstone weighed heavily on his thoughts. He wanted more of what had happened with the sightings. His return to the group was shadowed by his displayed enthusiasm. He never intended to see any of his former team members after Montana. The confrontation with Elise had proven to be his breaking point. The shock of his dismissal from the group paled in comparison to her phone call less than a year later. He remained stunned by Elise's invitation to return.

He missed his friends and even held distant feelings for Karen. The adventure and uniqueness of their purpose beckoned him, but it was the reason he kept hidden that truly enticed his return. Two more speaking engagements were all that remained on his contract with the university. With his book deal substantiated by hope and assumed expectation for success, he knew his time was running out. His lavish degrees in history and cultural studies proved his capabilities. He enjoyed the seminars and research of historical significances that made him valuable to the group. Their combination of Elise's gift, Gene's scientific prowess and the collective technology of the other team members accentuated his ability to enhance the historical value and explain potential situations.

But, with as many ventures experienced in his life already, the money was beginning to run out. He needed something new and exciting to rebrand his appeal and keep the attention of his benefactors. Competition for professors at the university was high. And with two of the three open positions filled, his opportunity for full-time employment was now in jeopardy. Gene and Elise were now a variable on his resume. The time he spent with them was no longer only for fun. He needed this to work and allow him the edge for employment in his field. Jeff knew that as much as he loved the history profession, it had few prospects that paid well.

"Gene, any longer in there, and we might as well settle for dinner," Jeff yelled. "Hurry up!" He clicked the next frame on his laptop and stopped. His eyes locked on the photo. Unsure of the image, he adjusted the settings and watched the enhancement. His mouth opened as he stared at the image.

"It didn't take me that long," Gene stated and walked out of the bathroom.

"Gene, take a look at this. Tell me what you see."

"What is it that I'm looking at?"

Jeff let Gene sit in front of the screen. "Pictures from yesterday, when Elise got sick out in the mountains. Look next to her…"

Gene yawned from his morning slumber and stared at the image. He sat on the edge of his seat and leaned closer to the laptop. "You've got to be kidding me!"

"Gene, this is Elise. Are you there?" The radio hissed with static.

Gene grabbed the device. "Elise? I can barely hear you. Why aren't you using a phone? Where are you?"

"This is a good test of our radios, because we are going to need them. You won't believe what I am looking at," Elise stated.

"You won't believe what I am looking at either, but go ahead."

"I found it. I found what I've been seeing in my dreams. It's a mountain. It is called Sunset Peak. Laura and I are going hiking for a while, just to see if I can provoke anything. It's the best revelation I've had."

"We may have you beaten on that one," Gene replied.

Elise took another look at Sunset Peak gloating with satisfaction. "What could be better than me standing in front of this mountain and knowing it is real?"

The radio crackled with Gene's response. "You standing in front of Poker Face yesterday."

The radio became silent. "I assume Jeff analyzed the pictures?"

"Yes, he did. Listen, we are transmitting in the open. Call me if you can get good reception. We need to talk." Gene's phone clamored next to him. "Wow, that was fast."

"It was Poker Face?" Elise asked. "So that is why I got sick."

"Possibly. But if that is the case, then we have a whole new hypothesis."

"Yes, we do. The hypothesis is who is this guy and what is he doing in Oklahoma when we just saw him in Arizona?"

"That's half of it," Gene replied. "It's not only who Poker Face is, but *what* he is. If this is a rip in time, why did you get sick?"

"I don't know," Elise responded. "But you don't think he is.."

"A ghost!" Jeff yelled in the background. "It's obvious. We are dealing with a ghost, spirit, apparition…call it what you want. Only the spiritual realm could remotely explain how he could be here. Look at the photo! He is standing right there. Come on you two, quit making this hard."

"Or you think he is standing there," Elise added. "If that is him, then he contradicts everything we thought was fact. Spirits don't wear clothes, remember?"

"Or do they?" Gene stated. He stared at Jeff and then looked out of the window in deep thought. "Honey, the rest of the group is coming in later today from Arizona. I spoke with Karen, and she and the guys have new information to share with us. This just might be a whole new experience that we have never seen before. Jeff and I are going to grab a bite and then head back out to that site. We are taking all of the gear. I know it is no-notice, but we are going to set up for an opportunity out there tonight. I'll stop by the refuge visitor center and get the proper approvals. With all that has happened with Jennifer's sighting, you getting sick, this new photo, and whatever else the group has, this could be huge."

Elise absorbed all of the information. "Yes, it could be. And I haven't even figured out this mountain in front of me yet. Since Laura and I are already out here, I want to go see this mountain up close. I don't know how long we will be. Let me know if you find anything." Elise stowed her phone and turned toward Laura. "Sounds like your Wichita Mountains have some secrets?"

Laura looked at Sunset Peak. "Maybe they do."

"Come on. It's just you and me now. Mind if we take a stroll on yonder mountain?"

"I know the perfect parking spot near the western slope."

"Lead the way!" Elise exclaimed.

They drove toward Sunset Peak and navigated around the western edge of the mountain. Laura parked in a small dirt lot and observed the surroundings. Elise grabbed her pack and stared at the granite chimney column rising up to form the top. They trudged through the dense undergrowth and plotted their way through the forest. The base of the mountain began to slope sharply in layers. They traversed the terrain and climbed their way near the peak. Laura led the excursion looking for direct routes with less natural obstacles. Every angle upward provided a higher view of the mountain range and the surrounding Great Plains.

Laura slowed her pace, allowing Elise to search the area and enjoy the panoramic view. The jaunt up the small mountain took less than an hour. They negotiated the landscape until Laura reached the top first. The wind tossed her flowing, brunette hair while she witnessed the scene. Elise caught up to her and sat on a boulder at the top. She remained quiet and stared at the ground.

"Are you okay?" Laura asked.

Elise caught her breath. "When I first heard people here refer to these hills as mountains, I thought that was funny. I've seen the Rockies, and these are no mountains compared to them. But climbing up this one has made me a believer."

"Considering you are on the Great Plains, anything with an elevation higher than a rooftop is a mountain around here," Laura replied.

Elise focused on Laura as though she was looking through her. "What do you know about this mountain? Does it have any history associated with it?"

"That would be a question for my father. If he would answer it. Why?"

"Just curious."

Laura sat near Elise. "You're not feeling sick, are you?"

"No, I'm fine. But I do sense something. I don't know. It's like there is something in-between here. I can't picture it. Not yet anyway."

"Do your dreams just come to you?" Laura asked.

"It's hard to say. Most of them come to me as a thought. It's kind of like how you might be sitting here and suddenly come up with an idea. Only I can feel when there may be a purpose or something more."

Laura watched Elise and heard the genuineness in her words. She looked across the range toward the horizon. The calming portrait brought peace to her apprehension. "Remember when I told you about my father and I hiking out here when I was young?" Elise nodded as Laura continued. "I was ten years old, and we were hiking over there by Crab Eyes. We went to pay our last respects to my mother. When we finished, I saw this huge herd of bison and begged my dad to go see them. We took off for them, and that's when everything started to go wrong. My dad fell and hit his head running from a mountain lion that was in a tree above us. We lost track of the daylight and ended up getting stuck out here overnight during the winter. I remember we found a small rock cave and stayed there for the night. I built a fire and fell asleep. When I woke up, I saw this strange man staring at me from the entrance."

"Are you sure it was a man?" Elise asked.

"Yes. I'm quite sure that was obvious."

Elise grinned at Laura. "What I mean is, do you think it was a spirit?"

"I don't know. I have wondered that for years. My dad claims he didn't see him. We were rescued shortly after that."

"You know, that's the second time you have told me that story. Why?" Elise asked.

Laura finally surrendered and chose to trust Elise. "Because whoever it was vanished right in front of us."

"Can you describe what he looked like? Did he have on a red and black checkered coat perhaps?"

"No, nothing like that. It was ten years ago, and I was young. It all seems blurry, even then. It was so cold and hard to concentrate. There wasn't much light either. I've questioned anything that I saw that night."

"Did you feel anything, like you were being watched?"

"I want to say I did. But I don't remember. I guess I was too scared. It all happened so fast, and I was really tired." Laura let the dialogue cease and readdressed Elise. "This gift of yours, does it allow you to see the dead or talk to spirits?"

"It varies. I might see the images of people or see them in a setting. It's almost like seeing a moment in time or a piece of an event."

"Do they talk to you, or can you summon them?"

Elise began to realize Laura's subtle intent. "No. I am not a medium if that is what you are asking. I do not interact with the dead. I may go weeks before getting a dream. I don't control it. It just happens."

"Oh, okay."

Elise addressed Laura with a comforting tone. "Hey, I don't mean to interfere with your feelings, but is this about your mother?" Laura did not answer. She fought to keep her sentiment calm. Elise placed her hand on her shoulder. "Laura, I am sorry for your loss. I can see that it is still an emotional part of your life. As perplexing as my so-called gift can be, I can't communicate with the spiritual world. I don't even know if that is possible."

"I know. I understand. I may not want to, but I understand."

"Look at me. Back when you were ten years old, you wanted that sighting you had in the cave to be your mother, didn't you?" Laura's eyes welled with tears. Elise moved and held her. Laura cried in her arms. She released her fragile pain in wrenching sobs that carried across the mountain. The comfort Laura felt with Elise invited her longing for an emotional escape that only her friend Sue could invoke. Elise provided an understanding that Laura had never felt before. She felt her tired soul find refuge in Elise's words and cried with the pain of many years. Elise continued to caress her. "It's okay, Laura. You will get past this. But you must let the pain in your heart go in order to allow the hope and peace to endure."

"I know. It's been so hard." Laura wiped her eyes and stood. "I didn't mean to cause all of this. I've held you up long enough."

"No, you haven't. I hope I've helped in some way."

"You have." The two ladies embraced, sealing a new bond in a developing friendship. "I feel like I have known you all of my life."

"Me too," Elise replied. "I feel the same way about your father, too."

"Ah yes, dear ole dad." Laura sniffled. "Let's get going before he becomes a conversation."

Finding Sunset Peak

Laura led Elise across the highest ridge of Sunset Peak. They boulder-hopped and traversed the slopes along the spine of the mountain. They paused often to observe the pristine view and watch for any wildlife in the valleys below. The rugged terrain offered little forgiveness for a wrong turn or miscalculated route. The granite rocks, boulders, and formations covered the peak with challenging obstacles to negotiate. The two women weaved through the undergrowth using any openings as a path to the next rise.

"What are all of these little brown balls on the ground. I keep seeing them everywhere," Elise asked.

"It's elk droppings," Laura answered.

"Elk? Good grief. There must be a thousand of them up here. Is this where they come to poop or something?"

"They like to come higher up. They don't care for people very much," Laura stated.

"Yeah. I've noticed there aren't any trails up here except for the animals. Why is that?"

Laura jumped on top of a boulder mound. "It is secluded. There is no easy way to hike Sunset Peak. Come up here with me. This is the second-highest point of the mountain. You can see the other side of the valley better from here."

Elise joined Laura at the top. "This is beautiful. These mountains are like islands in an ocean of land. You can see for miles. It's good that they protect this area."

"Yeah, it is. My dad says the refuge protects the mountains and keeps them looking the same way they did when our ancestors were here. He is really obsessed about our heritage and our affiliation to these mountains," Laura continued. "He comes out here a lot to hike and roam around."

"He probably does it to find his inner peace. From this view, I can see why." Elise observed a passing hawk. "What did you say your ethnic background is?"

"We are Wichita Indians," Laura replied.

"And your people lived in these mountains?"

"Yes. A long time ago."

"Do you know when your people lived here?" Elise asked.

"No, but my father would know. We think the Wichita people were the first to live here, which is why the mountains carry their name. But I'm not exactly sure. My father says these mountains have a connection with our people. He can get pretty far out there sometimes. And then, other times, he can be quite intriguing. He's a mixed bag, I guess."

Elise snickered. "I'll bet he is."

Laura flung a stick into some brush as they continued their hike. "Elise, I'm curious, but why do you all do your operations, or whatever it is you do, at night? Why not during the day when you can see what's going on like you did at Charon's Garden?"

"We call that the mystery question. We would love to operate in the daytime. It would be so much easier. But experience shows that the hours of darkness provide the most opportunities. Quite frankly, we do not know why the darkness is preferred. Hopefully, in time, the science of it will lead us to an explanation. But it does make it interesting."

"And scary," Laura added.

"Unfortunately, that can be the case, too."

"I'd stick with the daytime."

They continued their hike across the top of Sunset Peak. Their path led them to a rise in the higher terrain that narrowed along the ridge. The location provided a vantage point allowing them to view the east and west areas of the mountain with ease. The westward view extended toward the horizon, with the Great Plains stretching toward Texas. The eastward view presented a valley leading toward Elk Mountain.

Elise pointed at a location near the base of Sunset Peak. "Over there, do you see that little grassy area at the foot of that ridge? It's not that far from the road, and it looks like it has easy access. Can we go check that out? It might be a good place to set up operations if I can get Gene to agree."

Laura noticed the location. "Sure. It will be a challenge to get there from here, but we can make it."

"Oh," Elise sighed. "In that case, do you mind if we rest a bit? And I need to tie my hikers."

"Go ahead, take your time. I'm going to look over here for an easier way down."

Elise sat against a boulder and tied her shoes. She took a drink of water and stared ahead, relaxing with the view. She stretched her legs and observed the distant valley, watching the landscape while trying to calm her troubled mind. A slight breeze lofted across the mountain top, soothing her heated brow. She allowed the gentle wind to carry her thoughts across the mountain while she relaxed in the natural setting.

"It's time to go," Laura yelled from the ridge.

"I'm coming."

Laura continued leading them down the mountain. She angled her descent and navigated around the challenging obstacles of boulders, varied cliffs, and sloped ravines. A pair of elk jumped at their presence, fleeing across the terrain with ease. Both women watched the animals bound gracefully over the rocks and disappear through a forest. The midday sun highlighted the view of nearby Elk Mountain with its vast array of gray, tan, and rust-colored granite. The flat-topped mountain rose high along the eastern landscape, setting an elevated border to the valley below. The hints of the season were scattered across the scenery in shades of lime green and pastels.

Laura stopped near the base of the peak. "Wait here." She continued forward without looking at Elise. Elise observed the small area nestled between a steep granite slope and a large boulder pile. It led toward a rise that angled up the mountain.

"Laura, can I come over there now?" Elise waited for a response. The sun began to set behind the mountain. Its dense shadow crept over the land with a gradual pace. The rock-walled enclosure became dark. Elise struggled through the underbrush in pursuit of Laura. She entered the grassy area and stopped near the entrance. A coldness settled within the enclosure. She peered ahead to see the distinct glow of a fire against the granite. The light flickered against the rocks with a taunting gesture. She continued further in to the area and stepped around the boulder pile.

A bonfire burned with raging flames that tore at the night sky. The coals shimmered in white-hot heat that rippled in the air. Elise followed the flames upward to see Laura standing on the other side. The heat waves made it difficult to focus on her stance. She stepped closer to the fire feeling its intense heat billowing from the coals. She saw Laura standing near the edge of the fire with her head bowed toward the flames.

"Laura!"

Elise watched Laura slowly raise her head. She gasped at Laura's face. The flames reflected in her eyes with a sinister glow. A fiery red filled her eyes as she watched Elise with a slanted stare. Laura stood without expression and took a step toward the fire.

"No!" Elise screamed.

She watched, unable to move, as Laura walked into the fire. Elise fell to her knees in horror. She turned to see the mountainside consumed in a blaze. Flames ignited around the grassy area, surrounding her with no escape. Elise felt her soul yelling for help with no sound from her mouth. The flames engulfed the dry grass and rushed toward her in a consuming fury. She turned back toward the bonfire, searching for a means of escape.

A shrouded figure emerged from the fire and stood in front of her. Fear filled her heart as she watched the figure raise its arm and point at the mountain. The flames disappeared into darkness that engulfed the area. The bonfire remained as the only source of light. It illuminated the enclosure with flares of red and orange against the blackness. The figure turned toward her revealing a faceless head. She struggled to see a pair of slanted, glowing eyes from the darkened face. The figure pointed at Elise as the fire raged. It remained still as if to summon her toward it. Allowing the haunting moment to pass, the figure turned toward the flames. Elise stepped toward the fire in pursuit. A suffocating burst of heat rushed out of the flames and slammed her against the ground. She watched helplessly as the figure disappeared through the flames.

"Elise!"

Elise shuddered against the ground. "Wait, don't go!"

"Elise, it's me." Elise watched the fire disappear, and the surrounding darkness suddenly filled with intense light.

"Where am I?" Elise asked and shielded her eyes.

"You're here with me."

Elise struggled to see. "Who are you?"

"It's me, Laura. You're okay." Laura stood and blocked the sun from Elise's face. "You were dreaming. And from the sound of it, you must have been having a really bad one."

Elise began to regain her composure. "Are we still at Sunset Peak?"

"Yes. I left you to find a way down the mountain. You sat down and must have dozed off. I've only been gone for twenty minutes."

"Twenty minutes? Is that all?" Elise asked.

Laura helped her up. "Yeah. I heard you screaming and came back as fast as I could."

"I was screaming?"

Laura wiped her face with her sleeve. "From the sound of it, I thought you were being burned alive."

Elise stared at Laura. "What did you say?"

Laura observed the terror in Elise's expression. "Wait a minute. Were you having one of your dreams?"

Elise looked at the mountain. "It was so vivid. It was like I was there." She recalled her experience and told Laura. Laura listened to every detail. Elise began to react to her memories as the fear followed. Laura grabbed her hand and comforted her.

"Elise, it must have been a bad dream. Anything like that sounds like the end of the world." Laura helped her to her feet. "Come on, let's get you off of this mountain."

"I'd still like to go by that grassy area we saw earlier," Elise stated.

"Okay. It's along the way. You stay near me this time."

The two ladies walked together and started their way down the slope. Laura led them along a winding path to the base of the mountain. Dense undergrowth and shrubs covered the base as a natural barrier. Elise pushed through the thicket and stood near the opening of the grassy inlet.

"What is that?" Elise pointed to a bare dirt spot on the ground. She became hesitant as she observed the strange divot. "Is that a fire pit?"

Laura noticed Elise's apprehension and quickly calmed her. "It looks like one, but no. That is something you can find all over the Wichita Mountains. It's called a wallow. This is where bison lay down and roll in the dirt. They clean themselves that way. They make a huge cloud of dust when they do it."

Elise studied the dirt pile. "It looked like a fire pit. In my dream, I saw a bonfire here in this inlet. Good, I just wanted to make sure." Laura saw the relief on Elise's face. Elise observed the surroundings while Laura explored the back of the enclosure.

"Elise!"

Elise hurried toward Laura at the back of the inlet. Laura met her as she rounded the bend. "What's the matter?"

Laura took Elise by her shoulders and slowly turned her. "Look."

Elise gasped at the charred remains of an old fire pit. Seconds passed as she reached for her radio. "It looks like we are way beyond dreams now."

Chapter 8

Laura and Elise reached the truck and offloaded their belongings. They climbed into the cab and rested on the bench seat. Laura loosened her hikers and finished her remaining water. Elise tweaked her radio and set it on the seat between them. The two ladies exhaled from relief and exhaustion. The peaceful spring fauna accentuated the eventful day. They stared at the granite column rising above them and thought of their journey across Sunset Peak.

"When you look at it from here, it doesn't look that challenging. But you have made a believer out of me, Laura. The terrain here is unforgiving. After a hike like that, I'm wondering if I've ever been in shape at all!"

"These mountains can fool you. Hiking them can wear you out," Laura said. "I'm glad you came out here with me."

"Me too. Make sure you can get us back to that inlet. And please take the easier route, if there is one."

"How long do you think it will take them to get here," Laura asked.

Elise checked her watch. "After what I told him, I know Gene is motivated now. He should be here any minute. With them setting up on the other side of Charon's Garden, it shouldn't take them very long to get here. We can set up first and then decide if we should do split operations."

"Is Jeff coming?" Laura asked.

"Yes, I believe he is." She watched Laura nod slightly. "I saw you two after dinner last night. I'm guessing he asked you out?"

Laura turned toward Elise with harbored enthusiasm. She was hoping for the right moment to ask about Jeff. "Yes. We are having dinner tonight."

"Hmm," Elise mumbled.

Laura waited for a further response. Fearing Elise's sudden silence would end the budding discussion, she instigated the conversation further. "How long have you known Jeff?"

Elise adjusted her sock. "Long enough." Elise smiled. "Jeff is a character. He makes me laugh. He is full of life and has charm and personality. He is fun to be around, but he can also be the biggest jerk I have ever known."

"What happened? Did he do something to you?"

"Nothing that can't be forgiven. Karen might have something contrary to say about that. But things happen, I guess."

"Is Karen his girlfriend?" Laura asked with peaked interest.

"Ex-girlfriend. She's one of our team members. That's how they met. I'm no romantic, but Jeff is a tease. He comes across like a flirt with the romantic gestures, the suave look, and all the sweet-talking, but he tends to put Jeff first. I've seen him get pretty singular when it comes to commitment, even if it's just a date."

"You seem to know him rather well. What happened with Karen?" Laura inquired.

Elise noticed Laura's intrigue and chose her words with caution. "From what I know, he took an interest in one of Karen's friends, and it didn't end well for them."

"Oh," Laura replied.

Elise retreated from any further specifics. "In a lot of ways, he's just Jeff. But I can tell you this, he is a lady's man. Make no mistake about that. At least he thinks he is."

"Does he have a girlfriend now?" Laura asked.

Elise rolled her window down and leaned against the door. "For all I know, he has twenty girlfriends. Whoever captures that man's heart someday will probably get a medal for resiliency." She took a drink of water and faced Laura. "So, why all the questions about Mr. Finbow?"

Laura began to blush. "I think he's cute. We seemed to relate to each other while we were talking on the way to Charon's Garden. I know I don't know him that well, but from what I've seen so far, I like him. You're right though, he is quite charming."

"You don't know him at all. Don't rush anything. I don't mean to dash any hopes, but keep in mind that we don't plan to be here very long. Have fun, but don't hang your heart out there too far, no matter how charming he is."

Laura felt dejection creep through her. She disregarded Elise's words and continued reveling with warm infatuation. "I'll enjoy the time we have and see where it goes. Who knows, you all could be here for a while after what you experienced today."

"Sure, we could be, but Jeff can come and go as he pleases. I asked him along for historical reference, but he is not a full-time team member." Elise began to feel as though she had spoken too much. "Look, I'm not trying to turn you off to him. All I'm saying is be careful. You seem like a very nice young woman. I wouldn't want to see you get hurt."

"It's okay. I'm curious."

A vehicle repeatedly honked behind them. Startled, both ladies turned to see Jeff waving behind the steering wheel. He parked the car and motioned for the passenger to get out with him.

"That was fast," Elise stated. "Who is that with him? It doesn't look like Gene."

They watched the passenger slowly emerge from the vehicle. Laura gasped, "That's my father."

They exited the truck and met the two men between the vehicles. Elise welcomed both of them while Laura gazed at Jeff. She offered Wil a sharp glance and then returned her attention back upon Jeff.

"Where is Gene?" Elise asked.

"Mike and Tommy are on their way from the airport, so Gene stayed at the other site to wait for them. I did bring a surprise, though," Jeff motioned toward Wil. "We found this gentleman knocking on our doorstep at the cabin. Seems he is looking for a certain daughter of his and came inquiring with us. Which was a good thing for me, too, as I was looking for the same girl myself." Jeff grinned at Laura.

"That's fine, but what about setting up a site here? Did he change his mind?" Elise inquired. "We're wasting precious daylight."

"No. He was hoping you would consider Mr. Brooks as a volunteer to replace him. They talked it over, and Gene didn't think you would mind. Mr. Brooks sounds like he knows these mountains rather well anyway. Gene appeared to be very interested in the opportunity at Charon's Garden. He knows you won't go back there after getting sick. He said to radio him if you want to discuss it any further," Jeff replied. "If you all don't mind, I'd like to talk to Laura for a minute." Elise spoke with Wil as Jeff escorted Laura to the back of the car. Wil reluctantly watched her walk away while struggling to focus on Elise.

"Why did you bring him here?" Laura asked.

"Whoa, hold on there, ma'am. I'm just the delivery guy. He showed up asking where you were, and we offered to bring him to you. He *is* your father, you know. It wasn't like I was going to tell him no. I was kind of surprised to find out you were at our cabin and didn't want to see me," Jeff said.

"I needed to clear some things up with Elise. I wish you would have let me know my father was coming out here."

"What's the big deal? He wanted to know, so we told him. I heard you and Elise had an interesting hike this morning. I wish I could have muscled in on some of that time with you. Have I fallen to second place?" Jeff asked.

"No. We still have our date tonight though, don't we?"

"Uh, yeah, about that. It seems I've been volunteered to help out with the Charon's Garden site tonight. Gene wants to set up field operations, tents and all. But the good news is we are staying much longer than I thought, thanks to you and your new hiking buddy over there." Jeff pointed at Elise. "Can I get a raincheck on our date? Gene and Elise are paying my way, so I hope you understand. But I don't want to miss out on any more chances to be alone with those beautiful brown eyes of yours."

"Easy, Mr. Suave. I'm not so sure I want to forgive you for bringing my father out here. If you take him back, I'll consider that raincheck."

"Sorry, boss's orders on that one. And what's with this *suave* stuff? Where did that come from?" Jeff asked.

Laura laughed. "Long story. So that's it, huh? You tease me with a date and then dump me for some glorified camp out?"

Jeff leaned toward Laura. "If I can sneak over here later, I will. I'll make it up to you. I want every minute I can with you. I know it may seem rushed, but I don't know how much time we will actually have here. I want you to know that I think you are beautiful, and I can't wait to get to know you more."

Laura moved closer to Jeff. "Me too." Jeff took her hands and touched his lips softly against Laura's. She closed her eyes and welcomed the gentle moment. Her heart raced with emotion as they parted, still staring at each other.

"You are hard to resist. I'm really crazy about you." Jeff rubbed her forearms.

"I love…um, I mean, I'm crazy about you, too." Laura blushed and looked away. "I'm sorry, I didn't mean to say that. The first part, I mean." She began to get frustrated.

Jeff touched her chin and slowly turned her head. He kissed her again on the cheek. "Don't be sorry." Jeff calmed her embarrassment and led her back to the truck. They touched hands and intertwined their fingers as they approached Elise and Wil.

"I spoke with Gene. He wants to rally over there. He said Karen and the guys are due to arrive soon. He wants to hear what they have to say and determine teams after that," Elise stated. "Mr. Brooks, if you are serious about volunteering, I would really appreciate it if you would join me. I could use your expertise when we set up here."

Wil nodded. "Can it be the three of us?"

Elise turned toward Jeff and answered him. "Yes, it most certainly can be. Jeff, go on ahead and let Gene know we're coming. I'm sure you understand."

"It doesn't look like I have a choice." He faced Laura and then addressed Wil. "I guess the job has its demands. Mr. Brooks, it was a pleasure speaking with you on the way out here. Elise, try not to scare them half to death with your dreams of the apocalypse. And you," Jeff turned toward Laura. "I'll see you in a little while."

"I hope so." They squeezed hands in front of Elise and Wil. Jeff backed the car on to the road and waved. Laura waved in return as Jeff blew her a kiss.

Wil watched the romantic scene and stepped between Laura and Elise. "If you don't mind, I'd like to have a word with my daughter."

"Of course. I need to gather my things anyway. Take your time."

Laura glared at Wil and walked toward the road. Wil nodded at Elise appreciatively and pursued Laura. Laura crossed the highway and entered the woods without stopping.

"Laura, wait a minute," Wil said.

Laura swung around. "No, you wait a minute! What are you doing out here? I came out here to get away from you and how weird you've been acting. And don't even think about saying you're sorry. It would be a worthless gesture that you don't really mean anyway."

"Please, let me speak."

"No! How dare you burn mom's journal. That was just as much mine as it was yours. She wrote that journal for me. I've tried to ignore what you did and even go on as if nothing happened. But I can't. Not anymore. You are acting so strange lately and not even talking to me. But burning mom's journal? How could you do that?"

"It was a mistake. I didn't mean for it to fall in the fire," Wil stated. "It's difficult to explain. But if you would…"

"Explain? Explain what, dad? What is there to explain? Was there something I wasn't supposed to see? Did mom say something I wasn't supposed to know about? What?" Laura yelled.

Wil waited for her to calm down. "To some extent, yes."

"Yes, what?" Laura paused. "Are you hiding something?"

Wil remained silent. He observed his daughter with remorse. The developing pain of his decision and then accidentally burning all of Ayita's journal was now taking its toll. He knew this would happen with Laura, but the cost was becoming more than he could bear. "There are some things that are better left unsaid. And sometimes, finding an explanation or an answer can only make things worse. That is happening between us now. At the time, I thought I was protecting you. After your mother died, I only wanted to keep you from any more harshness. There were things in your mother's journal that I struggled with because they only brought more pain. Even the memories. But, some of what was written in there only brought confusion. I did what I did because I wanted to protect you. I didn't know what else to do. Even as I stand here, I still have not gotten over the loss of your mother. That was over ten years ago. I will try to do better. For you and for me." Wil looked up at the sky. "I've watched you grow up so fast. Now, you will go away to college and start your life to become an adult. I want to spend more time with you while you are here. Before the world takes you away from me, too. And I don't want anything to come between us."

"Dad, none of this makes sense. You, standing by the fire pit with her journal and then it falls into the fire? What were you doing out there with it anyway? That was the last little piece of mom that I wanted." Laura began to cry. "You may have burned it to protect me for whatever reason, but you aren't the only one that still misses her. I wanted that journal so I would *not* forget her. No matter how hard I try, I am starting to forget her. And it hurts so much."

Wil opened his arms. Laura relented and stepped to embrace. They cried together, sobbing with sheltered pain that transcended a decade. Neither answered each other to their satisfaction, but the verbal onslaught between them became too much. They contemplated the reality before them and decided without words to simply live for the moment.

"I am sorry I did this to you. You are my prized possession. I love you so much. I hope, in time, you will forgive me." Wil kissed her forehead and wiped her cheeks.

"I miss mom."

Wil choked with emotion. "I know, honey. I do too." They continued their embrace and silently surrendered to each other. They walked together toward the truck.

Elise saw them coming and greeted them with an avid welcome. "Good timing, you two. If all is well, I'd like to get some supplies before we make our way to the other site. I'm not that excited about going back over there, but we can get what we need for Sunset Peak. Mr. Brooks, I'm glad you are with us. I hope you and I can get to know each other better." Wil nodded his response.

"What exactly is your plan?" Laura asked.

Elise opened the passenger door and looked up at the mountain. "To go find some answers."

* * * * * * *

Finding Sunset Peak

The wind whistled through the trees beckoning the early onset of spring. Each branch portrayed a hint of green from the new fauna. Winter still held a finite grasp on the landscape with its variable temperatures. The warm days teased winter's end until another volatile cold front extended the season a few days. The unpredictable Oklahoma weather kept everyone guessing for what the day would actually bring.

Another gust barreled across a nearby pasture. The distinct flow of the changing wind became visible in the rolling waves of tan and brown grasses. Gene opened the tent flap and watched the surge impact the broadside of the canvass dwelling. He checked the straps on either corner and held on to the frame. He noticed two men approaching with large backpacks and cases in their hands.

"They're here!" Gene left the tent and hurried across the field to help with their gear. "I was beginning to think you all had gotten lost."

Mike and Tommy Blackburn extended their hands. "You weren't kidding when you said remote. How did you find this place?" Mike asked.

"We got the help of some locals. We will be putting your tech skills to the test out here. We're running split operations. Jeff is in the tent helping me cover the Charon's Garden area, and Elise will be on the other side of that mountain with those locals I told you about, Laura and her father, Wil. I'm feeling good about our chances here. This whole area has several windows of opportunity."

"It sure looks like you have been busy. Nice tents. Do you plan on inviting the Army? These things are huge," Tommy asked.

"I got them from a surplus store in town. Three should suffice. Two for work and sleeping and the other for supplies and the rental generator." Gene glanced across the field. "Where is Karen? I booked you all on the same flight."

"She's coming. She took a later flight. She kept going on about finding another source back at Tombstone," Mike stated. "She said it was worth the delay."

"It better be. Well, come on, let's get you guys to your tent. I'm anxious to hear what you have to say."

"Yeah, me too." Jeff exited the tent and greeted the brothers. "Come on in and drop your gear. What did my counterpart at the historical society have to say?"

"In a word, nothing," Tommy said. "And when we mentioned your name, he said he never heard of you."

"Hmm. I guess I was thinking of someone else. He said nothing? What do you mean?" Jeff asked.

"We showed him the still shots, each frame, one at a time. We didn't say how we got them or even who we are. He reviewed them and said they looked like cheap knock-offs from a theatrical play. He wasn't impressed," Tommy stated.

"No confirmation on Wyatt Earp or Doc Holliday, huh?" Gene asked. "What about Poker Face?"

"Karen handled that one," Mike replied. "But from what we saw, that historian didn't give her much attention either. He came off with an attitude as if he didn't want to talk about what we asked him. He did get strangely quiet when we first showed him the still shot of Poker Face but handed it back to Karen. Tommy and I left after that."

"What did Karen do?" Jeff asked.

"The historian continued talking with her. I don't know what they said."

Jeff sat back on his cot. "Another dead end. And that, gentlemen, is why I gave up on all of this last time. No leads, no references, no history."

"Not so fast," Tommy said. He reached in to his case and handed Jeff a plastic bag. "We did manage to buy this from the historian. He said it was a collector's piece and that he only had a few copies left. He was going to sell us two copies, but the other one had a page ripped out of it. And Gene, it wasn't cheap. You owe me forty bucks."

"Don't look at me! Your fellow historian right there in front of you has the checkbook on that one," Gene responded.

Jeff opened the bag revealing a hardback book. He read the title, "From Mines to Mysteries."

"The historian said it's about the early days of Tombstone and surrounding mining towns. Check out page 33," Tommy said.

Jeff thumbed through the pages. "Wait, is this…"

"Your map?" Mike asked.

Jeff sat silent and reviewed the detailed drawing. "This is it. It looks just like the one I have. Same size and everything. Where did that historian get this book?"

"I don't know, but that's what we thought when we saw the map," Mike stated. "When we saw the title of the chapter, we had a hunch it was your map."

Jeff read the chapter title. "Forgotten Maps of the Arizona Territory."

"What do you think?" Tommy asked.

"And you said that historian had another copy with a page ripped out?"

"Yes. He showed us. In fact, I think it was the same page as this map," Tommy said.

"Unreal." Jeff looked away in disgust. "It has to be the same map that girl gave me. I bet she ripped it out of that book." He focused on the hardcover. "Guys, you did alright with this. But unfortunately, it may be like the photos—another dead end. I searched southeast Arizona for weeks trying to figure out this map. None of the mountains, terrain features, or symbols matched anything in that area. And no one I talked to had ever seen or heard of that map." Jeff continued to study the page and narrative.

"We do have one more thing to show you in the book. This one will put your head in a spin," Tommy stated. He turned to the page and stepped away. "Check out this picture. Look at the guy standing to the left on the second row. The guy standing in front of him obstructs the view somewhat, but you can still see him."

Jeff stared at the black and white photo and held the picture in the light. "You've got to be kidding me. Poker Face?"

"Yep. That's got to be him. I know the photo is black and white, but his coat is plaid, and he has that same hat. You can see his trousers too," Tommy added. "This guy obviously didn't have a very big wardrobe. His facial features are very similar to the still shots we have from the Bird Cage Theater. It isn't undeniable, but the comparison is striking. The names are listed at the bottom of the photo."

Jeff read the name, "Owen K. Corr. So, Poker Face does have a real name."

"And it says in the reading that he was a miner there in Tombstone. He even struck it rich from one of his digs," Tommy said. "It says he buried his treasure somewhere in the Tombstone area, which is what the map supposedly leads to."

"That validates what Jennifer Tanner said, too," Gene stated. "Remember, she thought he might be a miner, only from this area."

Jeff became visibly upset. "After all the research I've done on this guy, all the time spent and all of the wasted effort only to find everything I ever needed to know about Owen K. Corr was right here in this book. Could someone please tell me how I could have missed this? I have never heard of this book before. Who is the author?" Jeff slammed the book shut and checked the front cover.

"I think it is Al Silver," Tommy said. "Who is also the historian we talked to at the historical society."

"It's the same guy? I don't know any Al Silver. Apparently, I don't know much at all. Gene, why don't you call this Al Silver and see if he can provide you some historical reference. Obviously, his stinking book has all of the answers!" Jeff threw the book on the cot and stormed out of the tent.

"You still owe me forty bucks!" Tommy yelled.

"Let's not let a little drama ruin the reason I have you all here," Gene stated. "Let Jeff cool off for a while. Do you guys remember The Little Bighorn?"

"How could we forget?" Mike asked. "Are you expecting that level of adventure here too?"

"Yes. Because this opportunity may be a lot like that one was. All on foot and completely mobile," Gene answered. "Be ready to embrace the variables of nature."

"Here? The Little Bighorn was grassy pastures with gentle rolling hills. The terrain here could eat that for breakfast. We saw the landscape coming in, Gene. Are you nuts? This place is as rugged as it gets," Mike stated. "This looks like the granite capital of Oklahoma."

"That's why we have you," Gene answered. "I know you can make it work. We will take you to the general location. It's not far. Tommy, you and Jeff will join me at the site while Mike and Karen operate from here in the tents. I couldn't go too far in from the main road, so this is as far as the base camp can go."

"Where's Elise?" Tommy asked.

"She's working another site with Laura and Wil. She may have her own opportunity brewing just on the other side of that mountain up ahead. She's had more dreams, so there's no stopping her now. They will be here soon. You guys get the gear ready and set up the mobile units. I hope you got plenty of rest on the plane. I want to get out there by sundown, and I plan on making this an all-nighter with shifts."

"We've been sitting most of the day. We're ready," Tommy said.

They unloaded their equipment and began setting up the base camp. Gene turned on the generator and provided instant power to their operation. Each team member executed their duties with routine precision. They enjoyed the experience of working outdoors. The level of excitement always seemed to escalate as compared to the typical encounters inside a building. The challenges of remote sites meant less equipment and indoor amenities. Their skills with adversity and ingenuity were constantly tested. They enjoyed the challenges of working outdoors and confronting the inevitable mishaps that nature always seemed to provide.

Mike and Tommy ran the cables and connected the communication system. Content with the field set up, Gene engaged the power switch and brought the tent to life. They checked each console and ran several diagnostics. Satisfied with their work, they began testing their mobile gear.

"One of you go yell at Jeff to come get his gear ready," Gene asked.

Mike leaned out of the tent and called for Jeff. "He's coming. He still doesn't look too happy."

Jeff threw the tent flap open and walked toward his gear. "I don't want to hear a word. Let's get going."

Tommy snickered behind Jeff's back. "Hey, Jeff. The next time you are in Tombstone, would you mind having Mr. Silver autograph that book? I'd really appreciate it." Mike, Gene, and Tommy erupted in laughter.

"Go ahead. Laugh your head's off," Jeff replied. Each man laughed harder. "You can't leave it alone, can you?" He looked at his mobile pack. "And why is my signal alarm going off? Did you guys mess with that too?"

"What are you talking about?" Tommy asked.

Mike grabbed Jeff's harness and checked his readout. "Did you run a diagnostic on your mobile gear today?"

"Of course. I got the best battery installed before you guys took them all," Jeff replied.

Mike adjusted Jeff's equipment and moved to the main console. "Tommy, check this out."

The two men stared at the large computer screen. "He's getting a reading." They looked at their own gear. "Switch them on." All at once, each mobile unit began to register individual readings.

Gene leaned over the console. "What is it?"

Tommy checked his digital map. "Either we all need to reboot, or this is the largest readout I've ever seen. Something big is generating a lot of energy around this area, northwest of here."

"A window?" Gene asked.

Tommy checked his readings again. "I don't know. It's too big to be a window. I've never seen anything like it. If the system is reading the signal correctly, the source is huge!"

"What is this dot? It keeps blinking." Gene pointed at the screen.

Mike and Tommy leaned closer to the screen. "That's a classic indication of a window, but that can't be. We don't have a motivator set up anywhere yet to detect one."

"Let's go." Gene wrapped his harness straps over his shoulders and secured his backpack. "Mike, you stay here and guide us to that location over the radios." Jeff and Tommy fastened their gear and ran out of the tent behind Gene. "Make sure you sync to the signal. Do you have an azimuth yet?" Gene yelled and ran toward the tree line.

"What about night vision?" Tommy asked.

"It won't be dark for hours. It shouldn't take that long. Come on!"

"Gene, radio check, over," Mike called over the radio.

"Loud and clear, Mike," Gene responded.

"Okay, I have all three of you on my radar. Your transponders are working well. Keep going north. You should be coming to a forest first, and then it gets rugged at the base of that first ridgeline."

"What about the window? Are you still reading it?" Jeff asked.

"Yes. It hasn't changed. It's still in what looks like a small cove surrounded by trees and a rock pile," Mike replied.

The three men hurried through the woods. They high-stepped over fallen trees and branches. The late afternoon sun began to lower along the horizon casting shadows throughout the forest. Thickets and dense undergrowth congested the forest floor causing the men to split up in search of easier routes. They reached the end of the forest and began negotiating the rising slope of the foothill. Large granite boulders lie scattered across the terrain. Each man spread out across the rise headed for the top. The wind began to increase as they ascended. They reached the highpoint of the ridge and observed the unobstructed view before them.

Massive rocky slopes rose high above the area. The mountains appeared as rolling waves of granite that continued upward, forming an impenetrable barrier across the region. The natural rock setting glowed in sunset hues of orange, red, and amber. Small oak trees and cedars shrouded the many valleys and ravines between the mountains. Several granite contours rose one behind the other. Each contour shared deep valleys with sheer cliffs. Giant boulders, scattered across the landscape, added to the natural obstacles of the area.

The three men caught their breaths. "Man, and I thought the Huachuca Mountains were tough to hike. This place is unreal. Look at how the terrain keeps rolling. It looks like there is one mountain, but there are actually four ridgelines. There is no way we can go mobile here at night, Gene," Tommy stated.

"It's rough. But think about it, guys. This is the perfect place for a window. It's remote, nearly inaccessible, and seems to have some apparent significance." Gene reached for his radio. "Mike, talk to me. How close are we?" Gene waited for a response. "Mike, come back. Do you still see the window?" The radio hissed with static. "Guys, check your radios."

Jeff clicked his transmitter. "Mike, are you there?"

The radio screeched a deafening sound causing each man to hold their radios away from their faces. Bewildered, they looked at each other as a scratchy voice yelled at them through the static.

"J...F"

"Did you hear that?" Tommy asked and held his radio closer.

"K...F"

"That sounded different than the first," Tommy stated.

Their radios transmitted a loud burst of static and went silent. The three men waited for a viable explanation from each other.

"Gene, guys, are you there?"

All three men shuddered at the sound of Mike's voice. Gene clicked his transmitter. "Mike, did you hear a voice on your end?"

"No, I thought my radio was dead. I changed the battery. Why are you guys still standing there? That window is east of you. You went too high. The larger signal is too far away, even for where you are now. Double back and stay on the channel. I'll guide you there."

"Are you taping our transmissions?" Gene asked.

"Yes, never stopped."

They hurried off of the slope and followed Mike's directions. They navigated the terrain to a level area near the refuge boundary fence as Mike continued to guide them toward the middle of a small field.

"Guys, wait..." Jeff stopped. "Gene, what looks familiar about where we are?"

Gene looked across the landscape. Out of breath, he appeared puzzled by Jeff's question. Suddenly, his expression became one of acknowledgment. "This is where Elise got sick."

Jeff pointed to a granite shelf ahead. "Up there is where she fell to her knees. And look, those cedars. I remember Jennifer Tanner saying something about a cedar grove when she saw..."

Gene ripped his radio off of his harness. "Mike, how far is that window from us now?"

"Maybe forty yards."

"Go!" Gene yelled. "Spread out and meet at that cedar grove. Start your video."

They ran toward the location of the signal. Jeff sprinted for the cedar grove while Gene and Tommy took opposite sides. Jeff bounded over the rocks keeping his sight on the trees. A small cactus tripped his stride, sending him crashing against a boulder. The cactus needles pierced his shoes and buried deep into his left foot. His harness camera lens shattered against the rock. He scrambled to his feet and hustled toward the cedars. Gene yelled at him to stop. Ignoring his call, Jeff pushed through the lower cedar limbs to the clearing on the other side.

A small man wearing a red and black checkered wool coat and brown trousers stood at the corner of the confined opening. A faded orange cap covered his face. Jeff observed the man in detail. His gray, wrinkled beard and dirty hands accentuated his rough appearance. He watched as the man slowly raised his head. Jeff struggled to see his face against the glare of the sun. The long bill of his cap lifted, exposing his entire face.

"Ah!"

Jeff turned to see Tommy staring at the man. The man turned toward Tommy. Tommy dropped to his knees, holding his face. "Tommy!" Jeff watched him fall to the ground with both hands over his face. He turned back to see the man standing in front of him.

"Jeff, help!" Tommy said.

Desperate, Jeff confronted the man with a spontaneous reaction. "Owen Corr!" The man slowly backed away in response to the name. His face remained directed upon Jeff. Jeff felt his face become numb. His eyelids and mouth became limp. His breathing became erratic as he fell to his knees, trying to overcome the confusion in his mind. He struggled to watch the man walk toward the granite rock shelf.

Gene stopped at the top of the shelf. Jeff observed the man face him and raise his arm. He pointed at Jeff. The man lowered his arm and moved away. As he neared the opening to leave, Jeff watched him disappear in front of him.

Chapter 9

"Stop! Right there, look. Do you see his face? He's right there!"

The group gathered around the computer monitor. "I don't see anything. The angle is bad, and Gene's camera was too far away. So was Tommy's camera. I'm sorry, Jeff. It isn't conclusive enough and enhancement won't work on something that far away," Mike said.

"Can you try running it through the filtering? Maybe the processing can…"

"We did that, Jeff. Neither camera had good angles of him. There is no way to tell for sure that image is Poker Face. Or are we calling him Owen Corr now?" Mike forwarded through the video.

"If I had not fallen, we could have had a close up of him. I was right there, Gene. I was right in his face!" Jeff said.

"Yeah, you ruined your camera. It will need to be replaced," Mike said.

"But it was still great footage of him as we approached," Gene said. "I would like to validate it with Jennifer Tanner. Let's see if we can get her out here to confirm it for us. Jeff, you still have her number, don't you?"

Jeff stared at the monitor trying to avoid Gene's questions. "Yeah, sure."

"It looks like you fellas have been busy over here. It's a good thing we came when we did. Play the recording from your radios. We want to hear it, too," Elise stated. Elise, Laura, and Wil moved closer to the speakers inside the tent.

"I haven't had a chance to clean it up yet. It has a lot of static and background noise. We each checked the feedback and no one was transmitting when this recorded," Mike stated. He played the audio several times as the group listened. They analyzed each word and questioned what the other heard for verification. Laura and Wil watched the team perform their research with precision. The experience brought them intrigue and some slight curiosity for the actual degree of sanity by each team member. Wil rolled his eyes with growing impatience. He checked his watch a second time as Laura nudged him to stop.

"What does JFKF mean?" Elise asked.

"I don't know. The voice said the letters very slowly," Mike answered.

"Did you all see anyone else out there when this was happening on the radio?" Elise continued inquiring.

"No. All we had was the transmission," Gene replied.

"It sounds scary to me," Laura whispered to Elise. "Could it be Poker Face?"

"We all thought that too, but I'm not sure how to prove something like that. What gets me is how it was said. He said it slowly, like he was reading the letters. I can't tell if he is saying two sets of letters separately or all together," Gene said.

Finding Sunset Peak

"So, you and Tommy felt like your faces became paralyzed and he backed away when you said his name. Did either of you feel like you were getting sick?" Elise asked.

"No," Gene answered. "Jeff said he might have, but nothing like what you went through. I believe that only had to do with you. I think it may be a connection he has with those that have a gift, like you, sweetheart. But then, how do we prove that?"

"Others have gotten sick. It's almost like there is a pattern, but then there isn't. It isn't consistent. If this were truly a window you three experienced, then all of this about faces getting paralyzed and spooky dialog on the radio would not have happened. It doesn't sound like science to me, but more like science fiction," Elise stated.

"Elise, don't start. Come on! You heard it yourself. Science or no science, we've got voices on the radio and some old guy up and disappearing right in front of us. How in the world do you expect any of us to prove anything scientific about any of this? Just because it may not be some *window in time* doesn't mean consideration can't be given to what you don't want to hear!" Jeff pushed the table and backed away from the group.

"Easy, Jeff. I know it has been an eventful day so far, but this is a good lead. All of them. Mike, continue washing that audio and try to isolate the voice. Tommy, get Jeff's camera replaced on his harness. I'm going to talk to Elise about her operation. Keep your heads in the game, and we will figure this out." Gene motioned for Elise to join him at the other table.

"Looks like we have a powder keg in here," Elise said.

"Jeff has been on edge since they brought in that book. And now that sighting seems to have pushed him over the edge. He saw Poker Face up close. He said he couldn't make out any facial features.

I think it scared him and he won't admit it," Gene replied. "He does seem frustrated, though. Almost like something else is bothering him."

"You never know with Jeff. Keep him with you for this one, okay?"

"Are you sure you want to do this? We don't even know Laura and Wil that well. Don't you think you are risking too much with them?" Gene asked.

"It's okay. Plus, it's not like we have much choice. We don't have enough to help out. But aside from all of that, I can't explain it. There is something about them that I can't figure out. Especially when I am around Wil. I think he knows something, but he won't let on. What's interesting is they both seem curious," Elise said.

"I don't like it. I know you are getting your dreams or whatever you want to call them now. But I don't know how solid this really is."

"Look. The signal is still coming from that direction. It's Sunset Peak. It's five times stronger than what you went after today. And the source of it is huge. I'm not passing this up," Elise stated.

"Alright, fine. You know we have a high potential opportunity right here. I'm taking all of the gear out to that cove Jeff led us to and see what we can find tonight. It will be dark in a couple of hours. You had better get going. You can take the mobile devices and see what you can come up with over there. If you get anything promising, let me know and I'll see who I can send over to you. Keep your radio close. Our phones are getting spotty reception out here. These granite mountains are impenetrable."

Elise rubbed her husband's hand. "This is what we live for. It's all about the science, remember?"

"I don't know," Gene answered. "I'm beginning to wonder if Jeff has a point. Maybe we are dealing with something beyond science. I know science is our foundation. But after all of this, I'm not so sure anymore. Be open to the possibility that the spiritual world may be conflicting with our pursuit of the science."

"If the science proves that's the case, then we will rule it out and move on. We don't deal with the dead, remember?"

"Yes, I know. But what if the dead are dealing with us? And we don't know it yet?"

Elise became flustered and thought for a reply that did not come. She changed her growing frustration toward a more obvious target. "If Jeff yells at me again, he's out of here. I'm not going to put up with his attitude again. It's always us having to tolerate his ego. Alive, dead, science or no science, I'm not going to relive another Little Bighorn with him."

Gene hugged her. "I'll talk to him. I didn't appreciate that outburst of his either. That was the risk we took inviting him back. You be careful over there. Science or no science, I want my wife back when this is over."

"I'll be fine. Now, tell me more about this signal you've found."

* * * * * *

Laura found Wil a chair and sat him at the corner of the tent. They watched the action unfolding from every team member. "I'm going to see what Jeff is doing. I'll be right back," Laura said.

"You're leaving me in the corner?" Wil asked. "Do I have to miss recess too?"

Laura ignored him and looked around the tent. "Excuse me, Tommy? Would you mind if my father looked at your book until we leave? We're waiting for Elise to finish and he's bored."

Tommy handed her the book. "Go ahead. There's a flashlight by the batteries if he needs more light."

Laura gave Wil the book and a flashlight. "Here, check this out. I'll see what is keeping Elise and then we will leave."

"Just stay away from that Jeff guy. He's trouble," Wil mumbled.

"Dad, read." Laura continued watching the commotion. Everyone scurried about as she moved next to Jeff. "Sounds like you had another experience today. Are you okay?"

Jeff tapped his fingers on the table, trying to calm his frustration. "Yeah. I get tired of Gene and Elise always having to prove everything. Listen to that! And they weren't there to stare at that guy in the face and watch him disappear. Some things cannot be defined by science."

"What did you mean when you told Elise that you don't want to hear it?" Laura asked.

"Ah, it was a jab at her that I will have to apologize for later on." Jeff checked to make sure Elise could not hear them. "Elise never wants to hear that some of our experiences could be nothing more than ghostly encounters. The spiritual world and science don't mix, according to her. Gene can be more accepting about it, but Elise doesn't want to hear it. She wants an explanation for everything, and it has to be proven by science. It's so odd. You'd think Gene, being the scientific one, would be that way. He's far more receptive to other possibilities than she is."

"If you all encounter things like you did today, I'll bet that can be frustrating," Laura added.

"Yes, it can be. Gene had a good point earlier; it was science that led us to the signal that we thought was a window. It was the same place we saw…" Jeff turned around toward Gene and Elise. "Hey! What if that actually was Owen Corr, and he passed through a window? The signal was there in that cove. It had energy. Maybe the window was there the whole time, and I didn't see it in the daylight?"

"Impossible," Gene responded. "That means he can pass back and forth through time. That wouldn't be a window, but more like a door, if there is such a thing. Sorry, Jeff. Even with our equipment and the science, no one can walk back and forth through time. All we can do is view time through the windows when we can find them."

"Okay, fine. Then say it, Gene. We saw a ghost. We saw a ghost walking around in the Wichita Mountains, and it spoke to us on the blasted radio. Go on, say it!"

"Jeff, you need to calm down," Elise said.

"Calm down? This whole thing has become a test of the obvious. There are no windows. There is nothing that gives a glimpse back in time, and there is no science! Not the science you're looking for. What if we are simply being allowed to look at the spirits of people from a time in history and that is all there is to it? After what we encountered today, maybe this is where we are at now. We find a place that others say is haunted, we check it out with some high-tech equipment and realize all we are seeing is a bunch of ghosts walking around with no purpose whatsoever."

Everyone remained quiet. Each team member absorbed Jeff's words for their own contemplation. Their experiences provided the only argument for wisdom to Jeff's dialogue. Each member knew Jeff was only verbalizing what was researched or pondered since the group's inception. The commonality was between them, but the decision to be made was how each member chose to confront it.

Gene approached Jeff as a mentor to his aggravated stance. "Everything you said is why we are here. To pursue answers. To ask *what if*. If that is all we discover, then so be it. That may be what you have to come to terms with, Jeff."

"That's great!" Jeff said. "If that's the case, then why don't we consult Mike and Tommy's precious book from their all-knowing historical society author? The book says it all! Never mind the years of research I did on this guy. But the mystery book has the answers!"

"Is this what you're throwing a fit about? That book? You're jealous of what some other historian wrote in some book?" Gene asked.

"Not just the book, Gene. All of this. One big dead end as usual, like that stupid treasure map. There is no science here, no windows in time, nothing. There never was. Come on, let me hear you both say it! We'll even use the facts of everyone's favorite, all-knowing book. Repeat after me…we are following the ghost of a dead miner named Owen K. Corr from Tombstone, Arizona that made a treasure map to nowhere!"

"Owen Keaton Corr wasn't from Tombstone. He didn't mine a day in his life, and that book you keep hollarin' about is nothing more than a bunch of lies and garbage."

A stunned silence filled the tent as the group turned in unison to see Karen Farris and an old man standing at the opening. Karen waved a joyous greeting. "Hello everyone! How's that for an entrance?" Karen ushered the old man toward the center of the tent. "This is Ed Silver. He's the source that I stayed behind for. It took some begging, but here we are. Sorry we're late."

Jeff approached Ed. "You're that guy from the Bird Cage Theater. You let me in the front door that night."

"Yep. I remember you. The cocky one. And you were late."

Jeff ignored his comment. "What did you say your last name is?"

"Silver," Ed replied. "And before you ask, yes. Albert Silver, the author of that book you were goin' on about, is my brother. He goes by Al to the select few that know him."

"Oh. Well, I didn't mean to say anything bad about your brother. I haven't had a chance to read all of his book, but I'm sure it is…"

"Garbage!" Ed interrupted and took a seat. "Al couldn't write his name twice correctly without help. Toilet paper has a better chance at gettin' published than that nonsense he put to print. And his book has the same purpose as the toilet paper." Karen giggled and covered her mouth.

"But Al told us it was published," Tommy stated.

"Far from it," Ed replied. "Al was so pig-headed about that book that he went out and started his own publishing company. He gave it some fancy name and used his influence in the historical society to gain attention. He printed all of fifteen copies of that worthless thing. Once folks realized he had no references and nothing to back his claims, he couldn't give the copies away. His so-called company went belly-up before the ink was dry on the pages. That book of his is worthless."

"Great," Tommy said. "Forty bucks for a limited first edition. A real bargain!" Gene and Mike snickered as Tommy scowled at them.

"Conned you out of forty big ones, eh? Don't worry, young man. I'll get your money back for you. It won't be the first time," Ed said.

"You said Owen Corr wasn't a miner?" Jeff asked.

Ed chuckled and slapped the table next to him. "Nope. The only thing that man ever dug was the hole he put his life in. He wasn't a miner. As far as I know, he never held a job. Very few people, with any kind of a reputation, hire anyone with a criminal record."

"Criminal?" Jeff questioned.

"Yep. Ole Keaton was a thief. And he wasn't a very good one at that. Oh, sure, he was around the mining business from time to time. But only long enough to steal about one hundred and sixty thousand dollars' worth of another man's find. That's why he's not from Tombstone. He got as far away from Tombstone as he could. The son of a gun couldn't show his face in town without the law or some bounty coming down on him. The man had about as much sense as the good Lord gave a pickaxe."

"If your brother's book is wrong, how is it that you know so much about Owen Corr?" Gene asked.

"And how do you know his middle name is Keaton? I didn't read that anywhere in the book," Tommy added.

Ed looked at the group with a prideful grin, enjoying his authority with the conversation. "Because Owen Keaton Corr was my great uncle. He hated the name Keaton. I use it out of spite toward my brother. Darn fool. Keaton ruined the family's lineage to this day and that idiot brother of mine tried to salvage it with that stinkin' book of his."

"And that is why I begged Mr. Silver to come with me," Karen said. "Oh, and Gene, we need to talk about his plane ticket and a few other credit card type items, if that's okay?" Gene expressed a glaring tone at Karen's feeble grin.

"That explains a lot then," Elise said. "You certainly helped clear a few things up for us, Mr. Silver. I don't mean to be rude, but my new team and I need to get back to Sunset Peak before it gets dark."

"No, wait." Jeff leaned closer to Ed, relishing the negativity about the despised book. "Your brother mentions a map in his book. From what research I have done, I believe it is a treasure map. After all that you have said, I'm willing to bet the map might involve those one hundred and sixty thousand dollars. What do you know about the map?"

"Nothing."

Tommy laughed. "I've heard that before. No offense, Mr. Silver, but you and your brother do have one thing in common…saying the word *nothing* to a serious question. At least you aren't charging us forty dollars for it."

"Tommy, will you shut up about the forty dollars? Go ahead, Mr. Silver," Jeff said.

Ed chuckled at Tommy and turned his attention toward Jeff. "Let me guess, you're a treasure hunter, aren't you?"

"No sir, just a historian trying to make his mark on the world," Jeff answered in anger. Elise and Gene looked at each other.

Ed noticed everyone in the tent was focused upon him. The old story-teller enjoyed the avid attention that beckoned for his every word. "So, you want to know about the map, huh?" Everyone waited without answer. "Young lady, will you hand me my satchel?" Karen handed Ed an old leather bag. Ed opened the satchel and took out an envelope. He lifted the sleeve and placed a faded piece of paper on the table. "This is the original map that is copied in that book. If there are any copies out there, they all came from this. My great uncle drew this map. Now, as to what it means, where it leads to, and what is there to be found, I don't know."

"Owen Corr never said anything about it?" Tommy asked.

"Nope. But this map is the only thing that I count as truly genuine. I've searched for years and never found anywhere that matches to what is labeled on this map."

"Where have you searched," Jeff insisted.

"All of southeast Arizona, that's for sure. I even took a peek down south of the border once. I thought I had a terrain match near a small town in Mexico. But it didn't pan out," Ed replied. "From what I know about his life and where he roamed, whatever this map leads to is most likely somewhere in Arizona. And as far as any treasure is concerned, I don't know what it could be. But I'd venture to say that any value on it today would be quite a handsome find."

"After all that you have told us, I am really surprised you don't have any answers on the map, Mr. Silver," Jeff commented.

Ed stared at Jeff with an offended look. He narrowed his eyes and then sat back in his chair with a devious sneer. "I recall a certain young fella once tell me that life is good." Ed continued staring at Jeff. "He also told me he was chasin' the *what if*. Well, here we are, young man. How good is that *what if* now?"

Jeff nodded, trying not to disrespect the aged man. "I remember I said that to you in front of the Bird Cage Theater."

"What else did I say to you?" Ed asked.

Jeff rolled his eyes. "You said life is always good when the answers go my way."

"And I wouldn't want to be there when you find the answers that don't." Ed reached out and patted Jeff's shoulder. "I also recall you said that you would call me when you don't find those answers. And here I am."

Jeff nodded again, unable to think of any further questions through his frustration. "Yes, here you are. Imagine that. So now what?"

Ed leaned near Jeff's ear and whispered only for him to hear, "Now, I'd say you've learned a lesson in respect. Do you agree?"

Jeff gave him a humbled nod. "I guess so."

"Good!" Ed rubbed his beard in thought and made eye contact with the team. "Now, it's my turn to ask a question. One that I have been reluctant to ask ever since this young lady convinced me to come along with her on this escapade."

"What question is that?" Jeff asked.

Ed offered a tone of confusion to his words. "Why am I in Oklahoma talking about Owen Keaton Corr in the Wichita Mountains?"

Everyone in the tent laughed. Jeff rushed over to the monitor and typed in an enlarged still shot of his encounter. "If you can identify this man, you might answer your own question."

Ed observed the attire of the man in the picture. He scrolled the image several times, looking at the enhanced details of his clothes. "I can't say the clothes are all that strange to me. If my memory serves, I believe Owen had a coat like that. Not sure about the hat. Can you make out his face any better than this? It's blurry."

"Unfortunately, no. His face has been rather difficult to see on more than one occasion," Jeff said. "Sometimes, I think it is intentional."

"We gave him the nickname of Poker Face because of that," Tommy stated.

"Ha! Now that's the most sensible thing I've heard all day. He certainly spent his share at the gamblin' tables. I have to say, the clothes do look familiar, but without seeing his face, this picture is no better than that sorry book of yours. Where did you get this?"

"I took this standing right in front of him here today," Jeff replied. Ed's face exhibited apparent astonishment. "There is also a photo in your brother's book with Owen's name on it. He's wearing the same coat and hat."

Ed rubbed his beard again. "Yes, I'm familiar with that picture, now that you mention it." Ed paused for a moment, still staring at the digital image on the screen. "I must say, this is all rather shattering. But I guess I am not gettin' my head around the obvious indication that you believe this is Owen's ghost?" Jeff looked back at Gene and Elise, hiding his satisfaction with Ed's comment.

Gene moved between Jeff and Ed and extended his hand. "Mr. Silver, I'm Gene Saige. I'm not sure if you remember me, but if you don't mind, we would like to show you some more evidence that might answer your question and maybe help us out on that topic at the same time. But first, can I offer you something to eat or drink?"

Elise grabbed Gene's arm. "Laura, Wil, and I are leaving. I'll radio you later. Have fun with this. I hope Mr. Silver can lead you to an opportunity. And good luck with Jeff. I know you're going to need it."

Gene gave his wife a hug. "Maybe Mr. Silver can help us figure out this mess. If anything, we can sit around and have story time with him. You be careful. Don't overdo it and take some extra sets of mobile gear. I'll feel better about you if Laura and Wil have some technology on their backs."

Elise said her goodbyes to the group and motioned for Laura and Wil to join her. Laura approached Jeff on her way out of the tent. "I guess we still aren't getting that date? You are a busy guy, Mr. Finbow. What does it take to get some time with you?"

"It's been nuts. I wish you didn't have to see all of that. Trying to get answers from people that don't see you as a priority can be very frustrating."

"Tell me about it," Laura joked.

"I guess I asked for that one. Look, I promise I'll see what I can do here and then get over to your site as soon as I can. I didn't expect this old guy to show up, so I'll see what else he has to say and sneak over to you later. I'm glad I got to see you, even if it was for a little while."

"Me too."

"I know Elise will have radios at your site. Get one and tune it to channel five. That's my private channel. We can talk, and I'll let you know when I can get over there, okay?"

"Sure. I hope it all goes well for you."

Jeff kissed her on the cheek. "You all be safe. Elise can get kind of crazy when she is doing fieldwork."

"I think I have seen some of that already. Bye." Jeff waved and went back into the tent. Laura ran with elation to join Wil and Elise in the truck. She beamed with excitement and looked back at the tent hoping for one more glance at Jeff. She felt the soft touch of his kiss and yearned to stare into his eyes again. Even with all of the interferences for his time, the heartfelt connection they were experiencing seemed to magnify with each encounter. She opened the driver's side door, thinking of how she could gain more time with

Jeff. The developing adventure with Elise was becoming more of a hindrance with her desire for Jeff.

"I was beginning to think Jeff had talked you out of coming with us," Elise stated as Laura started the truck. "Is everything okay with you two?"

"As good as it can be, I guess. I wish we had more time, but I know you all didn't come over here for me," Laura replied.

"Once Gene gets everything set up, maybe you two can get some time. If this signal is as strong as this readout indicates, they may be joining us instead."

Laura drove toward Sunset Peak. "What is that thing?"

"It's a device used for detecting high energy and static electricity microbursts. In other words, it's a gadget Gene developed for tracking potential sources for windows," Elise answered.

"And what exactly does that mean?" Wil asked.

Elise showed him the meter and display on the device. "It means there is a very large signal located right here that could generate enough energy for a rip in time."

Laura peeked at the small screen on the device. "Dad, doesn't that look like Sunset Peak to you?"

Wil stared at the readout. "Yes. If that is what this arrow thing is pointing to. It's in the direction of the Peak from here."

Elise held up the device and made some adjustments. "I appreciate you two trying to help, but there is no way the signal could be the entire mountain."

"Why not?" Laura asked. "You said it was a large signal. It looks like the whole mountain to me."

"That would require more energy than I have ever seen. These time rips are exactly that, small openings with a high energy outburst that last a few seconds. Which is why this is so puzzling. I've never seen one last this long before. Gene's equipment can be quirky at times, so I'm sure it's not the mountain," Elise replied.

The cab of the truck became silent as they continued the drive to Sunset Peak. The winding road crossed varied terrain involving valleys and high ridgelines that tested the peculiar signal. Each pass behind the facing mountains interfered with the signal until they passed by openings between the peaks. The signal jumped with intensity as they neared the highway leading toward Sunset Peak.

"What if it is?" Wil questioned.

Laura and Elise looked at Wil. Laura saw her father staring out of the window as he asked. Her long history with her father led her to know that any time he appeared to be looking away only meant he was mentally staring directly at you. Observing Elise's uncertainty, Laura knew to ask for his clarification. "What do you mean?"

"What if that signal is Sunset Peak?"

"Dad, she just explained it. She said it is too big to…"

"If all of that gibberish I heard back there at your tent is true and this Owen fella just up and vanished in front of them, then what's to say your signal gadget isn't reading Sunset Peak? Didn't it read that other location too?"

Laura waited for Elise to respond, realizing her father had made a curious point. Elise watched Wil with a renewed vigor, hoping this was the moment they could begin communicating together. "I'm not sure I have an answer for you, Wil. I guess all I can say is let's go and find out."

They approached the intersection to the road leading to their destination. Wil noticed the empty parking lot of the Wichita

Mountains Wildlife Refuge headquarters building. "Laura, pull in to the parking lot."

Laura pressed the brakes. "What's wrong?"

"Pull over, please. Park over by that small billboard." Laura drove through the vacant lot and parked near a refuge information kiosk. Wil addressed Elise, "I heard what you and your friends are doing out here. I don't fully understand it, but if you, and only you, promise to help me, I can help you and your friends in return."

Elise became intrigued. Sensing Wil's sudden willingness and unprovoked motion for trust, she engaged without hesitation. "Certainly."

"Do you promise? Only you." Wil stared at Laura while talking to Elise.

"Yes, I promise."

Wil gave a profound observation of Elise that left her feeling reviewed for testimony. "Okay then."

"Can I ask what you need help with?" Elise questioned.

"In time." Wil opened the passenger door and reached underneath the bench. He placed Tommy's book on the seat. "The young man that bought this said I could read it." He opened the book and showed her the map. "I listened to that older gentlemen. He was right about this map. And that Jeff character was right, too."

"Right about what? They said they have looked all over, and it leads to nowhere," Laura said.

Wil let a slight grin crease across his lips. "Exactly. It does lead to nowhere, if they're looking in Arizona."

"Huh?" Laura was confused. Elise remained quiet with an anxious curiosity.

Wil turned the book toward the ladies and pointed at the map. "It isn't the map that's wrong. It's where they've been looking." Both ladies gave vivid attention to Wil's finger as he guided it across the map. "Let's start with these mountains. Look at how they are contoured. Notice the landmarks in relation to the mountains and the valleys. Do you see how distinct they are? They practically hide themselves on the map if you don't know the area." Elise and Laura continued to observe with waning patience.

"Now, look at the map in this book and compare it to this." Wil turned around and held the opened book near the billboard. A trail map of the Wichita Mountains Wildlife Refuge was pinned against it in a plastic cover. He placed the two maps next to each other. Elise and Laura pushed each other out of the truck to get to Wil. "If you compare the features of the book map to these features located right about here," Wil pointed to an area on the refuge map.

Elise and Laura gasped. Elise grabbed the book from Wil and pressed it against the refuge map. The comparison overwhelmed her. "Unbelievable. The map in this book is the Wichita Mountains!"

"Yes, but look closer." Wil guided his finger along the book map again. "If these lines and arrows on the book map mean anything, I'll bet you a lunch anywhere in town that it's leading to right about here." Wil adjusted and slid his finger along the refuge map.

Elise watched his finger stop at a point on the map. She leaned eagerly toward the refuge map and compared Wil's location to the book map several times. She jumped hysterically and hugged Wil with liberating joy. "This is incredible! Where's my radio?"

Laura observed the discovery for her own validation. Convinced the dramatic scene was genuine, she faced Wil. "Elise may not ask you until she calms down, but I will. How did you know?"

Wil took the book and opened it to the map. He held it in front of Laura and pointed at a small feature on the outside edge of the sketch. "Look."

Laura squinted at the tiny drawing. "Crab Eyes?"

"I know of no other place on earth with a feature like that. I noticed it right away."

"Yes, I'm sure you did," Laura added. "And I know why." They looked at each other in unison as Laura reached for his hand.

* * * * * * *

"Good grief, Mike! Can't you pull up a lousy digital map on this thing?" Jeff asked.

"I'm trying to image the area. Give me a minute! It's not like we live here. I don't know this place," Mike replied. "Help me out with this one. Oklahoma is north of the Red River, correct?"

"You've got to be kidding me!" Jeff grabbed the mouse and directed the computer search.

"It's the Great Plains, Jeff. There's a reason they didn't call it the Great Obvious. You try to find a feature with no reference point. I think that's why they called this area plain, you moron." Mike watched Jeff struggle and then move in front of the monitor to prevent him from seeing his mistakes. "We're waiting, genius."

"Is this thing even working?" Jeff asked. He slammed the mouse on the pad.

"Do we want a topographic or physical map?" Tommy asked from the other side of the tent. "Would a weather map do? I've also got some highway maps on the table."

"Does it look like there are any highways out here? What good would that do us? Come on, guys! We could have the treasure of a lifetime just sitting out there waiting for us, and we're in here trying to plan a road trip to Houston!" Jeff yelled.

"Instead of standing there barking like some lost dog, why don't you and that giant ego of yours just shut up?" Karen demanded. "Contrary to whatever the voices in your head tell you, you are not the one in charge."

Jeff leaned over and whispered, "Karen, if you hurry, you can still make the last flight out of Oklahoma City. And if not, I'm sure we can find your broom."

Karen grit her teeth. "You're such a jerk."

Gene stood in the middle of the tent, watching his team erupt in chaos. He held the radio near his ear, waiting for an answer from the beleaguered group. Surrendering to the bedlam, he sat next to Ed Silver and propped his arm against the table. Both men watched the drama play out in front of them.

"You know, I've seen traffic accidents with more serenity than these folks. Is it like this all the time?" Ed asked.

"Only when they know we may be on to something big," Gene replied.

"I've got it!" Tommy shouted. "It's a topographic map of Charon's Garden. It's not very recent, but it will do. Where is Ed's version of the map? I can scan it and put them side by side on the monitor."

"We can do that later. Put your topo on the monitor," Gene said. The group gathered around the screen and compared the two maps noting each feature of the sketch to the detailed topographic digital map. "Okay, Elise. We're in business. What else can you tell us?"

The transmission crackled through the static magnified by the speakers plugged in to the radio. "Wil says the two rocks on the ledge are called Crab Eyes. They are the eastern-most boundary of the book map. From your location, that large mountain at the top of the page is Sunset Peak. That is where we are headed now. It is north of you. Wil says to not pay attention to anything south. He thinks the details are more numerous because Owen Corr came through the mountains from the north. He says this is a guess, but he thinks Owen may have traveled here from Meers. It was a mining town in this area about the same time as Owen came to Oklahoma. It makes sense if you think about it. Tombstone was a mining town, so maybe Owen really was a miner and came to Meers looking for treasure? Anyway, Wil says that's why you aren't finding anything where you are at. You are too far south. The map stops where Owen stopped."

"Alright, so what about those features and lines south of Sunset Peak? What are those?" Gene asked.

"Wil says those are valleys. If the sketch is accurate, he thinks Owen crossed through the Charon's Garden Wilderness Area and stopped on the southern side. He is quite sure that large peak in the middle is Charon's Garden Mountain. That shaded part is a ridge. He thinks those areas with the dots are grasslands or fields."

"What about that funny looking feature? The one at the base of the ridge by all the circles?" Gene asked.

"The circles are boulders. We all agree the blackened square is the treasure. Wil isn't sure if that odd symbol is a tree, a cliff, or what. It looks like a half-moon with something next to it rising out of the ground. He says it might be a terrain feature that you could only distinguish if you were looking at it," Elise stated. "Either way, he says it's not far from your current location. We are almost to our parking area. That is all that Wil could distinguish from the sketch. Radio back if you need us or if you find anything. We need to hurry and hike out to our location before dark."

Gene said his farewell and ended the transmission. Everyone in the tent remained quiet. Each team member studied both maps in search of clues. Their verbal silence and mounting desperation created the sounds of shuffling papers and busy keyboards that filled the tent with an office-like environment. Notepads became covered with ink and were passed around for more ideas and clarifications. The details of the digital map compared to the limitations of the sketch became a rising frustration among the group. The once noisy onslaught of bickering and temperament had become a chamber of refined thought and focused contemplation.

"Where did you say you supposedly saw my uncle?" Ed asked.

Everyone ignored him as Gene politely pointed on the map. "I think it was right about here. There aren't many landmarks to really locate it very well."

Ed thought for a moment. "On the way here, Karen told me about some other girl you all met that had some experience out here too. Now, it's just a hunch, but do you happen to know where she saw him?"

Everyone stopped in place. Jeff stood from the edge of the table. His eyes fixated upon Ed. Seconds passed as he finally mumbled a reply. "Ed's right. That's got to be it!" He stared at Gene, yearning for a desperate validation. "Jennifer Tanner's sighting, the place where Elise got sick, the location of our sighting…"

"It's where we last saw him," Gene answered with conviction.

"That clearing." Jeff's mind raced. "Give me a map!" He snatched a fully charged handheld radio and bolted through the front tent flap.

"Jeff, wait!" Gene yelled and watched the tent flap close. "Great!" Gene grabbed a map and looked around the tent. He thought for a moment while tapping his knuckle anxiously on his forehead. "It's just a hunch, but I need to make a quick call. Where's my phone?" Tommy reached across the equipment with Gene's phone. "Thanks. Now, let's see. Karen, you're coming with me. It will be dark soon, so grab some flashlights and night vision. Get enough for Jeff, too. Guys, stay and operate communications with Elise and us. Mike, contact Jeff and tell him I'm coming as soon as I can. Tommy, help me get some night gear ready and keep Mr. Silver company while we're gone." He exhaled sharply and turned to see Karen holding three flashlights. He punched in a number and held the phone to his ear. Gene exhaled from the rush of adrenaline and faced Karen. "Here we go again."

Karen loaded a backpack and set it next to Gene. "Promise me, if we should experience anything like we did at the Little Bighorn with Jeff and that horse, this time, don't yell for him to get out of the way."

Chapter 10

The sun sank behind a veil of clouds casting an array of color across the sky. The evening shades of violet, lavender, and blue highlighted an exhilarating contrast to the fiery swaths of red, orange, and amber that streaked across the lower horizon. The diamond-like brilliance of the first stars pierced through the fading light ushering in the foreboding night. The darkening sky appeared to collide against the rising tower of Sunset Peak. The view from the base began to hinder any precision of sight against the condensing blackness. The imposing granite slopes seemed to stretch beyond the atmosphere blocking the full view of the celestial display.

The small inlet flickered with hope as the developing firelight engulfed the woodpile. The orange hue from the flames danced across the dull granite walls illuminating the natural enclosure with a welcoming gleam. The hazy glow from the intensifying fire cast a ring of light around the camp. The radiance blinded anyone from seeing beyond the proximity of the fire. Elise continued assembling her equipment beyond the dense blaze while keeping a sharp eye on the time. Laura and Wil collected the last of a large pile of firewood. Satisfied with a bountiful supply, they gathered around the rock ring and watched the flames.

The relaxing moments turned to several long minutes with no conversation. Laura looked for Elise as a means of escape from the awkward silence emanating from Wil. He stared into the coals, watching the heat billow upward. She peeked at her father noticing his stern expression. Unsure of the situation, she stood to go find Elise.

"It seems like yesterday when I had to pull you away from a fire like this. Do you remember?" Wil looked up at her. "As soon as the wood started to pop and those flames began to lick the air, you would watch in amazement. You loved building a fire."

"I loved camping," Laura replied and sat back down. "I still do."

"It wasn't camping until the fire started. I've lost count of the campfires we've had."

"So many good memories," Laura said.

"So many good times." He looked toward the sky. "I miss those times. I miss time with you the most."

"I know you do. I miss it too."

Wil grabbed a broken branch and began to shuffle the hot coals underneath the logs. "I suppose this Jeff guy has been yearning for your attention?"

"Dad, don't start."

"Can't I talk to you without complication?"

"Yes." Laura rolled her eyes. "Just don't get so overly protective."

"Your mother used to roll her eyes at me that very same way." Laura wondered how he saw her from the other side of the fire. "I want you to be happy. That's all."

"I am," Laura responded. "I just met him. It's not like we are getting engaged."

"Just take your time. Don't rush anything."

"How interesting. I seem to remember you taking great pride in telling mom that you loved her eleven days after you met. Why would that be any different for me?" Laura knew her snide remark would cause an issue.

Wil leaned around the fire, "Because I knew I could go a lifetime with your mother. I may not get much right in this life, but I got that one perfectly."

"Yes, you did." Laura retreated.

"Honey, you've been through enough. I don't want to see you get your heart broken. Sometimes a father can see things. I know this may not be the right thing to say, but I am seeing things now. And I don't like what I see in this Jeff guy."

"You need to trust me."

Wil hesitated and then reluctantly continued. "I feel like he is not right for you."

"You think he is going to take me away, don't you?"

Wil began to get frustrated. "Be careful. That is all I am saying."

"I hope this isn't about mom. You aren't going to lose me like that. Not now or ever." Laura watched him struggle to speak. He rose to his feet and walked into the darkness. Laura saw him disappear down the embankment. Regret consumed her as she wiped her eyes. She despised his lack of approval toward Jeff and did not appreciate his quick judgment of him. The love still swelled in her heart for Jeff. The sudden attraction to him and mutual feelings filled the void she carried. She wanted the pain to go away. The happiness Jeff provided eased her anguish and offered a hope that she yearned for in her dreams. She felt remorse for her father but protected her feelings for Jeff with fervor.

"That should do it," Elise stated and sat by Laura. "For the equipment we do have, it's set up and ready."

"What exactly do you have?" Laura asked.

"Mostly video and audio. The basic load for a remote site. A video camera that captures any movement and some microphones located around our camp. Opportunities like this are mostly to see what can be experienced. If something occurs, then we bring in more of the big stuff, like Gene has at the other site." Elise looked around. "Where's Wil?"

"He's around. He walked off that way. We kind of got in a little fight, which we seem to do a lot of these days."

"Let me guess, you talked about Jeff?"

"Of course. And, of course, he doesn't like him."

"Now there's a surprise." Elise giggled at Laura. "The sure sign of a father's love for his daughter is to hate all the boys she dates. Hang in there. I'm sure it's not the first time. He's simply being a dad."

"He certainly keeps it interesting, for lack of a better word," Laura added.

"I would say interesting is the perfect word."

"What do you mean? I was kidding, Elise. I could think of a few other words I'd like to call him."

"Ah, come on. You'll get over it." Elise poked at the fire with a broken branch. "I find it interesting that he asked for my help."

Laura reclined against a rock and watched the flames. "He likes you. But if you're asking me what he wants your help for, I don't know. I've never seen him act like this before."

"Hmm." Elise's stick caught on fire. She raised the end of it above the flames and twirled it through the air. "It's strange that you say that."

"Why?"

"Did you notice anything about Wil when we parked the truck?"

Laura thought for a moment, "No."

"He led us directly to this location. Did you tell him where we were going?"

"He knew we were going to Sunset Peak. I thought you told him?"

Elise lowered her stick back in the fire. She looked at Laura without expression. "I never told him we were coming to this site." Laura stared back at her in silence. "He started hiking to this spot as soon as we crossed the highway. He led us the entire way."

Laura struggled to make sense of Elise's words. She recalled the journey from the truck to the inlet and could not remember any specifics. Her mind raced to find a simple excuse. "Are you sure?"

"I watched him the whole way. I never said a word to him, and he never asked. It's obvious he knew where to go. I watched you two while I set up the equipment. He seems so comfortable. It's almost like he has…"

"Been here before?" Both ladies jumped at Wil's voice from behind them. Elise placed her hand over her heart as Laura scolded him. Wil let them calm down and sat on the other side of the fire. He faced them with sternness. "Yes. I have been here before." Wil pointed at the old fire pit at the back of the inlet. "That fire over there was mine. I made it recently." He addressed Laura. "Your mother and I camped here once. I've been trying to find where you and I stayed that night we got lost ten years ago. Do you remember that small rock cave we slept in? I've never been able to find it."

"Is that what you need my help for?" Elise asked. "To find that rock cave?"

"No. That would be a waste of your talent. You say that your job is to find these windows that you and your friends have talked about, right?"

"Yes, something like that," Elise replied.

Wil gave her a convincing gaze, "I want you to see if you can find one here."

"Why here?" Elise questioned.

Wil sat back from the fire. "If all goes well, that answer will be provided to you."

"Dad, what are you talking about?" Laura asked.

"Not now, Laura."

Laura was surprised at his tone. He rarely called her by her name. "Wait a minute, is this about that fire again and the man we saw in the rock cave that night?"

Wil's eyes glistened in the firelight. "Not now."

Elise interrupted their escalating tension. "Wil, these windows don't just show up wherever we want them to. And if they do, we still may not get to see anything. Finding a window is extremely rare. It is not an exact science."

"You said your gadget was picking up a strong signal here. So, start with that."

"Yes, but getting a signal only means there is a certain kind of energy present. It doesn't mean a window may appear. A lot plays in to actually experiencing a window. The energy surrounding an area, the site itself, any historical significance, and sometimes even a humanistic signature about the location. And that's only what we think we know about them."

Wil crossed his arms and repositioned against a boulder. "You said you would help me."

"And I have. I set up some equipment to capture anything that might happen here tonight. Without really knowing if this place is an opportunity, it is, quite frankly, an educated guess. It's up to our equipment."

"It was never about your equipment, Elise," Wil replied. Elise was astonished to hear Wil use her name. "It is about you. I led you here because I need *your* help, not your equipment." Wil delayed his discussion to clear her mind. "Tell me, have you dreamed about Sunset Peak?"

Elise continued in her astonishment of Wil. His unexpected questioning both surprised and tantalized her interest. "Yes."

"Recently?"

"Yes."

"Was your dream rather peculiar about the mountain?"

Elise waited to answer. "I'm not sure what you're asking?"

Wil leaned forward. "Did you see a fire?" Elise remained quiet as confusion overwhelmed her interest. Wil noticed her reaction to his words and continued. "Did you see anyone standing by the fire?"

Elise shuffled to her feet. She began to tremble as she stood in front of the flames. Her mind swooned with confusion that suddenly alluded to fear. She lost control of reason and yelled across the fire. "What is going on, Wil?"

"If things go well, hopefully a confirmation."

"A what?" Elise asked. "Wil, you are really starting to scare me. How do you know about my dream? That is not possible."

"Oh, but it is. It isn't possible for all of your gadgets and equipment, but it is possible for you. You have a gift. You can see things. But sometimes, what you see can be obvious. Especially if the one that sees your gift actually experienced it. That, and a pretty good hunch."

"Dad, are you saying you knew what Elise dreamed about and experienced it?" Laura asked. Elise stood unmoving by the fire.

"I am saying that I know what Elise's gift is. She is a conduit with her dreams. The part about me experiencing it was, quite frankly, a guess." Wil grinned at Elise. "Is your equipment all set up?"

Elise still stood by the fire with mental fatigue. "What? Yes. Yes, it is. Why?"

"Good. Then I think I will turn in early for the night." Wil walked to his pack and untied his bedroll and sleeping bag. Elise watched him walk away. Still confused, she exhaled strongly and left to check her equipment a final time. Laura joined Wil by his pack.

"What's the matter with you?" Laura asked. Wil continued working on his bedroll. "Why did you ask her all of those questions?" Wil did not reply. Laura surrendered and turned to leave. "You are making it very hard to trust you anymore."

"And you, young lady, need to learn patience." Wil completed his sleeping arrangement and stood next to Laura. "If Elise is right, then questions will be answered in time. Until then, I am going to sleep. It's been a long day."

"It's too early to go to sleep. I might drive to the other site for a quick visit and see what they are doing." She waited for a reaction from Wil, knowing he would not approve of her seeing Jeff. Wil remained standing with no response. Frustrated at his stubbornness,

Laura continued her questioning. "What happens if Elise has no answers?"

Wil kissed her on her cheek. "Then that will be the answer."

* * * * * * *

A pack of coyotes barked in the distance. The increasing darkness carried their howls throughout the valley and echoed against the granite mountains. The moonlight cast a paleness over the land that deceived the eyes. Shadows magnified in the darkened forests and illuminated boulders and shrubs to appear larger than they were. The wind died, exposing a quiet that seemed to intensify any sound that occurred. The night closed in, sending the daytime inhabitants to slumber and awakening the restless creatures of darkness.

Jeff waited in the shadows at the edge of a forest. His sprint from the tent gave him the distance he desired from the group but left him exposed in an environment he knew nothing about. He was finished with the convoluted frustrations of the team. The lead from Ed Silver to explore their last sighting of Owen Corr was the answer he was waiting for. He needed a break. As much as he depended upon the team for answers, he wanted this opportunity for himself. Knowing time was against him and the team in full pursuit, he stepped from the trees and entered the sloping field.

Nothing looked the same in the darkness. He cursed himself for not bringing any night vision or a flashlight as he underestimated the rapid sunset. The rugged peaks cast their shadows that blocked the rising moon and dissipated its light in swaths across the refuge. What he thought he could recall from the daylight was now blackened with confusion. The terrain looked nothing as it did before. Unable to see his map in the darkness, he began to realize that his selfish departure had evolved into an unsettling observation. He was lost.

He traversed the ground at half his pace. He stumbled over loose rocks and tripped over branches and bushes. The noise he made from snapping twigs and crunching leaves carried across the land. The coyotes bellowed again. Their cries seemed closer than before. Jeff struggled to see in the dim moonlight. The cloudless sky helped, but the odd hue tricked his vision. A rustle in a nearby bush startled him. He stopped and focused on the undergrowth. An armadillo scurried past him without concern of his presence. Jeff continued up the slope relying only on the hope of his memory.

It was not until the faded resonance of a distant barred owl that Jeff felt the prickle of fear. The familiar calling of the winged creature carried a dreadful reminder of his experience at the Little Bighorn. The same sound occurred moments before his unexplained encounter with the horse and rider. The disturbing sight inflicted a scar upon him that he carried quietly in his soul. He kept the memory buried deep within his mind, but hearing the same owl again resurrected a dread that made him stop.

A giant, black object moved in front of him. A sound of grunting came from it. Jeff knelt, trying to see through the undergrowth. The object moved slightly but could not be determined in the dim light. A large exhale billowed across the ground. A branch snapped loudly as the object moved over it. Fear consumed Jeff as he froze in place, exposed in the open. Pondering any action with his few options, he backed slowly away from the object. He turned to see another object moving behind him. His heart raced. He fell to his knees and crawled to the side. He reached out and felt the rough texture of a granite boulder blocking his path. He climbed up the side of the rock and lay flat across the top.

The boulder elevated him five feet above the ground. His shoes scuffed against the coarse granite as he struggled for a safe position. The slight noise caught the attention of the object. His peripheral vision noticed the perception of four more objects nearby. He kept still and fought to control his breathing. A loud scrape against the boulder scared him. He jumped up and turned to look behind him. A large, curved horn scratched across the rock. Jeff squinted to see two horns rise within eye level of him. A sudden burst of air shot across his shoes.

"Ah!" Jeff yelled.

Hawwh!

The massive black object turned away and crashed through the brush. The distinct sound of hooves impacted against the granite. Another object approached the boulder and passed by. Jeff looked to see the swirled colors of black and white brush against the rock.

Hawwh!

Jeff watched several of the objects pass. He stayed on the boulder as they traversed the ridge and disappeared into the forest. Convinced the objects were real, he visually checked the area as closely as he could. No other sounds occurred. He slid off of the rock and strained to hear and see any other anomaly. Surrendering to the experience and curious as to why the team had not contacted him yet, he reached for his radio.

"Gene, are you there? This is Jeff." The radio was silent. He tried again with no resolve. He fumbled with some buttons, realizing that during his rapid departure from the tent that he failed to turn his radio on. He pressed the button and watched the screen brighten.

The radio hissed to life. He pressed the transmitter and called for Gene again. Static filled the receiver with the garbled sound of a return voice. He held the radio near his ear.

"JFKF"

Terror consumed Jeff. The same voice from before repeated the letters again. The owl beckoned its cry from the forest. Jeff backed against the boulder and sat on the ground. He made himself as small as he could. The mounting fear tore at him, causing him to fatigue and surrender to his escalating predicament. The letters repeated again. Jeff switched off his radio and peeked over the boulder. Desperation became his only recourse as he watched the valley. Realizing he had no options left, he stood next to the boulder and cupped his hands to his mouth.

"Help! Is anyone out there?"

Seconds passed with no reply. Jeff climbed on the boulder and yelled again. His voice carried over the landscape. He listened for any response. Refusing to turn the radio back on, he looked to the horizon. The distant haze of a town appeared dimly in the night. A radio tower beamed an intermittent red flash. He judged the distance to be many miles away as it dashed his remaining hope. With his sense of direction gone, he settled for the worst. He looked westward and saw the warm glow of a lantern swinging in step with the silhouette of a person.

"Hey! Over here!" He watched the lantern stop moving. "Over here!" Realizing the person could not see him in the dark, Jeff hurried toward the light. "I'm coming toward you." He navigated the terrain, keeping his eyes on the ground. The rising moon intensified its light, assisting with his treacherous pace. He paused to catch his breath. The light appeared to be moving toward him. He yelled again and continued forward. He tripped and fell down the slope. He stood and brushed off. The lantern continued moving up the slope. Jeff watched it swinging at the pace of its carrier. He weaved through the landscape obstacles and gained on the light. "I'm right here!"

The lantern stopped. Jeff raced toward it. Cactus and briars tore at his legs as he forced his approach. He pushed through a cedar grove and witnessed the full brilliance of the lantern. "Hello?" Jeff shielded his eyes. His vision slowly adjusted to the brightness. He regained his clarity to see a man wearing a black and red checkered coat crouching under a rock ledge. He gasped at the realization before him. The man stood and turned toward Jeff. His orange and black billed cap guarded his face. Jeff watched him hurry and gather some items near his lantern. The man reached for several bags on the rock ledge. He pitched the bags on the ground with each landing with a heavy impact. He took a tool and worked feverishly digging a hole under the ledge.

Jeff stood away and witnessed the display. The man continued digging and suddenly looked up. He dropped the shovel and reached at his side. Jeff noticed the distinct outline of a revolver appear in his hand. Jeff backed further toward the cedars and watched the man raise his arm. He aimed above the rock ledge and pulled the trigger. Expecting to hear the explosion of gunfire, Jeff observed the man fire three more times without a sound. He returned his revolver to the holster and finished digging. His urgency increased as he watched his surroundings and dropped the bags into the hole. He covered the hole and then quickly reloaded his revolver. Jeff watched him peek over the rock ledge a final time and then slowly back away. He crouched and ran for the opening of the cove. In an instant, he arched violently at his back and slammed against the ground. The revolver left his hand and hit the lantern. Jeff watched as the entire scene faded into the darkness.

He continued watching from the safety of the cedar grove, unsure of what he witnessed. The darkness consumed the area with only the moonlight to expose the landscape. Hearing no sound, he stepped from the trees and entered the clearing. He walked to the location where the man fell. Jeff searched the small area finding only grass, rocks, and undisturbed ground. Nothing remained of the event from moments earlier. His mind yearned to make sense of the situation. The darkness began to consume him once again. Feeling confusion combine with fear, he leaned against the rock ledge and sat down. Succumbing to despair, he accepted his remaining option and waited for morning.

The cool night air chilled him as he curled underneath the ledge. He rubbed his bare arms and looked across the moonlit view. His eyes adjusted to the night, allowing him to see objects and shadows that toyed with his perception. He noticed he was at a high elevation. The visibility from his position allowed him to see the rising mountains and hills around him. He observed the valley in the distance. A white light appeared at the opening of the cove, blinding his night vision. He shielded his eyes and squinted to see.

"Jeff, is that you?"

Jeff lowered his hand and stood. "Who's there?"

"It's Jennifer." She lowered her flashlight and hurried to him. "Are you okay?"

"Jennifer, who?"

"So much for my first impression. Jennifer Tanner. We met at BoomPa's Burgers, remember?"

"Yeah, I remember. I'm a little dazed. It's been a crazy night."

"How did you get up here with no flashlight?"

"That's a good question," Jeff replied. "What are you doing out here?"

"Gene called me. It's good for you that he did. They are looking for you. They waited for me to arrive, and then we split up to find you. Most of them got lost. I thought I heard you yelling from that ridge over there. I was on my way toward you, but I got held up by a herd of longhorns grazing near the forest."

"So that's what those were? I thought for sure I met Bigfoot."

"Why didn't you have your radio on? They've been trying to reach you since sundown," Jennifer asked. "We thought something had happened to you."

"You have no idea," Jeff answered.

Jennifer took her radio and called for the team. Some flashlights appeared in the distance. The light beams bounced through the darkness. Members of the team navigated the landscape and converged on them from different directions. The darkness slowed their approach while Jennifer attempted to guide them toward her location. The team entered the area and rested against the rock ledge. They upended their canteens and handed one to Jeff.

"It's good to see you are in one piece," Gene stated. He stood next to Jeff and lowered his voice. "Jeff, I consider you a good friend. But if you ever take off like that again, you won't be welcomed back." Jeff remained silent. "You risked the safety of the entire team tonight, not to mention nearly getting yourself killed by a herd of longhorns."

"Alright, Gene. I've got it. It won't happen again," Jeff replied. "I got excited."

"And stupid," Karen added. "But that's a given."

"It's a good thing Jennifer lives nearby and agreed to come out as quickly as she did. You could have spent the night out here," Gene continued. "Here's your jacket."

"Jeff, how did you manage to find this location in the dark?" Jennifer asked. "I've hiked out here before, and I still struggled to find you with my flashlight and GPS."

"What do you mean, *location*?" Jeff asked. "I got lost. I saw a lantern and followed it here. That's when I saw him again."

"Saw who?" Jennifer asked.

"Owen Corr," Jeff replied. The team stared at Jeff. "I thought maybe it was one of you, so I kept yelling. When I finally got here, I saw Owen Corr right there by that ledge. He was digging underneath it and then pulled out a revolver. I watched him shoot at something, but I didn't hear any gunfire. Then toward the end, I think I saw him get shot in the back. He fell right about here. That's when everything disappeared. Even the lantern light went out. It went completely dark."

"You saw Owen Corr, again?" Gene asked.

"Yeah. I thought maybe it was one of you with a lantern, and I followed it here. Then I saw him wearing the same clothes that he had on before."

"We don't carry lanterns, Jeff," Karen said. "Good grief, who carries lanterns this day and age?"

"I was in the moment, Karen! Okay? Can you give me a break? It's not every day I see some strange man carrying a lantern in the middle of nowhere." Jeff gained his composure. "Enough of that. We're losing time. How can we get back on track? He is out here. I can't be sure, but it looked like I saw a window. It was just like the Bird Cage Theater. Clear and detailed, like I was there. Did you all

Finding Sunset Peak

bring the equipment? If we can mark this location, we can find the original one and determine if there's a connection."

"You really don't know where you are, do you?" Karen asked.

Jeff stared in confusion. "What do you mean?"

Jennifer consoled him. "We're standing in the area where you last saw him. This is the original location. It's the same place I saw him when I had my experience, too."

Jeff turned around to see the granite ledge. "Of course, the rock ledge. And the cedar trees." He looked at Gene. "Owen led me back here."

"Or he saved you. I think you may have a connection with him," Gene said.

"Or he has one with you," Karen added.

"Unless it was an actual window, then he may not have seen you at all." Gene began to think. "Talk about coincidence. Where did you say you saw him digging?"

Jeff pointed near the granite shelf and then stopped. "Wait. You don't think he was burying the treasure…"

"Move." Gene unstrapped a case from his shoulder and removed a handheld device. He switched it on and began to sway it back and forth.

"A metal detector," Jeff stated. "Gene, you're a genius."

"You say that now. It took me forever to get permission from the Wichita Mountains Wildlife Refuge to have this out here. And if you had not rushed off so fast, we could have used you to help carry more equipment!" The detector beeped multiple times as Gene narrowed his sweep. "I think we have something. I have a small pickaxe and a hand shovel in my pack." Jeff grabbed the tools and hurried next to Gene. "The signal seems to be coming from underneath that rock ledge."

"Right where it was marked on the map," Jeff added. "This explains those odd features. And most of this vegetation wasn't here when the map was made. That's what was confusing us."

The detector made a long continuous sound. "X marks the spot! That's got to be it," Gene stated. He dropped to his knees and began digging next to Jeff. They moved several large rocks from underneath the ledge. Jennifer and Karen gathered around them, shining their flashlights. They dug carefully in the hardened earth, creating a wide hole. They moved several inches of dirt until they were nearly a foot deep. Gene felt the axe hit a hard object. "I hope that's not a rock." Everyone stopped as the sound confirmed their excitement. Gene cleared the dirt away and pushed the axe tip underneath the object. He pressed the handle downward and popped a rectangular bar out of the ground.

Jeff pulled the bar out of the hole and held it in front of everyone. Jennifer and Karen illuminated the bar with their flashlights. Jeff took a canteen and washed the bar, scrubbing it with his fingers. He wiped it off and put it in front of the lights. The bar was the length of his hand and three fingers wide.

"What is it?" Jennifer asked. She shined her flashlight closer to reveal a rough, gray exterior. Jeff turned it over in his hand, feeling the substantial weight of the object.

"I'm no metallurgist, but that's got to be the biggest ingot of silver I've ever seen," Gene stated. "It must be pure."

"It's got to be," Jeff answered. "It's heavy. It feels like the weight of a hammer." He faced Gene with a wide smile. "We've struck silver!"

"Is there more?" Jennifer inquired.

Jeff handed the bar to Gene and returned to the hole. He stopped in amazement and cheered. "You aren't going to believe this." He reached for the nearest flashlight and held it over the hole. One by one, Jeff tossed twenty-nine more silver bars from the hole. Some of the bars equaled the size of bricks. Everyone poured their canteens over the bars and cleaned away the debris. Jeff observed the bars with glaring satisfaction. He picked up the largest ingot and held it in front of everyone. "Who needs science when you have a treasure trove of silver in your hands!" He looked back at the hole and swept across the dirt with his hand. "That's it. There's just pieces of rotted bags and a rusted iron lock sticking out of the ground."

Gene took the pickaxe and shoved the tip through the lock opening. He pried the lock up, snapping the rusted iron in half. The ground by the lock shifted in the form of a square. "I don't think we're done yet." He reached down and grabbed the broken lock. Jeff assisted as they pulled up on the lock. The earth gave way around the lock and they lost their balance. Jeff hit his head against the rock shelf and let go. Gene reached with both hands and dislodged a metal box from the hole. He fell backward, slamming the metal box against a rock. The lid cracked open, spilling numerous pieces of clinking metal across the ground.

Karen and Jennifer shined their flashlights between them. Karen knelt next to the pile. "These look like coins."

Gene rolled over and held one in the light. He rubbed it with his thumb. "It is a coin. I think it's a gold coin." He lifted up the metal box causing more coins to fall between the group. He spread the pile with his hand. "These are printed. This is money."

Karen read an inscription on one of the coins. "1880. And it has a face on it. It looks like it spells *liberty* across the forehead. I think these are American gold coins."

"Wow! How many do you think there are?" Jeff asked, rubbing his head.

"It looks like a hundred or more of them." Gene piled the gold coins and lined each silver bar side by side. The team stood together and admired the impressive hoard.

"What do you think all of this is worth?" Karen asked.

"I don't know," Gene replied. "But I do know that we are way beyond science now."

* * * * * * *

The night carried a slight chill in the darkness, with a thin layer of condensation forming on the tent. A strange silence continued inside while the group gathered around the center table. The hum of the heater made the only sound. Ed Silver sat in the middle of the tent, teasing his beard with one hand. His eyes narrowed upon the stacked bars of silver and gold coins in front of him. He observed the treasure for several seconds without any words. Everyone waited for his first response, happy to be in the warm tent and away from their earlier ordeal. Eager to pursue the moment, Gene sat next to Ed and sipped his coffee.

"You never thought this could happen, did you?"

Ed placed one of the bars back on the pile. He sat back in his chair and continued twisting his beard. "No. I sure didn't. And I don't know what is more unbelievable. The fact that Owen Corr had a real treasure or that you all found it."

"Yes, it is rather unbelievable," Gene responded. "I'm sure it is also quite vindicating for you."

"It certainly puts a frustrating story to rest. The only thing I wonder now is if I'm staring at a trove of stolen gold and silver. There's no tellin' where Owen got this from. That silver looks original and smelted from the ore. It probably did come from a mine. But those gold coins have got to have come from a bank. The only question there is if the withdrawal was legal," Ed snickered.

"And there's no tellin' what all of this is worth," Jeff added. "Those gold coins alone have got to be worth several hundreds of thousands of dollars. I still think it's interesting that we counted exactly two hundred of them. A bank would be that exact, so maybe you're right, Ed."

"Explaining it won't be easy, but the historical significance of it will be what matters now," Gene said.

"What are you talking about?" Jeff asked. "Who are we explaining to? We found it. There's your explanation. Like Ed said, end of story."

Gene leaned over the table. "Explaining it to the Wichita Mountains Wildlife Refuge Manager is what I meant. Like it or not, our treasure was found on government property."

"What?" Several of the team members exclaimed at once.

"Why are you all acting so surprised? This isn't our first time working on government land. That was the stipulation when I got permission to use a metal detector and treasure hunt. It was allowed under stipulations of scientific research. They made that quite clear. I have to report this." Gene sat back down.

"You've got to be kidding me!" Jeff yelled. "Forget them. We won't say anything."

"It's not that simple, Jeff. Come on, you aren't new to this. Remember the Little Bighorn? Anything discovered on government property is under their jurisdiction. It's the same thing here."

Ed crossed his arms and mulled the conversation. "I'll see if I can file an appeal. It may not go anywhere, but it's worth a try. If anything, all of this may end up in some museum, most likely in Oklahoma since the map led us here."

"Forget that," Jeff replied. "We don't have to claim anything. They will never know. We found this in a wilderness area. I could leave with it right now, and how would they stop me?"

"I would tell them tonight or when they show up here in the morning for their daily report. It was part of the arrangement to allow us to be here. Let it go, Jeff." Gene watched Jeff continue to get angry about the discussion.

"That's stupid," Jeff stated.

"We get the credit for finding it. That's really what we're after, right?" Gene asked. Jeff picked up another bar and gripped it tightly without a reply.

"Either way, your story of how you found the treasure is quite interesting. That's the strangest thing I've ever heard, that's for sure." Ed took a large gulp of his coffee and hinted for more. "You all have quite the mystery on your hands. I'm sure more will come of it. I still can't believe there was treasure there. And from what you said about Owen firing a revolver makes me think he was neck-deep in trouble."

"Or he was murdered," Gene said.

"Yep. That very well may have been. It would explain how he died. No one in my family really knows how or where he died. I guess that treasure map of his proves he got around to places other than

Arizona. I'll have to visit this Meers you were talkin' about earlier and see what I can find."

"About all you will find there are some really great hamburgers and cobbler with ice cream. It's a restaurant," Karen stated.

"Sounds even better!" Ed laughed. "I guess I'll leave that mystery for you all to solve. You sure seem to be good at it. But until then, if you don't mind, I'd like to catch some shut-eye before the rooster crows. I know it's still early for all of you young'uns, but us old folks need our rest. I trust you are going to keep this cache in a safe place?"

"Yes sir. I'll call it in shortly. I'm assuming they will keep it at the refuge headquarters," Gene replied.

Everyone said goodnight as Karen escorted Ed to the sleep tent. Gene watched Ed depart and walked toward the monitors. He motioned for Mike to join him while everyone exited the tent to make ready for the night.

"What's up?" Mike asked.

Gene rested his leg on an empty chair. "Did Jeff tell you how all of this happened, the full extent of it?"

"Yeah. I noticed you didn't go in great detail in front of Ed."

"Ed doesn't need to know. All he needs to think is we saw Owen's ghost. And I hope Jeff will keep his mouth shut in front of Jennifer too. I'll be sure to talk to him. We don't need this getting out to anyone other than the team."

Mike shook his head with a ponderous smile. "Good grief, Gene. Do you know what this means? We found a real treasure, and Jeff may have watched a murder through a window. How in the world is that possible?"

"I don't know. It's too much to comprehend at once."

"It raises a question none of us want to ask, especially Elise when she finds out." Mike looked around the tent. "Are we dealing with a window in time, or is this really Owen K. Corr's ghost?"

"If he's a ghost, then why is he reaching out to Jeff?" Gene added. "This is going against everything we ever thought we knew." He tapped his forehead with his knuckle and thought. "Look, Mike. I need you to keep this quiet until we can figure a few things out. Help me keep this under control, and don't let anyone talk outside of the team. I'm not giving up on the science of this just yet. Get some sleep and then take Karen in the morning and go back to that site. Set up everything we've got and see what you can research. Take enough food for the day. I want to rule out some questions before we go any further, okay?" Mike nodded without a reply. "Are you alright?"

"Yes. But it seems like this has gotten complicated. It's nothing like we've ever encountered before. I'm wondering how much of this is really about the science anymore."

Gene coughed a fake laugh, "That's what you are going to find out."

Chapter 11

The moon continued toward its apex in the night sky. The brighter stars shimmered as crystals through the white lunar reflection. The pale glow highlighted the feeble path from the tent site to the parking area at the refuge highway. Jeff and Jennifer stomped through the prairie grasses avoiding the dark unknowns of the scattered forests. The illumination prevented any shadowed encounters with more refuge inhabitants. Due to their longhorn experience earlier in the evening, Jeff ensured ample distance from darkened features. They traversed the landscape at a cautious pace and reached the parking area. The pavement appeared luminous in the moonlight. Jennifer stood by Jeff next to the vehicle with her keys in hand.

"That treasure is bothering you, isn't it?" she asked.

"The whole thing bothers me. It ticks me off how by-the-book Gene has to be. That treasure was a group effort, and now we have to give it up to someone that wasn't even here? Stupid. Just plain stupid."

"Like Ed said, maybe he can get an appeal, and you all can keep the treasure. That has to be worth a fortune, especially with the historical value."

"It's not the money. I want the credit of finding it," Jeff said.

"But you did get the credit. Gene said so too."

"No, Wil Brooks found it. He figured out the map, the location, the symbols, everything. And he wasn't even at the site! Without him, the treasure would still be lost. The only credit any of us really get is wiping the dirt off of the silver bars."

"Why does this mean so much to you?" Jennifer asked.

"I needed this treasure. I needed to find it. This would have boosted my standing with the university several times over, not to mention my speaking on the history circuit and my book deal. The historical significance of this would have set me for life. And now it's nothing more than folklore for children's bedtime stories."

Jennifer took his hand. "Jeff, you were there. You played a vital part in the whole discovery. If that was Owen Corr's ghost that led you to the site, then you found it. No one else can say that. That speaks for something, no matter who you are. And what a cool story."

"This is shared credit. I want full credit. It's a missed opportunity, just like all the ones before this. Everyone back there, they are in it for the science. I don't care about that. Not anymore. What matters to me is that it is my name in the history books."

Vehicle headlights appeared in the distance. The high beams cast a brightness across Jennifer's car. Jeff shielded his eyes as Jennifer leaned closer to him. She caressed his face and held him close. "I'm sure it will work out for you. Give it some time." She kissed him softly across his lips. He lowered his hand to her waist, surprised by her move of affection. She released from the kiss and nudged him with her nose. The vehicle stopped at the end of the parking area with its lights still shining on them. Jennifer turned around as they both protected their eyes. "Who is that?"

"It's probably someone from the wildlife refuge. I'll bet Gene called them about the treasure as soon as we left the tent. I'd better go speak with them."

"Are we still going to have that hike you talked about at the restaurant?" Jennifer asked. "That's really the only reason I came out here tonight. That and to help find you."

Jeff thought desperately to remember talking about hiking with Jennifer. "Yeah, of course. Let me straighten up a few things, and I'll call you." They waved at each other as Jennifer entered her car and backed on to the highway. Jeff watched her drive away and walked toward the parked vehicle with its headlights aimed at him. He held his hand over his eyes and approached the driver's side window. He adjusted his eyes from the glare and noticed the window was down. "Hey buddy, you're blinding us. Turn your lights off." The driver dimmed the lights. "I guess you're here to see the big find?"

There was a long delay before the driver responded. "No, I've seen enough." Jeff stepped near the driver's side window to see Laura Brooks staring through the windshield.

"Laura! I thought you were someone from the refuge. What are you doing here?"

Laura slowly faced him. "Elise told me about the treasure. I thought I would come over and congratulate you. But I can see you are busy celebrating with that other woman."

"Oh, she's a part of the team. She came out to help us, and we were saying goodbye."

"By kissing her on the lips with your arm around her?"

"She's a friend. It was a gesture. It's been quite an emotional night. You see, when we first got to Oklahoma, we met her at a restaurant, and she helped us out. She was with us from the beginning. Once we…"

Laura shifted her truck in to drive and swung it around. She yelled out of her window as she pulled on to the highway, "Don't let me interrupt your emotional night, Jeff. And you can forget about having any more *friendly gestures* with me!"

* * * * * * *

Wil rolled to his side and faced the fire. It roared with a well-fed base of dried branches and fallen trees they dragged from the forest. The fire crackled with life, consuming the wooden fuel at a steady pace. The flames rose high above the base and licked at the sky. The coals glowed orange and shimmered from the intense heat. The towering blaze reminded him of the bonfires he fashioned for Laura on their camping trips. The thought of Laura bothered him. He yearned to talk with her more and make everything right. He tossed under his quilts and finally threw them aside. The night sounds provided soothing tranquility that his troubled mind would not accept.

He rose from his mat and stretched his aching back. He warmed near the fire and noticed a dim light inside Elise's tent. He thought of their previous discussion and knew he confused her. Still not convinced of a reliable trust, he kept Elise at a safe distance with his knowledge. He needed her ability and keenness for science, but not at the expense of his instinct. Eventually, he knew all would have to be revealed between them if there was to be any hope of discovering an answer to the mystery that he carried within him.

Wil saw Laura's empty bedroll. Assuming she was with Elise, he strolled toward her tent. The fire highlighted a tripod outside of the tent. Wil observed the high-tech camera mounted at the top. Several cables and an antenna protruded from the device. The wiring led to Elise's tent as Wil noticed the white glow of a small monitor. He walked around the tripod and stooped to look through the eyepiece. The infrared feature magnified the heat signature of every object within the viewing area. The brightness of the fire blinded him. He looked away and rubbed his eyes. He stared in to the darkness trying to regain his vision. The moon assisted his attempt to focus as he turned away to listen.

All at once, the crickets stopped chirping. The night sounds ceased, leaving the fire as the only noise. The stillness of the night air seemed to thicken in the dense silence. Wil remained motionless, encountering the rare but experienced feeling of being watched. Unable to fully regain his night vision, he leaned slowly toward the camera and peeked through the eyepiece again. The warm silhouette of a person stood next to the fire. Wil raised his head and saw a man standing by his bedroll.

The flames shrouded the man from view. Wil stepped away from the camera and felt the sharpness of a cold blade press against his throat. He remained in place and felt a hand on his back pushing him forward. His knee brushed the tripod, turning the camera away from the fire. The person behind him forced Wil toward the fire. The man near the flames approached Wil bearing a knife in his hand. His face was blackened with a camouflage that covered his features. He observed Wil with a curious expression and felt the collar of his shirt. The man backed away and motioned to the person behind Wil. Wil yelled as the blade left his throat, and he was shoved to the ground by the flames.

* * * * * *

Laura stopped at the sudden outburst. The echo drifted across the foothills of Sunset Peak. Judging the direction, she needed little verification to know the distinctive tone of a person's intensified voice. Certain there were no other men in the area, she felt confident she heard her father. The moon cast its rays over the terrain providing enough visibility for her to run. She bounded over the land watching for any object that could cause her to stumble. She stayed in the grassy flats along the edge of the mountain slopes away from the dense woods. Her flashlight lit the unknown path as she saw the glow of the fire.

"Dad?" Laura hollered. "Elise?"

Elise stood over Wil's bedroll and met Laura by the fire. "I heard Wil. I came out to check on him and he's gone. Did you see him?"

"No, I just got back from the other site."

"I thought maybe you had changed your mind and took him with you. I didn't even know he was still here."

"Did you see anything?" Laura asked.

"No. I was sitting in my tent radioing the team to check out for the night and heard him yell. I looked out and saw nothing."

"Where did you last see him?" Laura asked and checked his belongings.

"He was getting his bedroll ready, but that was much earlier."

Laura looked around the site. They checked the nearby foliage and lower slopes of the mountain with their flashlights. They called for him several times with no response. Concerned for the passing time yielding no results, they met back at the fire. Laura checked his bedroll again and then looked around the fire. "What's this?"

Elise aimed her flashlight at a spot near the fire. "Is that Wil's footprint? It looks like he dug his heel across the dirt."

Laura observed the mark across the ground and hesitated, "Or he was dragged."

"Dragged?" Elise walked to the opposite side of the fire. "There's nothing over here. The ground is too hard and rocky." She noticed the mounting worry on Laura's face. "Let's check the camera." They hurried to the tripod. Laura reached to remove it from the base. "Wait!" Elise grabbed Laura's arm. "Something's not right. This camera's been moved."

"Why would he do that?" Laura asked. "That doesn't make any sense."

"Maybe he didn't."

Laura's eyes widened as she began to look around the campsite. "There's no way we will know now."

"Actually, there is." Elise rushed toward the granite embankment. She climbed along the rock slope and reached above a small ledge. She held up another camera and turned toward Laura. "It's our protocol to have a backup system."

"Did Wil know you put that there?"

Elise answered without reservation, "No. And I intentionally didn't tell him. Sorry, but I wanted to be sure in case something happened."

"I guess you were right. Something did."

They went into Elise's tent and connected the camera to a monitor. Elise started the playback, and they watched each frame. She forwarded through the footage and stopped abruptly on a specific scene. "Who is that?" They studied the image and waited for it to focus. "There, on the other side of the fire. It looks like someone staring at Wil." They continued watching the video. "Someone else is coming in to view." They noticed two more people enter the picture.

"That's Wil, but who is that behind him? It looks like he has something across Wil's throat."

"Can you zoom in?" Laura asked. Elise stopped the video and started her computer. The software opened, allowing her to magnify the frames in slower motion. They watched Wil get pushed down in front of the fire with the stranger behind him. The other person walked next to Wil, exposing his face to the camera.

"Who is that?" Elise asked.

Laura leaned closer toward the monitor. "Oh my gosh." She sat back and remained entranced upon the monitor. Her mind flashed back to memories of her childhood. A rush of emotion collided with her thoughts. "It's him."

"Who?" Elise asked.

"The man from the fire."

"What are you talking about?" Elise looked at the monitor to see the man wave his arm above the flames. The fire magnified with an intensity that blinded the camera lens. The bright flames lasted several seconds before the lens could refocus. "What just happened?"

"No!" Laura screamed and tore open the tent. She ran to the fire and looked at the coals. "I don't see anything."

"Laura, wait. Come here. You have to see this!" Laura searched around the fire for remains and ran back to the tent. Her eyes streamed with tears as panic began to overwhelm her emotions. Elise grabbed her by the shoulders and steered her to the monitor. "Look."

"He's dead. He's dead, isn't he!"

"Look at the monitor!" Elise played the video back. They watched to see the two men step around the fire before the flames intensified.

"Where are they going?" Laura reached for the tent flap.

"Laura, wait," Elise held her in the tent. "Calm down. I need you to think. Breathe."

"My father's dead," Laura said and cried uncontrollably.

"No, he's not. Look at the video." They watched the replay several times. Each time Elise pointed to the moment with Wil by the fire. They observed him before the brightness of the flames blinded the camera lens. "It's obvious they went around the other side of the fire and into the woods. It only looks like he fell in the fire. The flames kept the camera from seeing them at that point. It couldn't be anything else. We will find out where they took him. But to do that, I need you to settle down and help me, okay?" Laura began to breathe at a slower pace. She nodded and continued watching the video. Elise backed the footage to the beginning. "Here. You said something when you saw this part, something about a man from the fire? What did you mean?" Laura observed the first man while Elise slowed the motion. "I can't tell if it is the light distorting the picture, but that looks like a man. You're right."

Laura kept her attention on him, "He looks like an Indian."

Elise addressed Laura with confusion. "How can you tell? It's hard to see any features to distinguish anybody in that darkness."

"Because he looks like the man from the fire. The fire I remember when I was ten. The man I saw then looks like that man there." Laura began to feel fear.

"How do you know?"

"Because that man was an Indian too."

"Laura, there are many people around here that are American Indians. That doesn't really tell us much," Elise stated.

"That's not what I mean. Can you zoom in on his clothes?"

Elise became puzzled. "No, I don't have the equipment here for that kind of detail. The scene is too dark, and the firelight contrasts against the camera lens. Do you see something?"

Laura stared at the monitor. Her memory collided with the scene before her. "His clothes, they're different. I remember. He looked different. Not like someone from today."

Elise observed the scene again without clarity. "From today?"

"He looked...like he was from a different time."

Elise observed Laura in question, unsure of what to say or ask about her comment. "Are you saying he looked like someone from the past?" Laura nodded. Elise thought for a moment. "I'll see if Gene and the team can clean this up on their computers. Maybe they can get more detail, but that will take a while to get all of this to them."

"It's him. It's who my father would not let me talk about. Not even to the police. He made me keep it a secret."

"Why?"

Laura hesitated to respond and then surrendered to years of frustration. "Because he didn't want anyone to know."

"To know what, Laura? What is it you are not telling me? You and your father know something. What is it?" Elise's frustration began to mount.

"That there are Indians in the Wichita Mountains that no one knows about. And we saw one ten years ago."

Elise did not answer and continued analyzing the video. Laura became bewildered. Her thoughts twisted together in a mindless confusion that tore at her soul. Her ability to reason reduced as she reached for Elise's arm. "Are you sure my father is not dead?"

"If he had fallen in to that fire and died, we would have found his remains still there. Nothing could burn up that fast in a fire that size. Something else is going on here. I don't know what it is, but I need you to stay with me, okay?"

Laura watched the scene of Wil by the flames again. "We're not alone out here. Those men took my dad. What should we do?"

Elise switched off the monitor and sat next to Laura. She stared at her with a determination that provided no sympathy to the moment. Her own memory of a dream began to recollect as she gave Laura a demanding look. "What you should do is stop playing games with me and let's come to terms with all of this right now. Before I radio the team for help, I want some answers from you."

"What are you talking about? What answers?" Laura asked.

Elise leaned closer to Laura and continued with a firm voice, "I think it's time for you to tell me exactly what you and Wil saw that night when you were ten. What about this *Indian* you keep referring to?"

Click, click.

Elise and Laura sat motionless in the tent. "Did you hear that?" Laura asked. Elise nodded and held her index finger near her lips, indicating to Laura to remain quiet. She pointed at the tent wall and shut off the interior light. The firelight illuminated the silhouette of a person standing outside of the tent. The shadow cast a grayish outline across the tent. Both ladies watched the shadow pass slowly toward the back. Laura faced Elise with a horrified expression and pointed at the rear of the tent. Elise motioned for her to stop and held up a nine-millimeter pistol from her sleeping bag.

"Shh," Elise whispered. "Follow me." She reached for the tent flap and prepared to open it. Her eyes widened at the sudden darkness that engulfed the tent. Laura reached for her as Elise held her close. "Someone put out the fire."

"What do we do?" Laura asked with a frantic voice, struggling to whisper in the blackened silence. Elise waited to respond as the sound of a sharp blade slowly cut through the back of the nylon tent.

"Do you have your flashlight?"

"Right here," Laura replied.

"Get ready to shine it as soon as we leave the tent. And stay behind me."

"What am I shining it at?"

"Whoever's at the back of the tent." Elise tore open the flap and rushed outside. She pointed the pistol in the darkness, unable to see anything. Laura frantically pursued and tripped on the netting. She fumbled the flashlight across the ground and watched it roll near the brush. It stopped with the intense beam shining toward the woods. Laura hurried to retrieve it as Elise grabbed her arm. "No, wait! What is that?"

The bright light illuminated a dark cloaked figure standing motionless between the trees. Its shrouded head bowed toward the ground. Elise raised her pistol and struggled to aim from her trembling. "Who are you?" The figure remained still. "Don't make me shoot you!" Both ladies watched as the figure slowly raised its covered head, revealing two slanted, glowing eyes reflecting the light from the flashlight toward them. A sudden movement whisked by Elise's face from behind and slammed in to her wrist. The pistol flew from her hand and disappeared in the darkness. The force of the attack knocked her against Laura sending them falling.

Elise held her arm in pain as they watched the flashlight begin to move. It rose above the ground and turned toward them. The bright beam highlighted a second figure standing over them. An identical pair of slanted eyes shimmered in the light as the figure reached out and struck Elise across her face. Laura watched her collapse against the ground. Before she could yell, a third figure emerged from behind and bound her mouth. She writhed to break free as she was pushed to the ground. The twinkling stars outlined the dark shape of a hooded figure standing over her. Its slanted eyes glistened with a sinister stare. The haunting sight was her last as her hands and feet were bound, and a black cloth sack was thrust over her head.

* * * * * * *

The sun breached the horizon and cast its rays across the Wichita Mountains. The morning took hold of the day with more indication of Spring's arrival. The changing season proved to be the most indecisive with its cool nights and warm days. The turbulent winds gathered at random times to form violent thunderstorms that appeared without notice. Forecasts became unpredictable for any percentage of accuracy. Threatening weather rolled in from the west, bringing a cold front that stirred the atmosphere with a variety of precipitation and gusts. The bright welcome of the morning became subdued with the gray, creeping presence of churning clouds.

Mike worked on the last of the equipment to finish setting up the site. Karen checked their gear and ran diagnostics on their field monitors. Their early arrival provided them precious time to arrange their equipment for one last opportunity at the treasure site. Karen watched the weather drift in and stir the terrain with its windy effects. Mike struggled against the breeze. The varied gusts tossed his equipment across the ground, making it nearly impossible for the gear to stand alone. He stopped his feeble attempt against nature and called for reinforcements.

"Karen, can you bring me the support straps and a hammer? I need to secure these sensors against the wind," Mike asked.

"I told you we should have checked the weather." Karen searched the packs and carried one to Mike. "Good news is we have several straps and plenty of stakes. Bad news is we forgot a hammer."

"That's okay. Find a rock. I'll bang them in place with that."

Karen walked the ground and found a piece of granite that fit her hand. She kicked the rock out of the earth and handed it to Mike. "Where do you want to anchor the stakes?"

Mike pointed to some areas around the site. "Wherever you can. I'm sure there is rock all around us. You may have to dig to find a spot with no granite."

Karen used a hand shovel and dug small pits in the ground. Granite fragments and rocks prevented a thorough digging. "This is impossible. There are rocks everywhere."

"Try using that metal detector in my pack. It has a feature that can detect solid objects in the ground. It might help."

Karen pulled the metal detector from his pack and began scanning the sight. She found several clear spots in the ground and began pounding in the stakes to anchor the equipment. She tied several straps and worked her way around the enclosure. She reached the opening of the inlet and searched for the remaining spots to dig. She walked over the ground swaying the metal detector back and forth.

Beep, beep!

She stopped over the spot. "What does it mean when it makes a noise?"

Mike tied another strap to her stake. "If it sounds off, you've found something metal." He turned around from his work, "Check it out. Maybe it's another silver bar." He smiled and continued tying the strap.

"Are you kidding? Jeff scoured this entire area. There's nothing left."

"He only checked under that granite shelf where the treasure was," Mike replied. "I guarantee there is nothing left to find over there."

Karen dropped to her knees and began digging at the spot registered by the metal detector. "If he had not found that treasure, I doubt we would be here right now. The energy signal has weakened, and we found the treasure. I know Gene wants to be sure, but I think any opportunity here is gone. Jeff saw the window. I think that's enough."

"Ah, come on. You know Gene is going to make sure we don't miss anything. He's ruling everything out before we pack up. And you've got to admit, that treasure was quite a find. We've never found anything as cool as that before. Who can say that they got to be a part of discovering buried treasure? That tops everything we've ever done."

"Mike, come over here."

Mike finished tying the strap and glanced at Karen, "What is it?" Karen did not answer. He dusted off his pants and walked over to her. "Did you find us some more buried loot?" He knelt next to her and looked in the hole. "What is that?"

Karen cleared away some loose dirt. "I think it's a bone."

"It's probably an animal. I saw pieces of a deer's skeleton in the woods. This place is full of bones."

Karen cleared away more dirt. She angled the shovel underneath the bone and pushed down on the handle. The eye socket of a human skull raised out of the ground. She backed away and dropped the shovel. "That's no animal. That's a person's head!" Mike observed the skull and studied its features. "What are you doing? That's a dead body!"

"I know, Karen. And it might be the body of Owen Corr." They stood in silence over the skull. Mike picked up the metal detector and turned it on.

"What are you doing with that? Skulls aren't metal," Karen said.

"Yes, I know that too. You found the skull using the metal detector. But something metal triggered it." Mike moved the metal detector slowly over the skull. No sound registered. He backed away and surveyed around the skull in a circular pattern. Karen walked next to him as he widened the circle around the skull.

Beep, beep!

"There!" Karen shouted.

"Grab the shovel."

They both dug at the spot. Karen passed the detector over the site several times. Each time the sound registered a strong signal. Mike dug at a steady pace. The edge of the shovel scraped against the ground. He reached in the hole and cleared away the loose dirt revealing a white, curved bone. He dug for several minutes, clearing the earth away from the smaller bone. Karen passed the detector over the site and concentrated on one location. Mike worked feverishly to uncover the source of the signal.

"I think I feel something. Something metal." He took the shovel and gently pried the bone out of the ground.

Finding Sunset Peak

"Oh no, it's an arm! Mike, we've found an entire body. Stop digging! This must be a grave," Karen yelled.

Mike held the skeletal arm in his hands. He angled it to observe its length and watched a solid object slide away from the wrist. He removed the dirt-covered object from the arm bone and cleaned it off. Karen handed him a canteen. Mike washed the impacted dirt away and held the object between them.

"It looks like a watch. A metal wristwatch."

Karen took the watch from him and turned it over several times. Her hands began to shake as she covered her mouth. "No, no! It can't be! Mike, there is no way this can be real!"

"What is it?"

Karen stared at the watch with a horrified expression. She looked at Mike with her eyes consumed in shock. "This…is Jeff's watch."

"What? Our Jeff?" Mike took the watch and examined it again. "How do you know?"

Karen began to pace back and forth. Anxiety overwhelmed her emotions. "The back! Look at the back of the watch."

Mike turned the watch over and rubbed the metal backing. "It looks like worn letters."

Karen grabbed the watch out of his hand and pointed at each letter in front of him. "JFKF. They are the initials for Jeff Finbow and me, Karen Farris. I had them engraved on this watch. The same watch I gave to him three years ago when we were dating. It was a Christmas present."

Mike stood dumbfounded. He looked down at the skull and dropped the arm bone next to it. He backed away from the bones and looked around the small enclosure. Uneasiness began to fill his mind. His vast propensity for computer technology, the sciences, and physics complimented his superior intelligence. Known as the more studious of the group, along with his brother Tommy, Mike applied the scientific and reasonable approach to questions or problems that the others saw differently. He knew the importance of research to any situation and enjoyed the personal challenges he encountered working with Gene and Elise. But for the situation lying on the ground in front of him and the watch in Karen's hand, he realized this challenge was more than he could bear alone.

"I think we had better call Gene," Mike said.

"Here," Karen handed him the watch. "I don't want this. I don't want anything to do with it. I didn't sign up for this. It's one thing having to tolerate looking at his face every day since Tombstone. I promised Elise I would put up with him as a favor to her. But that watch, that watch was special." Karen began to tear. "I can't do this anymore."

Mike took the watch and moved Karen to the granite ledge. They sat together and stared at their grim discovery. Mike hid the watch under his pack and took his radio. "Karen, I'm not going to lie to you. I have no idea what is going on right now. This is where Gene comes in. I say we contact him and get out of here. This is far more than I bargained for, too."

Karen wiped her eyes and calmed herself. She exhaled and looked beyond the bones and in to the horizon. "I loved him, Mike. It really hurt when he cheated on me. I did all I could to forget him. And now he just keeps coming back in my life, like a tease. I try to get over him, and he keeps showing back up. He won't go away. No matter how hard I try. And now I find the watch I gave him for our special Christmas trip to the Grand Canyon three years ago on the arm of a skeleton in Oklahoma." She paused and looked at the ground, "I told him I loved him there." She wiped her eyes.

Without thought or pretense, Mike placed his arm around Karen. "Jeff is a fool and a heartless coward. Everyone knows that. You deserve so much better than that two-face. Any respecting man would love to have you in his life." Mike took a breath and went with the moment. "I know I would." Karen sniffled and turned toward him. Her large, tear-swollen brown eyes melted his heart. His pulse quickened as he met her glance, "Stop wasting your love on someone that doesn't know what love is."

Karen snickered and nudged him. "And this whole time, I thought you were just a computer nerd."

"Well, I am an active member of two very prestigious online dating sites. I've had to turn down a few hopefuls in my recent days," he looked away with a fake grin.

"And exactly how long have you been a member of these sites?"

Mike cleared his throat. "It's a yearly renewal, thank you very much." Karen laughed. She glimpsed at his eyes and kissed him softly on the cheek. "Thanks, Mike."

He took her hand and presented the radio. "What do you say we contact Gene and get this over with?"

Karen stared back at the skull. "I have a feeling this is only the beginning."

Mike reached up and lightly touched her chin. He turned her toward him and presented a wide smile. "I certainly hope so." They looked at each other with accepting acknowledgment as Mike clicked the transmitter, "Gene, this is Mike."

"Go ahead, Mike."

"Karen and I have made a discovery. I think it would be best if you were on-site for this one, over."

"Good, then I didn't hike up here for nothing. Look in front of you." Mike and Karen glanced ahead to see Gene, Jeff, and Ed Silver approaching them.

"What are they doing here?" Karen asked.

Mike saw her reservation and shoved the watch in his pocket. "You stay here. I'll talk to Gene. It will be okay." Karen agreed as Mike approached the group. "I'm sure glad to see you guys. We've had a slight detour on our work here."

"Yeah, I heard about your little stealth operation. Sounds like we've got separate agendas going on throughout the team," Jeff said.

"What are you griping about now?" Mike countered.

Jeff confronted Mike with a surprised expression. "What's your problem?"

"You're everyone's problem. You don't know how to shut your stupid, arrogant mouth. And quite frankly, we are all tired of it." Mike stood his ground, trying to embrace his newfound boldness.

"What are you getting at, Mike? Those are strong words to say without anything to back them up. I guess you've found life beyond your computer screen, eh?"

"Jeff, that's enough. We talked about this," Gene stated. He stood between Mike and Jeff. "What's going on, Mike?"

Mike pointed at the skull and arm bone. "We were setting up our equipment when the wind storm blew in. We tried to anchor everything down and discovered this." The group walked next to the bones.

"What's wrong with Karen?" Gene asked.

"She's not feeling well. I think she's tired." Mike increased his volume and directed his response toward Jeff. "Tired of unwanted reminders of the past!"

"What's gotten into you?" Gene asked.

"I'll tell you later."

Ed Silver knelt by the skull. He observed the arm and pieces of the hand bones. "It has to be Owen. Nothing else could explain it. He must have died right here."

"I don't think it's much of a grave, Ed. We didn't dig that deep. The holes for our anchor stakes are shallow. Karen found him. We stopped digging and radioed you. This wind has not let up since it started. We didn't get very far with the setup," Mike said.

"When I saw Owen fire his revolver, it looked like he turned and fell. Maybe he got shot and died here?" Jeff stated.

"Maybe," Ed replied. "I'm not leaving till I get some answers. If this is Owen, I want to give him a proper burial. He may have been a scoundrel in his days, but I'll make sure he gets a resting place."

"Either way, we have to report this to the refuge authorities. They will know what to do," Gene said. "Gather up the equipment. I don't want to disturb this site any more than we already have."

"Gene, can I see you for a minute?" Mike asked. "In private?" Gene followed Mike around the cedar grove. Mike led him far enough away from the group so he could talk without interruption. He reached into his pocket and pulled out the watch. "This is another reason Karen is upset. We took this off of the arm bone. The soil was rocky, and we used the metal detector to find soft ground. It registered this. We dug it up, and it was on the wrist."

"This looks modern, like a watch worn today," Gene said. "What are these letters on the back of it?"

"You don't miss much. Karen said those are initials. JFKF. Jeff Finbow and Karen Farris. She gave this watch to Jeff as a Christmas present three years ago!"

Gene raised his head, his eyes widened in astonishment. "What?"

"I know. It's hard to believe, but Karen knew. I didn't want to say anything until I showed you. What does this mean?"

"It means Jeff has some explaining to do." Gene kept the watch and walked briskly back to the group. He rounded the cedar grove and approached Karen, Jeff and Ed waiting at the granite shelf. "Mr. Silver, something has come up, and we need to get you back to the tents. I'll call the refuge manager and have him out here as soon as possible to address this site. Mike is going to escort you back. We will be along shortly."

"Gene, shouldn't I stay here and…"

"I'm not asking, Mike. Get moving. Jeff, Karen, I need to see you both." Gene waited for Mike and Ed to depart. They weaved their way off of the ridge and disappeared through the forest. "Karen, Mike told me everything." Gene opened his hand and presented the watch to Jeff. "Does this look familiar?"

Jeff took the watch and observed it. "Yeah. It's mine. I lost it at the Bird Cage Theater when the equipment malfunctioned. Where did you find it?"

"How do you know it's yours?" Gene asked.

Jeff checked the back of the watch. "It has my initials on it. See, right here."

"I'm surprised you still wear it," Karen said. "It has my initials on it, too. Or have you deliberately overlooked that?"

"No, I haven't. I just didn't want to say anything to upset you. You look upset already."

"Shut up, Jeff. Like you care. You only wear that watch because it's your favorite and you got it for free. I know it has nothing to do with me. I'm surprised you didn't have my initials buffed off of it."

"You know, Karen, contrary to what you might believe, I really don't have anything against you. What do you want from me?" Jeff asked.

"You ended it, Jeff. None of it meant anything to you. You left. But you keep coming back. You ask what I want? I want you to leave and never come back." Karen pushed off of the ledge and stormed away.

"You seem to forget that I was invited back, Karen."

"Not by me!" she replied without looking at him.

Jeff watched her depart. "I don't know what I ever saw in her. Gene, I know Elise wanted me back with the team, but after all of this, I think I might have to end our time together soon. I've had enough of her."

"That might happen sooner than you think," Gene said.

"What?"

"Are you telling me the truth about this watch?"

"Yes. I lost it at the Bird Cage Theater. Where did you find it?"

Gene leaned against the rock ledge and watched for a reaction from Jeff. "Karen found it on the wrist of that skeleton, buried in the ground."

Jeff's mouth opened as he inhaled with a stunned appearance. He backed away from the skeleton and stood next to Gene. He looked at the watch and then back at the bone. "Gene, I promise. It flung off of my wrist when the equipment jammed. You mean you didn't find it at the theater?" Gene shook his head. Jeff thought for a moment and paced a few steps. "It must have come off of my wrist when the window appeared in the theater. The playback, when we saw Owen bend over. He must have been picking up…" Jeff stared at Gene, "Do you know what this means?"

"Your watch breached the window," Gene replied.

Jeff started laughing. "It went back through time! Owen Corr found my watch! He bent over and picked it up. We saw him do it. Holy cow, Gene, that wasn't a window. It was a door. This is unbelievable!"

"Yes, it is. And for now, it's going to stay that way. You are not to say anything about this to anyone, do you understand? Especially Ed Silver. We need to get our heads around this before anything goes public. I'm trusting you on this."

"Calm down, Gene. This is so big I doubt anyone would believe it anyway. At least not yet. This is amazing. Can I keep it?"

"It's your watch. We may need it for some tests, so don't lose it again. Come on, let's catch up to the others." Gene watched Jeff eagerly observe his watch with silent reservation.

Chapter 12

Gene stood in front of the patrol car and waved at Ed Silver sitting in the passenger side seat. The old man appeared tired and distraught from the eventful day. He returned the acknowledgment and waited for the driver. Gene observed him with trepidation. The situation tore at Gene's conscience, filling him with regret. Watching Ed writhe in confusion taunted his decision. He had never withheld vital evidence before, but this experience beckoned his unwavering call to pursue the science that he so desperately yearned to explore. He thought of how to make the moment right with Ed and avoid exposure of the truth that would only lead to more questions. It was his protection of that fragile truth that kept him from telling Ed about the wristwatch. In his self-justification, he did not have answers to the questions he knew would be asked of him. Until he did, the truth would remain shrouded in the science needed to determine any answers.

"You and your friends had quite a day today. I'd say you earned an extra day on that permit." Refuge Manager Russell Riley stood next to Gene. "Are you okay?"

"No sir. I've been better," Gene replied.

"I could see why after all of that. Your friends in there seemed rather spooked. Finding that skeleton out there the way you did would bother most folks. I still don't fully understand what your business is out here, but I think you and your crew need to get some rest. Finding that treasure and now this? You all have got to be worn out."

"What are you going to do about Mr. Silver?" Gene asked.

"We will take his statement and call in a forensics team to see what they can determine. It will be a process, but I think the passage of time has worn out the welcome on this case. It will mostly be for any attempt at identification and rule out some protocols."

Gene swallowed and hoped for the best. "Officer Riley, it is rather difficult to explain, and I don't have the answers at the moment, but if I can attempt to determine the identification of that skeleton scientifically, would it be wrong of me to take some needed time to do it?"

Officer Riley chuckled. "Now that is the best verbal attempt to withhold evidence that I've heard in a long time." He walked toward the driver's side door. "The forensics team will be here in the morning. It should take them most of the day to exhume the remains. What do you say you clear your conscience by tomorrow evening? We can discuss that treasure too. Would that do it?"

Gene smiled at Officer Riley's cunning wisdom. "If it keeps me out of the backseat of your patrol car, then yes sir, that will do it."

Officer Riley gave him a thumb's up and started the car. Gene watched them drive away and faced the path leading to the tent. The winding stroll gave him time to think about the impending formalities that awaited him with the team. Their encounter today provided an ending to their investigation that was consumed in complexity.

He knew his team would have questions. It was the debate leading to the answers that he dreaded. The science of the entire situation was becoming overshadowed by simple speculation. He despised the thought of guessing. His pursuit of truth through science was his mainstay, but this latest opportunity was daunting. For the first time in his peculiar profession, he was clueless for an explanation.

He opened the tent flap to a surprising quiet. Karen sat by the radio observing a monitor while Jeff, Mike, and Tommy sat on the tables facing each other. Gene noticed looks of dejection on their faces. He grabbed a chair and sat on it backward, crossing his arms over the seatback. Everyone remained silent with their own reasoning. Gene acknowledged each of them and exhaled in a resurrection of memories while he stared at the floor.

"I used to think our experience together at the Little Bighorn was the one. I really thought that opportunity was the one that would explain it all. The science, the analysis, the research…all of it was everything we could have ever asked for. To tell you the truth, I thought that whole event would justify our work and put us on the map. Then we went to Tombstone and the Bird Cage Theater. After that whole revelation, I just knew we were set. The scientific community would welcome us with open arms and shower us with accolades and proven justification of our mission. We would finally be respected as pioneers of the scientific community in our field of study." He looked up to see everyone watching him. He smiled with gleaming fascination and then let his expression slowly fade away. "And then we came to the Wichita Mountains Wildlife Refuge." He paused to filter his next words for appropriateness but submitted to the genuineness of the moment. "And quite frankly, after what I saw today, I have no idea about any of this now."

The silence remained before Mike pierced the stillness. "We have one overriding fact right there on the table." He pointed at Jeff's watch. "It breached the window and went back in time. Owen Corr found it, and then we found it on him several decades later. It's not a window, Gene. We discovered a door. A portal through time that everyone in this room thought was not possible until we came to the Wichita Mountains."

"But what about the radio, hearing that voice mention the initials?" Tommy asked. "The same initials on that watch. If this opportunity we've discovered here is a door and we have proof of a portal in time, then how do we explain that voice?"

"That's easy; it was Owen Corr," Jeff answered.

"Using a radio?" Mike asked with a condescending tone. "They didn't have radios back in his time."

"We're going to do this again? Fine. I'll say it one more time since no one else wants to approach it. It was his ghost. Call it a spirit, apparition, shadow, or a lousy reflection from space, I don't care. You all need to face this fact since we're talking facts. It was Owen Corr's ghost that spoke over the radio."

"But how?" Tommy asked.

"I don't know!" Jeff yelled. "Maybe that's our new mission. Like it or not, it happened."

"You saw his ghost and followed him up to the site? You watched his ghost get killed? You stared his ghost in the face? What about all of that?" Mike asked.

Jeff waited to respond. He looked at Gene and contemplated with obvious anguish. "You want my opinion? I think we have been dealing with both. The spiritual and the physical. His ghost and a window in time. It can be the only answer. As to how to get that answer and prove it, I don't know."

"Like I said," Mike stated. "The watch passed through the window or the door or whatever you want to call it. We know that. If it can happen at the Bird Cage Theater, it can happen here. That's what we should study first. I hear you about the ghost and all, but you can't deny what we have discovered with that watch. That watch is our new mission and our new question. It must be explained."

"Exactly!" Jeff stood from the table. "Gene, I say we go back out to that site and investigate one more time. You said it yourself. You don't have any idea about any of this now. Well, let's gear up and go change that. Let's go get some answers."

Gene exhaled again and glared at Jeff without remorse. "The refuge authorities are conducting an investigation up there. As of now, the site is off-limits."

"What?" Jeff asked.

"Calm down, Jeff. You seem to forget that we found human remains there. That supersedes anything we do. Besides, Tommy confirmed there are no longer any readings coming from that site. It's over," Gene replied.

"My watch passes through time in Arizona and shows up buried on a dead guy in Oklahoma, and you think this is over?" Jeff asked. "We have the potential of a lifetime here, right here! We have discovered the ability for a person to go back in time, and you think this is over?"

"Whoa, now wait a minute, Jeff. An object somehow passed through that window, not a person. Keep your facts straight. That goes for all of you," Gene responded.

"A watch, a person, what's the difference?" Jeff countered.

"It's a huge difference. We have no idea what this is capable of. We can only fantasize. A living person is not the same as a lifeless object. We don't know."

"All the more reason we need to get back up there and give this one more shot, Gene. I can't believe you are being so stubborn!"

"Jeff, this discussion is over," Gene said. "We have one day left here. We need to use it to pack up. Maybe, in the future, we can see what else we can do. But for now, we need to pack and go link up with Elise. Let's get moving."

"No."

Gene faced Jeff. "Excuse me?"

"I'm not going back empty-handed. First the treasure and now this. I didn't join back up with you for some sight-seeing tour in the mountains. We all have our reasons, Gene. And I have mine. I need this discovery, and I need you to understand that."

"And I need you to understand that we are out of options. Our time is up. Now get your things together and let's go."

"Not me. I quit." Jeff grabbed his pack and brushed by Gene as he walked away. "I'll get a ride to the airport." Everyone watched Jeff throw the tent flap open and exit. He kicked the flap closed, leaving the tent in silence.

Karen lifted the flap slightly and waved, "Have a nice flight!"

Everyone laughed and rallied around Gene. He stood quietly and focused his attention away from Jeff. "Alright, everyone. The drama is over. We have work to do, and now we are a hand short. Let's get this over with. I'll deal with Jeff later." Mike and Tommy began disconnecting their equipment as Gene approached Karen. "Have you heard anything from Elise yet?"

"No. She missed her second report time. We haven't heard from her since early yesterday evening. The radios are working, and phone coverage is spotty."

Gene rubbed his chin. "That's not like her. Come on, let's get packed up and get over there before sundown."

* * * * * * *

"Laura, wake up."

Cool water splashed across her forehead. Laura slowly opened her eyes at the gentle touch caressing her face. Intense daylight caused her to turn away from the brightness. She noticed granite walls around her. The confined space appeared as a small cave. She looked about the enclosure and rubbed her head. "Where am I?"

"You're with me. Drink some water."

Laura guzzled the water and focused her vision. "Dad?"

"Yes. You're safe. Lean against the wall while I tend to Elise." Wil propped her up and then assisted Elise. She moaned and held her hand against her jaw. Wil offered her water, and she emptied the canteen. He checked them over and gave them some food. They enjoyed the nourishment and finished the remainder of the water. "There. You both look much better. You had me worried for a while."

"How did you find us?" Laura asked.

"I was led to you," Wil answered. "How do you both feel? You're not hurt anywhere, are you?"

Laura ignored him. "Is this a cave?"

"No, it isn't. It's that rock-dwelling we stayed in ten years ago. Remember? The one we spent the night in during the winter? They found it and led me to it. That's how I found you both. I'm guessing they put you in here. I hope they weren't too rough on you."

Elise continued rubbing her jaw. "That's debatable. Who is this you keep referring to?"

Wil sat between them and held Laura's hand. An eagerness Elise had not seen in him before was very obvious. Laura watched his odd demeanor and waited for his response. He acknowledged Elise and turned toward Laura. "Honey, do you remember that man we saw that night, the man by the fire?" Laura nodded. "I've waited years to tell you this. I've wanted to, but I didn't want to say anything without proof. Now I've got it, I've got proof. It's also what your mother and I witnessed too. We couldn't explain it then, but I can now. I've seen them. They're out here. They have been all along."

"Who?" Laura asked.

"Our people." Wil observed their confusion. "Wichita Indians."

"Is that who took you from the campsite and then attacked us last night?" Elise asked. "We should report them to the refuge authorities."

"It's not that simple," Wil stated.

"Why not?" Elise questioned. "I have video evidence of them taking you. All the police need to do is find them and arrest them."

Wil stared into Elise's eyes. "Remember when you said you would help me?"

Elise gazed back at him with the sudden awareness that Wil meant more than what she realized. "Yes."

"Good. Because I need your help now." Wil looked behind at the entrance to the granite rock enclosure. "It's late afternoon. It should give us enough time to get their attention again, if they are here."

"The Wichita Indians?" Elise asked. "Are they coming back?"

"I don't know. I don't know how to explain it, but maybe you can."

"You want me to explain that there are Indians in the Wichita Mountains?"

"Yes. But they are not like us. Not like people today." Wil no longer felt compelled to reserve his secret any longer and looked at Laura. "They are from the past." The enclosure became quiet as Wil continued, anxious to involve them. "I don't know where they go, but they're out here in the mountains. Your mother and I saw them once, and we couldn't explain it then either. It happened again when you and I were here that winter. I didn't want you telling anyone because I wanted to see if they were real. And I wanted to protect you. I've been searching for them for a long time. I realized I was getting obsessed with it, which is why I decided to take that part out of your mother's journal. I never meant to burn the entire book. I wanted it all to go away."

"But why? You could have just told me. Why did you burn mom's words?" Laura asked.

"I know, I was wrong. But I was scared. I didn't want any more turmoil in your life. You had already been through too much. It was all so confusing. I was ready to give it all up, and then we met Elise and her friends. Once I realized what they do and what I heard them talking about with that treasure, I thought that maybe she could help us. I wanted something more. I wanted to know if what our family saw was real."

"Did these same Indians take you away from the campsite?" Elise asked.

"Yes. I'm not sure where they took me. It seemed odd. I was still in the mountains, but there was something different about it. I can't explain it."

"That's not who visited us last night," Elise said.

"What do you mean?" Wil asked.

"I don't know who they were. They were all around us. They cut through Elise's tent and then surrounded us. They even pushed us down," Laura stated.

"And it was their eyes," Elise continued. "They had these slanted eyes that reflected the light. They didn't look like Indians at all."

"I didn't see anything like that," Wil said. "For a time, I almost felt like I was somewhere else when they left me."

"They left you?" Elise asked.

"For a while, and then they came back. When the sun came up, I wasn't far from here and recognized these rocks. That's how I found you."

"They wanted you to find us," Elise stated. She thought for a moment and became restless. "I need to get out of here." They crawled out of the enclosure and welcomed the fresh air. "Where are we?"

"We're on the southeastern side of Sunset Peak. I was up there, toward the top of the mountain," Wil said.

"Show me," Elise said. They traversed the foothill and angled up the rocky slope. The mountain rolled in various slopes disguised by the thickening foliage. They followed Wil horizontally to a small clearing on the other side of the slope. "This is well protected from being seen below. How far are we from our campsite?"

Wil pointed across the mountain. "It's over that way. It's far."

Elise observed the clearing and kicked some charred wood, "Was this your fire?"

"No. It was here when they left me. They must use it at night."

"It's enormous. It's more like a bonfire than a campfire." Elise looked around the area and continued thinking. "Why would they take all three of us away from our campsite? It's almost as if they didn't want us there."

"Or they wanted us further away. More remote. But why?" Laura asked.

"It's so they could watch us. Look." Wil pointed toward a grove of trees enclosed by thick shrubs. Crouched underneath and blended perfectly with the landscape, a brown face observed them in the stillness. "Don't move. Let him know that we see him." Wil knelt slowly and placed his hands on the ground. He then motioned for the observer to come forward.

"Wil," Elise stated.

"It's okay. Just keep still. He's sizing us up. It's three to one."

"Not if you count the two behind us," Elise added. They turned around to see two men standing with knives drawn. The man in the bushes emerged in an instant, surrounding them in the center of the clearing. They observed the men in detail. Their thick, black hair fell against their tanned skin. Their clothing consisted of rustic leather coverings that appeared weathered and used. The exposed skin revealed slender, muscular bodies with agile frames. They appeared as capable outdoorsmen with military-like precision to their statures. They observed Elise, Wil and Laura with an anticipated stance. "Amazing."

Wil made eye contact with all three of them. He spoke in a language that was not English. The three men reacted to his words.

The two standing near each other spoke in low tones. Wil spoke again. The larger of the two acknowledged him with a few syllables. Wil smiled and placed his hand on his chest, and spoke to Elise and Laura. "I look like them." He pointed to Laura. The second man uttered some words and indicated Laura's long hair. Wil spoke again and motioned to Laura. The men reacted with understanding.

"What did you tell them?" Laura asked.

"That you are my daughter." Wil spoke again and directed their attention toward Elise. "I told them you are our friend that is here to help us." The dialogue continued in short sentences. Wil struggled at times to pronounce some words but kept their interest in the feeble conversation.

Confusion became apparent upon their faces several minutes in to the fragmented discussion. Wil struggled to reply at times, unsure of his pronunciation.

"What's wrong?" Laura asked.

"They want to know why we are here and where we come from. I think they also want to know what kind of clothes we are wearing. I do not understand some of their words. I know they are speaking in the tribal language. I'm not as fluent as they are. I don't understand what they mean. It's the part about 'where we come from' that is confusing me."

"They want to know where we live?" Laura asked.

"Or what time we're from," Elise stated. "How could they be living out here for so long undetected by anyone? These mountains aren't the Rockies. They are not that vast."

"I think they are asking where the others are," Wil said.

"Are they lost?" Laura asked.

"I think they are confused. They keep saying they want to go back through the mountain. They don't know what to do."

"That goes for me, too," Elise said.

* * * * * * *

The taxi stopped at the departure entrance to the Lawton / Fort Sill Regional Airport. Jeff pulled his travel case through the door and waited in line. He checked the time and reviewed his itinerary. The small airport allowed him to see most of the main mall of the terminal. His patience became short for any further stay in Oklahoma. Knowing he was departing with nothing to show for his investment in time, he was eager to return to Arizona and salvage as much of his career as possible. The agreement with Gene and Elise angered him as he could not share his experiences with anyone outside of the team without legal approval. The culmination of events from Tombstone to the Wichita Mountains offered him no resolve toward the dire situation with his university employer.

He thought of the entire experience in the mountains. His temper flared as he recalled the numerous events that could have benefited him. His frustration with Gene to not pursue the potential of the opportunity at the Owen Corr site tore at him. He knew the potential of that discovery could motivate his career down a path of complete job security, fame, and fortune. The interference of science and the authorities aggravated him. He looked at his watch and let go of his travel case. He unlatched it from his wrist and turned it over. His engraved initials, along with Karen's initials, remained visible on the backing. He thought of her and shook his head. The sudden thought that his watch was once strapped on a dead man's arm surpassed his threshold for tolerance. In a mild fit of rage, he balled up the watch and threw it at a nearby waste can. The watch hit the opening with a loud impact against the metal lid. He stared at the can without remorse and reached for his travel case.

"Having some issue, Sir?"

Jeff turned to see an airport security guard standing next to him. The encounter startled his momentary lapse in judgment. "No, officer. Just a long-overdue goodbye to the past."

The officer observed Jeff with scrutiny and asked for his flight reservation. "I see. In the future, please make sure your goodbyes are less dramatic. It will avoid any unnecessary attention. Enjoy your flight to Arizona."

"Believe me, I will. I won't ever be coming back here. Can you tell me where the men's room is? I need to make one last contribution to my time here."

The officer glared at Jeff. "Down the terminal and to the right, just before the service gates."

"Great. I definitely don't want to miss my flight."

The officer turned away and mumbled, "I don't want you to either."

Jeff checked his travel case and received his boarding pass. He hurried to the restroom and turned the corner without looking. He slammed in to a large man exiting through the door, knocking his belongings against the wall.

"Watch where you're going, you idiot."

"Sorry about that," Jeff replied.

Three more men stopped in front of Jeff as the larger man picked up his items. "Yes, you are." The man swung at Jeff and knocked his travel bag out of his hand. "You can be sorry for that, too." He pushed Jeff out of the way and kicked his bag across the floor. The three other men joined the man and walked out of the restroom. Jeff rubbed his shoulder and picked up his bag. He watched the four men stop at the baggage claim area. He noticed Ed Silver walk through the arrival entrance.

"Mr. Silver," Jeff yelled and approached him. "I didn't know you were flying out today. I guess you've had enough of Oklahoma too?"

Ed glared at him with uneasiness. "Uh, yeah. It's time to go. It's been quite an adventure, that's for sure."

"Did you get Owen Corr's remains worked out with the authorities?" Jeff asked.

"Yep. We got him all dug up and taken care of."

"That was fast. I thought the forensics team wasn't supposed to be out there until tomorrow morning?" Jeff asked. "That's one of the reasons I'm leaving early."

Ed looked around the terminal and then back at Jeff. "I guess they got out there earlier than expected. Say, your friend Gene, when is he leaving?"

"Their last day is tomorrow. They were packing up to go to the Sunset Peak site and meet his wife there."

"Is this guy bothering you?" Jeff swung around to see the same four men gathering around him. The larger man walked to within inches of Jeff. "You sure like to get in the way, don't you?"

Ed stepped between them. "No, this young man and I are talking. He is filling me in on some information. Excuse us for one minute." Ed pulled Jeff to the side. "Ignore them. I must say, I am surprised to see you here at the airport. I thought you were a part of their team?"

"Not anymore. Let's just say it was time to part ways. I'm headed home," Jeff said.

"That's too bad. It must be frustrating to leave and not have anything to show for it." Ed observed Jeff with a curious tone and watched him react to his words. "That friend of yours, Gene, sure seems to be in charge. You know, Jeff, after all that happened out there at the site, I can't forget that ole Owen Corr is still family to me. And family is family, do you know what I mean?"

"Yes sir. Family is important," Jeff replied.

"Yes, it is. And I hope to preserve Owen's legacy, however messed up it may be, as best I can. As a man of history, I'm sure you can appreciate that. Am I right?" Ed asked.

Jeff found himself succumbed to the one-way conversation. "Uh, yes sir."

"Good. I never got to ask him before I left, but is there any chance you know what Gene did with the treasure?" Ed asked. "That will go a long way to solving the confusion surrounding Owen's troubled past. I'd appreciate any help you could offer."

"I'm not entirely sure. He was supposed to give it to the refuge authorities for them to hang on to, but I don't think he did yet. Finding my watch changed everything. He probably forgot."

"Finding your *what*?" Ed asked.

Jeff's face became flushed as he realized what he said. Panic consumed him as he quickly tried to recant his statement. "Nothing. They got busy. I would guess the treasure is still with them at the site."

Ed smiled. "That's good. Thank you. Well, you had better get on your plane."

"Aren't you coming? This is the last plane out for the day," Jeff said.

Ed became nervous. "Sure. You go on ahead, now. Don't wait for me. I've got a little business to tend to in the men's room. You take care."

Jeff shook hands and walked toward the departure gate. He observed the four men gather back around Ed. They approached the rental car counter and waited for the attendant. Ed signed several pages of paperwork and checked his watch. He grabbed his belongings and rushed down the terminal. Jeff watched the attendant slide some keys and a map to the large man. He shoved the items in his pocket and walked out of the terminal with his three companions.

"Sir, please step forward," the airport agent directed Jeff.

Jeff turned around and handed her his boarding pass. He looked back at the exit and down the terminal as his mind raced from the confusing observation. A feeling of uneasiness began to overcome him as he thought to make sense of what he witnessed. "Actually, I need to check on something. I'll get back in line." He took his boarding pass and flung his travel bag over his shoulder. He approached the rental car attendant. "Excuse me, where is your rental lot located?" The attendant circled an area on the airport map and handed it to Jeff. He ran out of the terminal and stopped at the curbside drop off area. Vehicles and taxis passed in large numbers as he perused the road. He looked across the rental lot and saw the backdoor of a white van slam shut. Jeff noticed the large man open the passenger side door. All four men were in the van as he watched them drive away.

Jeff returned inside the terminal. The intercom buzzed with the final announcement of his departing flight. He hurried to the gate—

the last of the passengers filed toward the restricted area waiting to board. The mix of people made it difficult to see through the crowd.

"Last call, sir," the attendant stated.

"You didn't happen to see an older gentleman board for this Arizona flight, did you?" Jeff asked.

The attendant gave him a frustrated look. "I'm not privy to that information, sir. This is a full flight, and they are beginning to board." Jeff looked down at his boarding pass. He slapped it against his hand and looked back down the terminal. "We're closing the gate now, sir. Are you boarding?"

* * * * * * *

Wil Brooks observed the horizon with a solemn feeling to the moment. The late evening sky began to transition in an array of colors that seemed to emulate the mystery before him. The deepening blue spanned across the distance in hues of azure to indigo. Shades of fiery orange and red intermingled with the fading wisps of clouds casting an aerial glow that accentuated the landscape below. The southwestern setting appeared perfect, except for the lone thunderstorm building along the remote skyline. The rising anvil-shaped cloud crept in from the west. Its menacing presence brought wonder and concern to those watching it develop from the top slopes of Sunset Peak.

Wil watched the formation gain in strength. An occasional glimpse of lightning flashed from deep within the cloud. It highlighted the expanding storm against the dusk, making it appear more ominous. All around the area, in every other direction, the sky remained undisturbed. The vastness of the clarity combined with the expanse of the Great Plains gave the storm cloud the appearance of a lone island. Just as the anomaly that sat before him, the atmospheric feature strangely did not belong.

He continued observing the electrical display within the distant cloud and returned his attention upon the men. They whispered among themselves with curious expressions. Wil entertained occasional discussion with half phrases and muttered interpretation. He deciphered what he could of their language, but he knew much of the attempt was in vain. He motioned several times about the mountain. The men spoke of its rolling slopes and boulder-covered terrain with obvious awareness. Wil tried to describe the mountain with specifics hoping to determine where the men were from and what they kept referring to as home. With each try, confusion led to frustration as Wil yearned to understand them.

"What do they keep pointing at?" Laura asked.

Wil spoke to them and stood. He looked eastward and nodded his head to encourage a vague confirmation with the men. "The black path. They aren't sure what the black path is or where it goes."

"The road?" Laura asked and pointed.

Wil chuckled at the words from the taller of the men. "They want to know what it is that runs so fast on the black path."

"Vehicles? They don't know what vehicles are either?" Laura became perplexed.

One of the men pointed upward and spoke to Wil with a fearful tone. Wil calmed him and appeared to struggle with a reply. "He is asking what makes the lightning move so slowly in the sky. What is the white line in the sky?"

Everyone looked up as Laura spoke first. "The airplane. They're wondering what the airplane is. How could they not know these things? What does this mean?"

"I don't know. They act as if they don't know." Wil paused and thought. "But the one thing they keep referring to is the mountain. They keep saying they are from here when I ask them," Wil said.

"Here, as in Sunset Peak?" Laura asked.

"The valley, the area, all of it. They don't know the name of the mountain, but they know the mountain. What I have trouble with is something about the mountain burning. They keep referring to it as hot or burning."

"The mountain is on fire?" Elise asked. "Can you ask them if that is what they mean?"

"It is what they mean. I just don't understand how they mean it. They are saying something about a burning mountain and their home. It doesn't make any sense," Wil stated.

"It does to them," Elise replied. The three Indians continued mumbling between them. They pointed to the sky and waved their arms as if to include the mountain and the valley below. They stared at Wil, Laura, and Elise and spoke quietly among themselves. Their expressions portrayed a sense of importance with their words. "Can you tell what they are saying?"

"I think they are deciding to accept and trust us. They have not spoken to anyone like us before. They are curious and want to know more," Wil said.

Elise watched their determination and reacted to the moment. "Ask them if they have seen anything else strange on the mountain. Ask them if they have seen anyone else on the mountain that has eyes that glow at night."

"I'm not sure how they may react to that. If I can't explain an aircraft to them, how in the world am I going to explain a question like that?" Wil asked.

"Just do it, Wil. See what they say." Wil got their attention and asked about the slanted eyes Elise and Laura had experienced. All at once, the three men acknowledged Wil with stern faces. The same man that responded to Wil before held up his hand with his fingers spread open. He moved his hand up and down in front of his face.

The bushes moved behind them. The three Indians stood as Wil, Laura, and Elise looked around in fear. Another Indian dressed similar to the other three emerged from the foliage. He was camouflaged to the terrain with streaks of black across his face and arms. He walked around the group and joined the three Indians. They spoke briefly, and without warning, three of them ran through the undergrowth and up the mountain. The one Indian remained and spoke a few syllables to Wil. Without acknowledgment, the Indian turned and followed the other three men.

"What's going on?" Laura asked.

Wil thought for several seconds before responding. "I think he said someone is coming. Back at your tent site. I think someone is there."

"It must be Gene and the team. It would take them about this long to get here. We still have some time. Come on, let's follow those men," Elise said.

"Why?" Laura asked.

Elise looked at Laura with a perplexed expression. "Why? To find out more about them. Don't you see what this could mean? We may have found a lost tribe of people out in these mountains. All of this is incredible. Hurry! Let's go." They took off after the four men and plowed their way through the thick vegetation. The dense growth slowed their pursuit as they pushed through the bushes and branches. The trees gave way to a more angled slope covered with granite and boulders the size of cars piled on top of each other. They reached the top of a lower slope and searched the area for the Indians.

"Do you see them anywhere?" Laura asked.

"I smell something burning. This way," Wil directed. They followed him across a granite outcropping to the other side of a higher peak. The view became more expansive as they reached the other side of the granite wall. A large bonfire burned in front of them. The flames tore at the darkening sky as they descended next to it. "They were here." Wil pointed at the footprints in the dirt. They looked around the area and were able to see much of the terrain.

"Where could they have gone? There is nowhere else to go but up the mountain. And we could see them from here if they did," Laura said.

"They sure are fast," Wil replied.

"Almost too fast," Elise added. "Look at this view. We can see everything from up here. There is no way they could have gotten this far ahead of us and we not see them."

"Maybe they hid as we went by them?" Laura asked.

"No, Elise is right," Wil said. "That would not explain this fire. They had to have built this earlier."

Elise leaned against the boulder. The fire crackled with a voracious appetite as it consumed the piled wood and branches. The hotbed of coals shimmered in the failing light. "This fire has been here a while. They didn't just build this." Elise continued to think. "Ten years ago, you two had a fire going when you saw that Indian too, didn't you?" Wil and Laura nodded. "And then there is the energy we saw on our instruments that is emitting from this mountain. And now we have Indians disappearing."

Wil approached her next to the fire. The heat billowed from its intensity. "And they have been watching us. That fourth man came out of nowhere. They knew we were here." He waited for Elise to respond. "You said you would help me. What do you think?"

"I think I need to get down to Gene and the team as fast as I can. And don't worry, I'll be discreet. It will be dark soon. They built this big fire for a reason, so maybe they will return. See if you can find them or any other clues and then meet me at the tent site before nightfall. I need to check with Gene before this goes any further."

"At least tell me you have some idea to this?" Wil asked.

"Not yet. I need to get some science involved. Then we can narrow this down. But until then, we need to protect these people as best we can. No one needs to know about this until we can better communicate with them." They agreed with their plan and separated. Elise started off of the mountain toward her tent site. Remembering a moment from before, she turned around and yelled. "Hey, Wil. When you asked that Indian about the slanted eyes, what did he mean when he passed his hand over his face?"

Wil yelled in reply, "I think he was trying to say a mask."

Elise followed the contoured slope off of the mountain. Her eyes and feet navigated the terrain with developing endurance, but her mind raced with the dilemma and mystery of the Indians. Until now, everything had been a culmination of experience and emotion. Interaction with limitation had been the only recourse for her and the confounding situation. She knew the needed variable was science. She trekked across the landscape with the expertise of a trained hiker. The fading sunlight proved invaluable as she guided herself with confidence toward the tent site.

She thought of her dreams, remembering the visions of fire, the mountains, and the faces that had no clarity. She contemplated their connection with everything they had experienced. The intrigue of the Indians dominated her mind. Frustration ensued as she turned from reason to her comfort zone of science. She processed the events from her scientific approach and envisioned everything under that purview. The team's experiences at the other site with the treasure and the windows absorbed her thoughts about her experiences at Sunset Peak. Finding the mountain from her visions proved to be her joy and confirmation, but now the science was needed to establish proof and answer the difficult questions. Above all, she wanted to help Wil.

Elise traversed the last foothill before the valley. She stopped suddenly as her mind froze in revelation. *The fire!* She jumped in elation and ran toward the site. She bounded through the remaining trees before reaching the inlet. People gathered around her tent. All she could think about was discussing everything with Gene and getting back to Wil.

"Hey everybody! It took you long enough to get here. Where's Gene? I was beginning to think he had run off with the treasure!" Elise said.

"I hope not. That wouldn't be good for either of us." Elise stammered to a stop. A large man wearing a camouflaged boonie hat and black bandana emerged from the tent.

A second masked man stepped from behind the tent and moved toward her. "You look tired."

The large man opened the tent flap. "Why don't you have a seat. Then you can tell us about that treasure. We would really like to hear your story." Two other masked men stepped from the trees.

Elise noticed pistols hanging on the hips of each man. The large man motioned for her to enter. "Don't make me ask again."

Chapter 13

Wil and Laura sat together watching the bonfire. The wind calmed for the late evening sounds of nature to be heard. Their view portrayed the rugged beauty of the Wichita Mountains. Wil observed Elk Mountain bathed in the shades of orange, red, and gold. The valley between them awakened with nocturnal hunters. He saw his favorite rock formation. Crab Eyes appeared small from Sunset Peak; the twin rocks were barely visible in the distance. His keen knowledge of their location allowed him to locate them. He watched them become shadowed and thought of his late wife, Ayita.

He glanced at Laura and knew the moment had arrived. Unsure of what was to come from their encounter with the Indians, he yearned to repair with Laura and strengthen their bond. Tired from the confusion of the entire ordeal, he reached for Laura's hand. Laura felt his touch. She noticed his angle away from the fire. She followed his stare and realized the focus of his attention. She placed her other hand over his.

"It's a good view, isn't it?"

Wil wiped tears. "Your mother loved to write. She used to say it was her escape from reality." Wil laughed. "What she meant, but never told me, was that it was her escape from anything interfering with her happiness. She said the fulfillment of her writing was not the ending but the journey to get there. Sometimes she would write a story and not know how it would end. She let the story take her on a journey. That was the fun part, she used to say. She told me that she would simply clear her mind when she could not think of something to write about and ask God for the words. She had strong faith." Wil exhaled deeply. "I never knew joy like your mother had. I put my joy in her. And when she died…" He turned toward Laura. "You are my joy now. You are all I have left. I love you and never wanted anything to hurt you. I've been so confused. Meeting Elise and having this encounter with these people has been more than I expected."

"Dad, what is it? What's bothering you?"

"All of it."

"All of what?"

"Trying to make sense of all of this. From when your mother and I saw that man the first time to why I tore the pages out of her journal. I didn't want a lot of questions asked or a reminder of it. I didn't want the police to know, and I was tired of searching for answers. I reached the point that I wanted it to go away. Until I met Elise. And now we have the discovery of these people living in the mountains. I have proof that I didn't have when I accidentally burned the journal."

"Is that why you are upset? You have regret that you burned the journal?" Laura asked.

"I had regret that very moment." Wil stared at the bonfire. He calmed in recollection. "When the people took me from the campsite, it was still dark. I must have passed out. When I woke up, it was day. I was still here on Sunset Peak, but it was different. It even felt different."

"In what way?"

Wil pointed toward Elk Mountain. "I looked across the valley. It didn't look like it does now. It was overgrown. Nothing was burned from previous fires. Everything looked different." Before Laura could respond, Wil looked northward. "And I didn't see the road."

"It's hard to see it from here anyway," Laura said.

"You don't understand. It wasn't there. It was gone." Wil envisioned the memory. The unknown became more visible as he thought of reason. He looked at Laura with renewed vigor. "We need to protect these people. Something is happening here that I can't explain, but we need to make sure these people are safe no matter what. I don't want them becoming part of some half-witted college experiment like I saw at that other site."

"But you asked for Elise's help. There are going to be others, dad. The whole team will be involved. They are good people," Laura stated. "Whatever you experienced here, they can help figure it out. You need to trust them."

"No. These people have to remain a secret. We found them, we spoke with them. They are us. Even your mother knew it. I see it now. I don't know where they are from or what they are doing here, but they reached out to us. The first time was with your mother and me. Then they reached out to you and me ten years ago. It's happened again. We have to protect them." A hint of anger resonated in his voice. "Come on, help me put this fire out."

"How will they find us without the fire? It's getting dark. Don't you want to see if they come back?" Laura asked.

"We can build another fire. Hurry, we have to stop Elise."

* * * * * * *

Jeff Finbow stared at his boarding pass. He watched it bounce on the passenger seat of his rental car. He exhaled with unease and returned his attention upon the road. He sped along the highway leading toward the nearest entrance to the Wichita Mountains Wildlife Refuge. His mind wrestled with his reasoning to leave the airport and pursue the odd encounter with the four men. He wanted to board the plane and go home to Arizona, forgetting his entire experience in Oklahoma. But he knew he would be going home empty-handed. And irritating him more, no matter how he tried to ignore it, was Ed Silver. Jeff had the feeling that something was wrong.

He recalled the scene of Ed speaking with the four men at the airport. Nothing about the observation appeared coincidental to him. He knew his hunch was risky, but he acted on impulse. He held hope that he could salvage something from his time in Oklahoma and benefit his career back home. His time was nearing an end, and he knew he had to provide new material to keep his lucrative job with the university's history department.

He regretted his departure from the team and did not want ill-feelings from them. He knew it was time for him to leave and his tolerance of the entire situation was over. He despised not getting more accessibility to the treasure and not being allowed to further investigate the gravesite of Owen Corr. The incredible occurrence with his watch rivaled every frustration. The limitations on the unique experience drove his anger to ignite his temper and quit without notice. But driving his curiosity above all of those occurrences was seeing Ed Silver at the airport.

Jeff noticed the exit to the wildlife refuge and prepared to turn. He wondered how to get another attempt at some answers that would benefit him. He needed facts to launch his career. The situation at Sunset Peak was in question, and he was curious about what had become of Elise, Laura, and Wil. The rental car shuddered. Jeff jolted from his thoughts and gripped the steering wheel. The car pulled toward the right as he resisted to stay on the road.

Jeff passed the billboard, reading its welcome to Cache, Oklahoma and the Gateway to the Wichitas. He took the exit as a warning light flashed on the dashboard. He slowed and parked the car on the shoulder. The road stretched in to the distance leading toward the Wichita Mountains. The setting sun illuminated the granite slopes casting a southwestern appeal.

Jeff opened his door and inspected the vehicle. The car leaned oddly from the back-right tire. "No!" he yelled and kicked the gravel. The rim rested on the asphalt. The tire was partially shredded with a distinct odor of heated rubber. "I don't have time for this," he voiced and opened the trunk for the spare. The distinctive chirp of a police siren sounded and stopped behind him. Jeff watched as a tall, imposing officer exited a Cache patrol car.

"Hello there. I'm Sheriff Ken Stockton, Cache Police. It looks like you need some help, young man."

Jeff extended his hand and introduced himself. "Yes, I sure could, Sheriff. Rotten timing for a flat. I'm in a hurry and need to get to Sunset Peak before sundown. I'm trying to find the jack and get started."

Sheriff Stockton checked the trunk. "I don't think you need to bother with that." He pushed against the spare. Jeff watched his hand sink into the tire. "That's not going to work."

"Great," Jeff said and stared toward the mountains. "The one time I don't inspect the rental."

"Can you call the company and get a tow?"

"I don't have time for that, but I guess that's my only choice," Jeff replied.

"What's the hurry on Sunset Peak? It's a little late for hiking, isn't it?"

"I need to check on some friends out there. It's a long story. I want to make sure they are okay," Jeff said.

"Why don't you call them? You can get reception out there sometimes."

Jeff thought before answering. His situation was becoming complicated. Unsure of where the conversation would go, he continued. "It would be better if I saw them in person. Call it a hunch, I want to make sure they are alright."

"Are they staying in the wilderness area? I hope they registered with the refuge headquarters."

"I'm sure they did," Jeff said.

Sheriff Stockton narrowed his eyes in observation of Jeff. His towering presence made Jeff feel obscure. Jeff noticed his change in demeanor and tried to appear casual. The sheriff walked beside Jeff's car and looked in the back. He checked the front seats and strolled next to Jeff. "It sounds like you're in a situation." Sheriff Stockton glanced at his license tag and wrote down the number. "Why don't you lock up your vehicle, I'll call it in, and we'll go check on your friends. How does that sound?" The sheriff stood between Jeff and his car with an expression that provided the answer for him.

"Uh, yes sir. Thanks for the offer. I don't think I have much choice."

"Good. Have a seat in the front." Jeff entered the police vehicle and watched the sheriff activate his vest radio. He remained outside for a few moments and opened the driver's side door. He switched the radio to his car and drove forward. "Headquarters, this is Stockton. I'm going 10-23 to the refuge. Follow up on previous transmission, over."

The radio crackled back in acknowledgment. The sheriff increased speed and addressed Jeff. "Mr. Finbow, why don't you tell me what all of this is really about? I'd hate to waste taxpayer-funded gasoline."

Jeff realized his ploy to appear casual had failed. Not willing to risk anything with a sheriff, he told him everything about the four men and Ed Silver. He kept his response brief and limited the details of the team and their experiences. Careful not to ramble, he concluded his response explaining his involvement in the situation and his feeling about Ed and the four men. Sheriff Stockton remained silent as they approached the entrance to the wildlife refuge. They rumbled over the cattle guard as Sheriff Stockton slowed the vehicle. Jeff watched him reach for his radio and contemplate a transmission.

"That's an interesting story, Mr. Finbow. You seem to have a lot going on out here that no one is aware of."

"It's been an interesting couple of days. But like I said, I just want to be sure. What are you doing with your radio?"

Sheriff Stockton glared at him. Jeff felt as though he had violated some protocol with his question. The sheriff returned his attention through the windshield. "I want to be sure, too." He clicked the transmitter. "Refuge headquarters, this Sheriff Stockton. What's the 10-20 of the refuge manager, over?"

* * * * * * *

"There's their vehicle," Karen Farris pointed ahead.

"Park next to it," Gene Saige said. "Everyone, get your gear and be ready to go. I don't want to waste any time. Anything from Elise on the radio or phone yet?"

"Nothing," Tommy replied.

"Make sure you have your flashlights. I know it's nearly dark, but move as fast as you can," Gene stated. They gathered their gear from the trunk.

"Gene, what about this?" Mike pointed at the two sacks of silver bars and gold coins in the trunk.

"Ah! I forgot about the treasure." Gene thought and looked around the area.

"We can't leave it here; it's too risky," Mike stated.

"No, we can't do that." Gene became desperate for a solution. "How heavy are those sacks? Can we carry them?"

"Across that terrain? No way," Tommy said.

"I'll stay with the vehicle and watch over the treasure. I can cover the radio in case Elise calls," Karen stated.

"Thanks Karen." Gene motioned for Mike and Tommy to go ahead. He walked next to Karen. "Take this." He handed Karen a small pistol. "Elise and I got special permits. You're alone on a wildlife refuge at night. I'll feel better about your safety. Do you know how to use it? It's loaded."

"Better than you do," Karen smiled. "Thanks, Gene."

The three men hurried across the road and through the woods around the base of Sunset Peak. The forest became dark from the setting sun and the canopy of leaves blocking the remaining light. They skirted the foothills and pushed through the foliage, often stopping to check the directions to Elise's campsite. The terrain was different from their previous site. Sunset Peak rose sharply near their route with thicker undergrowth and larger granite obstacles to negotiate. Identical in remoteness to the Owen Corr site, each team member began to notice the difference in effort to traverse the ground.

"Why did Elise pick this part of the refuge? Nearly sixty-thousand acres to choose from, and she comes here?" Tommy asked.

"She didn't choose it. It chose her," Gene replied. "We're getting close. Keep moving." They continued toward the campsite at a slower pace. The darkness consumed the area as dusk set in. The dim light played night tricks with their eyes making it difficult to see the terrain. The vegetation became dense. Unable to see ahead, Gene led them around the foliage and up an embankment. The team traveled along higher ground to avoid the thick undergrowth below. They weaved between boulders as the incline increased.

"Gene, I'll be the first to say it. Are we lost?" Tommy asked.

"No. We're getting some elevation to see where we are going," Gene replied.

"Can we stick to flat land? I'd be happy with a best guess at this point," Mike asked.

"And I'm about to pass out," Tommy added.

"Would you rather be trudging through that forest in the dark? Quit whining, and come on." Gene started forward as Mike pulled his arm.

"Wait, listen. Do you hear that?" Mike asked. The team stopped. The distinct sound of footsteps on granite were coming toward them. They aimed their flashlights in the direction of the sound. "I hear talking."

Gene aimed his light up the ridge. "Elise! Is that you?"

"No. It's Laura and Wil Brooks. Who are you?"

"Laura! It's Gene. Elise's husband. The whole team is here."

Laura and Wil emerged from the top of the ridge and waved in the light. They descended to the team. "What are you doing here? You're a quarter the way up Sunset Peak."

"We're trying to find Elise. Is she not with you?" Gene asked.

"She went back to the campsite to meet you. You haven't seen her yet?" Laura asked.

"No. We're trying to find the site."

Laura snickered. "Look behind you." The team turned around and saw a bright fire illuminating a tent at the base of the mountain. "Good thing we found you."

"Yeah, way to go, Gene. You elevated us right by it," Tommy stated.

"Come on, let's get down there," Gene said.

The group descended toward the camp. The elevated view made it easy to plot a course. They walked to the inlet and stood by the fire as Gene rushed toward the tent. "Elise?"

"I'm over here," Elise replied. She stepped from the trees.

Gene noticed a strangeness about her. "Are you okay?"

"That all depends on you and your friends." A voice from behind Elise answered in a stern manner. "Move over by the fire, all of you!" The man emerged from the trees, joined by three other masked men blocking the entrance to the inlet. "Get over there." The large man wearing the boonie hat and black bandana shoved Elise next to Wil. "I'm going to make this simple. As to how hard it gets is up to you." The man rested his hand on his holster, ensuring everyone noticed his sidearm. "I want that treasure. I know you didn't turn it in, so where is it?"

The group kept silent. Tommy glanced at Gene and then looked at the ground. One of the other men shoved him in the back. "What are you looking at him for? Answer the man!"

"I…I don't…"

"Hit him again," the large man said. "This time, make it count."

"Wait!" Gene yelled. "I have the treasure. I know where it is. But please don't hurt anyone."

"Keep talking, and I won't have to," the large man said. "Where is it?"

"It's back at our vehicle, parked by the road," Gene replied. "One of my team is there with it."

"What? There's another? I thought you accounted for everyone?" the large man asked his counterpart. The other masked man shrugged his shoulders. The large man paused and then drew his handgun. He walked closer to Gene and raised it in front of his face. "Take us to your vehicle." He motioned to his men. "Everyone will follow this guy, single file. Put the two women and the old man at the back of the line." He pointed at two of his men. "File in behind these two." He walked next to Gene and pointed his pistol at his side. "Lead the way. And don't be a hero."

Gene aimed his flashlight and led the group forward. The large man followed behind him, with Tommy and Mike trailing. Two of the masked men walked behind them with Elise, Laura and Wil being followed by the last of the masked men. Gene's team used their flashlights to avoid the scattered obstacles. The dense undergrowth and darkness complicated their journey, causing them to trip often. Gene struggled to find a clear path away from the mountain. The large man shoved him repeatedly, threatening him to hurry.

Tommy tripped on a branch sending him crashing in to the large man. Mike stopped to assist his brother as one of the masked men shoved him to the ground. The large man stood and kicked Tommy in the chest. "Don't let that happen again!"

"He didn't mean to," Elise shouted.

The trailing masked man struck Elise across her face. She lost her balance and collided against Laura. Both women fell to the ground. "Shut up and get in line."

"How dare you!" Wil yelled and rushed to help them. "You heartless coward."

"Coward?" the masked man asked and aimed his pistol at Wil.

"No!" Elise grabbed her flashlight and directed the beam in the masked man's face. He covered his eyes with his free hand as Laura grabbed a dead tree branch. She stood and swung the heavy wood against the man's head. The branch cracked in half as it impacted across his skull. The man fell and discharged his weapon. The shot exploded through the darkness and ricocheted against a boulder. Elise reached for Wil and Laura. "Run! You know these mountains better than anyone. Get out of here!"

"What about you?" Laura asked.

"Go!" Elise hurried next to Wil and whispered, "The Indians and the fire. There's a connection. I hope you find it."

"What's going on back here!" the large man high-stepped toward them. Wil acknowledged Elise as he and Laura sprinted through the darkness.

"They hit me," the masked man replied. "I shot at one of them."

The large man grabbed him by his collar. "And you missed. Get after them!" He pointed at the other two masked men. "One of you go with him. Take their flashlights. I don't care what you have to do. Don't let them get away."

Wil and Laura bounded across the terrain at a careful pace. They stayed together, helping to guide each other over the landscape. Laura looked back to see two flashlight beams bouncing in the darkness toward them. "Dad, they're coming."

Wil guided Laura toward the lower slope of Sunset Peak. The darkness of the ridge contrasted against the hue of the starry sky. He noticed the slope contour to a level area before it rose sharply up the mountain. "Run over there. We can get out of this brush and hide between the boulders." They hurried across the terrain and heaved heavy breaths against the rising slope. Exhaustion tore at them as Laura helped Wil along.

"Just a little bit further," Laura said.

Wil felt his body give out. He placed his hands on his knees and stopped for a breath. "What's that?" He pointed ahead. An orange glow illuminated the area in front of them.

"You have to come on." Laura grabbed his arm and pulled him forward. They rounded a pile of granite boulders and stopped. A huge bonfire lit the area with flames reaching toward the sky. The established base burned bright with red coals. The heat billowed in every direction as Laura watched in bewilderment.

Wil steadied his breathing and took Laura by her arm. He looked into her eyes and forced a desperate smile. "Run. Get away. And no matter what happens, I want you to trust the moment. Believe in what may not be believable." Laura observed her father with confusion. Rather than bombarding him with questions, she simply nodded.

"Both of you stay right there!" said a voice from behind them. The two masked men approached. "You move fast for an old guy. And that pretty thing with you cuts a quick trail too. Why don't we take a rest?"

The second man replied with a congested laugh, "Yeah. Pretty lady, you come over here where I can keep an eye on you."

"Stay away from my daughter!" Wil yelled.

"Aren't you the cocky one? If I remember, you called me a coward. Let's see how tough you are now."

"You take care of that ole buzzard. I've got this one." The second masked man stepped toward Laura and grabbed her arm. Wil lunged at the man and struck his face. The other man punched Wil in the back, knocking him to the ground. "Cold cocking me in the dark. That's dirty pool, mister." The second man kicked Wil in the chest. He moaned and fell in the dirt.

"He's mine." The first masked man snatched Wil by his hair and jolted his head upward. "How did you like that?"

"Leave him alone!" Laura shouted. The second man pulled her toward the forest. She kicked and hit at him. "Let me go!"

He back-handed her in the face. Dazed from the blow, she fought to keep her balance. "That should shut you up," the man said and dragged her to the tree line. She tripped over the foliage. "Let's see that pretty face again." The man grasped Laura's jaw and raised her head. She felt dizzy as the man knelt in front of her. Through her blurred vision, she noticed a movement in the woods. A dark silhouette stepped from a tree behind the man. Laura strained to see the figure raise its head. A pair of slanted, glowing eyes stared back at her from underneath its hood.

The man leaned close to her. "What are you lookin' at? I wouldn't bother with trying to run off again." The man laughed and exhaled in her face. His pungent breath caused her to gag. "There ain't nothin' back there," the man said. He placed his hand on his pistol and turned to mock her. The dark being loomed over him. Horror filled the masked man's eyes. He shoved Laura away and reached for his sidearm. A sudden movement raced passed his face, slashing his arm with a powerful swipe. The menacing figure thrust forward and grabbed the man by his throat. It lifted the man above the ground and threw him several feet from Laura. The masked man rolled across the grass. Unable to locate his weapon, he held his wounded arm and ran for his counterpart by the fire.

The first masked man struck Wil again. He pulled Wil to his feet and stood him in front of the fire. He raised his weapon in Wil's face and cocked the hammer. The man placed his finger on the trigger and aimed. "No one calls me a coward." Wil closed his eyes.

Shh…thump!

The fire's crackle became the only noise in the area. Wil heard the strange silence and opened his eyes. The straight shaft of an arrow penetrated halfway through the masked man's extended forearm. Stunned, the man stared at his arm. He looked toward the direction of the arrow and saw a dark figure standing among the trees. The light from the flames reflected from its sinister slanted eyes. The man's arm began to shake as he aimed at the figure.

Shh…thump!

"Ugh!" The man turned to see the second masked man standing behind him. An arrow protruded from his right shoulder. He fell back against the ground.

Consumed in fear, the first man stepped away. The dark figure moved next to him. With blinding speed, the being spun around and kicked the man's legs out from underneath him. The masked man hit a rock with his head and fell unconscious. The figure approached the second man. He wailed in pain and began to yell as the figure stood over him. "Help, help me!" The figure crushed its fist against the man's face. He blacked out from the impact.

Wil dropped to a knee and observed the dark figure. Laura rushed up from the woods and knelt next to him. They watched as the two figures assembled in front of them. Wil and Laura noticed their shrouded faces appearing as nets with shards of glass embedded for eyes. The mirrored surfaces reflected the firelight with a hellish glow. They watched as one of the figures raised its arm and pointed behind them.

Wil and Laura turned to see another figure emerge from the fire. It stood before them untouched by the flames. The heat had no effect as it remained stationary. With a welcoming gesture, the being motioned them toward the fire. Wil and Laura remained silent as they watched the figure disappear through the blaze. The two remaining figures stepped closer, insinuating their movement forward.

Laura held Wil's arm. "Daddy…"

Wil looked at Laura's frightened eyes. Recalling a similar situation by a fire ten years ago, he saw his daughter's same innocent expression. A comforting smile emerged as he whispered to her. "Just believe." Laura began to cry as they approached the edge of the fire.

"Believe that you will be okay…" Wil continued as they closed their eyes and stepped through the flames.

* * * * * * *

"Where are they at? They should have caught up to us by now," the large man with the bandana asked his counterpart. He stopped the group and grabbed Gene by his shirt. "How much further?"

"We parked up ahead. I can see the highway," Gene replied.

"This is far enough." The large man approached Elise, Mike, and Tommy. "Here is how this works. You three are going to walk back the way we came from. My associate is going to watch you. You won't know where he is. If any of you get the notion to follow us, you won't see this guy again." He placed his hand on Gene's shoulder. "Leave your flashlights on the ground."

Mike and Tommy started walking away as Elise faced her husband. "Gene…"

"It's okay," Gene said. "Go."

"Move it!" the second masked man shoved Elise. They departed into the darkness.

"Take me to your vehicle. And it better be the shortest route," the large man said. He motioned for his counterpart to follow. They continued through an oak forest and reached the highway. Both men watched for oncoming traffic and then escorted Gene across. "Go on ahead. Have whoever is waiting in the vehicle to exit and open the trunk." The large man stayed behind and raised a handheld radio to his face.

Gene approached the back of the vehicle and called for Karen. The door opened, and she stepped outside. "Gene?"

"Yes. Listen, I need you to do exactly as I say. Open the trunk and then throw me the keys."

Seconds passed before she leaned in and pushed the button for the trunk. She looked at Gene before throwing him the keys. Her suspicion became obvious. "It's open. Is everything okay?"

"It is now," the second masked man replied from the front of the vehicle. He pushed Karen toward Gene. "Both of you get against the car. Don't move." The second man took the keys and threw them into the brush.

Gene and Karen faced the vehicle as the two masked men searched the trunk. The second man voiced his satisfaction as they shined their flashlights into the bags. "Looks like it's all here," he said and ran his hand through the gold coins.

The headlights of an approaching vehicle lit the parking area. The large man stepped back from the trunk. "Grab the bags." The second man reached in the trunk as the large man approached the highway. Gene watched him turn away and nudged Karen. With both hands, he slammed the trunk door on to the head of the second masked man. It hit his skull and crushed him against the sacks of treasure. The man pushed away from the trunk and stumbled backward.

"Hey!" the large man yelled and ran toward his counterpart.

"Karen, run!" Gene yelled and ducked along the side of the car.

"Stop!" The large man pointed his flashlight at Karen. He pulled his pistol from the holster and aimed. Dazed from the injury, the second man collided with the large man and reached to break his fall. His hand grabbed at the large man, pulling the bandana off of his face. The flashlight turned upward, revealing the large man's exposed facial features.

Karen saw his face. "You're the man from the historical society. You're Al Silver!"

"You clumsy idiot!" Al shoved his counterpart away and aimed his pistol at Karen.

Bam! Gene shuddered and saw Al grab his leg. He looked back to see Karen's extended arm holding a pistol.

"Run, Gene!" Karen yelled and ran to the front of the car. Gene raced after her as a white van skidded to a stop behind their car. Al limped to the trunk and grabbed the two bags of treasure. He tied the bags together and flung them over his shoulder. He struggled to the van and pitched the heavy bags through an open window.

The masked driver got out and fired several shots in the air. Gene and Karen hid at the front of the car. The driver shoved the second man on to the center seat of the van and slammed the door shut. "Where are the others?"

"I don't know. Let's go," Al replied.

"Did you get shot?" the driver asked.

"It grazed my leg. Drive!"

Both men saw police lights appear in front of them. They noticed the distinct features of a wildlife ranger's lettering on the vehicle. The officer stopped in front of them and opened his truck door. He drew his weapon and aimed. "Turn off the engine and get out of the van!"

"I've had enough of this." Al leaned out of his window and fired at the officer. Bullets rained across the officer's truck, missing him as he dove across the seat. Two of the shots found his back wheel and exploded the tire. The truck sat on its rim as the officer crawled over the front seat to the other side. He rested his arms along the bed of the truck and returned fire. "Let's get out of here!" Al yelled at the driver. The van tires churned up dust and pebbles as it found traction on the asphalt and sped away.

The officer watched the van disappear in the darkness and reached for his radio. "This is Refuge Manager Riley. Suspects are in a white van heading east on highway forty-nine. They are armed, and shots have been fired. Requesting immediate backup and pursuit, over."

The driver reached seventy miles an hour and continued along the narrow two-lane highway. The unforgiving terrain forced him to keep his attention on the road. Al tended to his wound and wrapped his leg with a torn shirt. "How far till we turn?"

"It's the next right. On the other side of that ridge up ahead," the driver replied.

"Where did that ranger come from? I thought you had this place staked out? So far, nothing has gone right with *your* plan. And what about my men? We left them back there. How do you figure on getting them out? I knew you would jack this up," Al said.

The driver ripped off his bandana. Al stared at the angry face of his brother, Ed Silver. "Say that again, and you'll be joining them!" Ed swerved to keep the van on the road as they passed the sign to Caddo Lake. "You obviously didn't search everyone like I told you to. Where did the girl get that pistol? Did you even know she was in the car? If you had followed my plan like I told you to, you wouldn't have gotten shot. As long as your men know to be at the west gate before sunrise, we will pick them up as planned. What happened to them?"

"I don't know. That old man and his daughter took off. My men went after them. It shouldn't be a problem," Al replied.

"There had better not be any killing. We don't need that kind of attention," Ed said. "What about the treasure? Is that all of it?"

"From what I could tell, yes. It's heavy enough," Al said. "We may have one problem, though." Al looked out of his window.

"What?" Ed asked.

"The girl back there recognized me."

Ed reached across the seat and pulled Al toward him. "What!" He cocked his arm and hit Al in the face. "They can identify you now! I ought to…"

"Watch out!" Al yelled and pointed ahead.

Ed slammed on the brakes. Both men saw bright police lights suddenly turn on in front of them. A police car was parked sideways in the intersection, blocking both roadways. Ed gripped the steering wheel and released the brakes. He stepped on the gas pedal and increased speed. "Hold on."

"What are you doing? That's a sheriff's car," Al said.

"I don't care who it is, that's the right turn we have to make, or we're finished," Ed replied.

Jeff Finbow leaned out of the police car. "Sheriff, I think they're going to hit us."

Sheriff Ken Stockton stood outside of his vehicle. He watched the white van increase speed and aimed his shotgun. "Jeff, get out of the car. Run to that ditch on the other side of the road." Sheriff Stockton waved his flashlight at the oncoming van and remained by his vehicle. The van showed no indication of stopping. "Here, take this." He pitched the light to Jeff. He aimed his shotgun and fired.

"He's shooting at us!" Al stated.

Ed turned the van violently toward the right and slammed sideways across the police car. The impact pushed the car toward Jeff. He jumped out of the ditch as the car fell sideways in the shallow ravine. He shined the flashlight at Sheriff Stockton and then toward the driver's door of the damaged van. The stunned driver looked out of the window at Jeff.

"Ed Silver?" Jeff exclaimed.

Ed noticed Jeff and looked away. He regained his composure and turned the wheel. Metal twisted and scratched between the vehicles as the van broke free and drove past the refuge headquarters.

"Are you okay?" Sheriff Stockton asked. "That was a near miss."

"That was too close," Jeff replied. He dusted off his pants and looked at the wrecked police car. "Looks like we need another tow."

Sherriff Stockton lowered his shotgun and watched the tail lights of the escaping van depart around a curve. He stood in front of Jeff with rising anger. Sheriff Stockton exhaled with visible frustration and spoke with a furious quiver in his voice, "Who is Ed Silver?"

Chapter 14

"Is he following us?" Al Silver asked and adjusted his leg bandage.

Ed Silver peered at the rearview mirror, "I don't see anyone. I think we're okay. Are you hit again? I think he fired a shotgun at us." Ed noticed a gaping hole in the windshield.

"My leg is killing me. Are you sure you know where you're going?" Al asked.

"This is the same road they used to get to their site. It's close to where we found the treasure. It leads off of the refuge. We're almost there," Ed replied.

"Where are we?" the second masked man sat up in the middle seat. "What happened?" He pulled his mask off and rubbed his head. Blood trickled across his face.

"You're safe, son," Al stated. "Wrap this around your head to stop the bleeding." Al leaned near Ed. "He may need to go to the hospital."

Ed rolled his eyes. "I think you hit your head too. Both of you sit back and shut your mouths. Aaron, check that treasure and make sure those bags are tied tightly together. I don't want them ripping open." Ed had a smirk on his face as he saw the sacks of gold and silver. "Over a hundred years of family searching, and we finally found it!"

"We're rich!" Al said.

Several minutes passed as they continued down the refuge highway. "This is it." Ed turned along another road. The road narrowed from the thick forestry and vegetation on each side. He slowed and switched on the high beams. They passed a sign for Post Oak Lake and drove to a small parking area. A gray four-door truck was parked at the lot. Ed stopped opposite of the truck and looked at Al and Aaron. "Alright boys, that's our new ride. Aaron, here are the keys. Help your father over there and get it started. I'll get the treasure and set this van on fire." Aaron opened his father's door and helped him to the truck. Al's leg worsened as Aaron tried to rebandage it. He secured his father in the front seat and hurried back to the van. Ed grabbed his pistol and a box of ammunition. He opened the side door and pulled the bags of treasure to the edge. A long, thick cord bound the two bags together, separating the gold coins from the silver bars. Ed admired the loot. Aaron rushed to the other side of the van and opened the door.

"We need to get going," Aaron said.

"Grab that roadmap on the dashboard," Ed said. "Get anything else that can identify us."

Aaron opened the driver's side door and reached for the map. "Uncle Ed, look." Aaron pointed through the windshield. The headlights brightened the sage grass field in front of them. Ed squinted ahead. A man wearing a black and red-checkered coat stood in the middle of the field.

Ed braced himself against the door. He rubbed his eyes and noticed the man moving toward them. "Owen Corr." His hands began to shake as he pulled his pistol from the holster. "Aaron, get back to the truck. Now!" Ed stepped away from the van and aimed at Owen. "I don't care what you are. If you come any closer, I'll shoot!" Owen kept coming. Ed fired three times at Owen's chest. He watched as Owen stopped. Ed placed his other hand on the pistol. Owen was close enough for Ed to see his orange cap and brown pants. He watched as Owen slowly began to raise his head.

Aaron drove the truck behind the van. Al looked out of the window and saw Owen standing in the field. "Ed, come on! It's not worth dying for. Get in the truck!"

The van headlights flickered and shut off. Darkness engulfed the area. The stillness of the night surrounded Ed as he tried to see. He grabbed the two bags of treasure and slung them over his shoulder. "I'm coming!" He turned to see Owen standing between him and the truck. Ed backed away to the front of the van. He watched as the truck spun its tires and drove away. "Wait, you fools!" The light of the night sky began to illuminate the area in a dim hue. Ed wrapped the cord across his shoulders and held each bag. Owen moved around the van toward Ed. Ed hurried toward the railing of the Post Oak Lake dam. He tripped over the jagged granite terrain and felt his way forward.

He saw Owen still approaching. Ed fell against the railing of the concrete walkway. The dam rose high above the cavernous ravine on one side and the still blackness of the water on the other. The narrow walkway curved to the other side of the ravine along the top of the dam. Ed shuffled across the walkway, holding on to the railing with each step. He saw Owen moving toward him.

Fear began to incapacitate his thinking. Out of breath, he stopped at the center of the dam and looked over the railing. Darkness filled the chasm as he fought for breath. He watched Owen continue to move. Ed surrendered to the moment and spoke to alleviate his dread. "I've searched for this treasure my whole life." Anger began to swell within him. His words became his weapon as Owen neared. "My grandfather told us what you did. This treasure belongs to the family." He waited as Owen stepped within feet of him. To subdue his mounting fear, he lost his temper and yelled, "He should have shot you in Arizona!"

Owen Corr raised his head. Ed stared at his lifeless black eyes. He felt his face paralyze. His breathing became erratic as he fell to a knee. He let go of one of the bags and reached for his pistol. "You aren't taking me!" The sudden shift in weight caused him to lose balance. He reached for the railing and missed as the bags twisted around his neck. Screaming as Owen stood over him, he fell backward in the water. The laden bags plunged through the black depths pulling Ed toward the distant bottom. He flailed with his arms trying to reach the fading surface. The heavy metals impacted against a layer of thick silt. The bags sunk in the mud and anchored Ed's lifeless body deep underneath the murky bottom.

* * * * * * *

Wil and Laura stood together by the bonfire. The wind blew gently across their faces. The rising sun cast its warmth across the landscape as they observed the spring day with its vibrant colors and emerging life. They stretched from their night time slumber by the fire. The view from their elevation on Sunset Peak allowed them to see most of the area. Elk Mountain and the Crab Eyes area awakened in the morning array. The contrast of color to the deepening greens of the vegetation highlighted each feature of the scenic beauty.

Laura faced northward. A puzzled expression complimented her curious stare. Wil noticed her interest and joined in the view. They watched the northern grasslands with a sense of confusion. Wil knew she was attempting to define the sight before her with what her mind could not explain.

"Amazing view, isn't it?" Wil asked. Laura remained silent. Wil continued to console her. "When they took me through the fire the first time, I saw this same view. I couldn't explain it. Part of me didn't want to. It was confusing. But at the same time, it felt right. As if I was supposed to see this, but I did not know why." Laura kept looking ahead. "What I dreaded the most was how I was going to explain it to you."

"And now you don't have to," Laura said. She paused to continue absorbing the panoramic. "It all looks so…"

"New?" Wil asked.

"Perfect."

"And wild," Wil added.

"Where is the highway?" Laura asked. Wil did not respond. "The northern boundary fence, where is it? Caddo Lake is not there either. Up here, that fire from two years ago. Nothing is burned. It's overgrown. I don't remember the trees being so big."

Wil realized Laura was becoming anxious. "Go ahead, I know you see them."

"I assume those are dwellings around that creek? I do not remember that creek being there."

Wil tried to embrace her as she pushed him away. She ran to the other side of the rise and looked westward. "Where is the ranch house? The one that I wish we had? I don't see any farmland. Nothing is plowed. No radio towers. No towns."

Wil walked toward her. "Honey, it will be okay. We will figure this out together."

"This is what you saw? Is this what you hid from me? Is this why you burned mom's journal? What is this? Where are we!" Laura yelled. Her confusion turned to frustration.

"Wherever this is, whatever that fire does, how in the world we are even able to stand here is why I did what I did. All I know is we are here. As to why we are here and how it happened, I don't know. But we can find out together." Wil extended his hand.

Laura's eyes welled with tears that she fought to harbor. Her voice writhed through the emotion that choked her words. She cleared her throat. A long pause lapsed as Laura stared at Wil. "Could this be heaven?"

Wil gave Laura a bewildered reply. "No, Laura. It's not."

"But what if mom is here? What if this is a pathway to the next life, to heaven? What if she's here?"

"Honey." Wil became filled with remorse.

"No. What if this is? This could be heaven."

"Stop, Laura. Don't try to find a resolution in this," Wil stated.

"How do you know?"

"How do I know what?" Wil asked.

Laura became angry, "How do you know this is not heaven!"

Wil grabbed her arms and pulled her close, "Because last I read, you don't need a *bonfire* to get there!" He paused. "Do not make this something that it isn't."

Laura released her tears. "I want her back." They embraced and held each other. Neither cared for their situation, but only to find consolation in their shared ordeal. The moment meant something different to each of them. But together, it no longer mattered. Laura sobbed in her father's arms. She looked across the small clearing to see an Indian standing by the fire.

They walked toward the fire and approached the Indian. He stood adorned in his finest of dress. Leather skins appeared sheen with a colorful assortment of dyes. His hair flowed down his back, exposing his face. He had a kind, welcoming demeanor that exuded wisdom. His presence alluded to one of expectation, as he did not appear to be surprised by Wil and Laura. They watched each other without words for several seconds. The Indian motioned behind him. A woman emerged from the trees. She stood by the man and observed Wil and Laura. Seconds became minutes before everyone gathered by the fire.

They spoke for hours, gesturing with their hands and mimicking various items that they could not speak. Laughter, at times, brought smiles to the group as Laura played along. When Wil could not understand the conversation, they reasoned for explanation. The time spent led to a new and unique relationship. Laura remained patient. She had many questions and yearned to be included, but let her father continue the communication. She took satisfaction in the joy Wil expressed with the couple.

Time passed, and the Indian couple stood. Wil nodded his head and addressed Laura. "This is truly amazing."

"What are they doing now?" Laura asked.

"They are inviting us to eat with them. They have a village at the base of Sunset Peak. They hunt here," Wil said. He spoke to them, and they stepped aside. "I asked them for a moment with you." He took Laura's hands. "I know you have questions. We will talk soon. I am going with them to their village. I will see if I can get some answers."

"What have they said? Can't you tell me anything?" Laura asked.

"I asked them about the fire and how we are able to pass through it." Wil contemplated his words. "They said the mountain is of the people. That the people and the mountain share a bond. They said the fire is power." Wil laughed and continued. "I thought of Elise when they said this. They said the fire is like a door through the mountain. I thought that maybe there is a burial site here or something similar, but I'm not sure."

"A door? Did they say how it works? How are we able to pass through and not get burned?" Laura inquired.

"They tried to explain it, but I couldn't understand them. They kept talking about a bond with the mountain. From what they said before, I think they mean a belief."

"Is that why you told me to believe when we walked through?" Laura asked.

Wil thought for a moment. "Yes, that must be it. From what I can tell, not everyone can pass through. They asked a lot of questions about us after that. Why we are like them but don't look as they do. I know we are in a different time. But as to what time that is, I'm not sure. I had to get a bit creative with some of my answers to their questions. After all that they said, I think I have a new appreciation for Elise and what her team is trying to do."

"Why do they wear those masks?" Laura asked.

"They know the time is different when they pass through. The same as when we did not see the road, they wondered what the road is. They kept calling it the black scar on the land. They do not want to be seen. They said the masks protect them. I believe they think it is spiritual," Wil said. "There is more I want to talk with them about."

"Good," Laura said. "Let's go."

"No," Wil replied. "I want you to go back. They will be looking for us, and there will be questions. You can put an end to this. Tell them what you must, but do not say anything about what we have experienced. I want to protect these people."

"What about us?" Laura asked. "Are you coming back?"

"Of course, sweetheart. Please understand how much I need this. Whatever this is, I want to know it. And so did your mother. Let me do it for her, too."

Laura looked at the Indian couple. "They are magnificent, aren't they."

"They are our people. They are us."

Wil stoked the fire and walked Laura beside it. The flames intensified from the fresh wood. The Indian couple watched as Wil and Laura shared their parting words. Wil got Laura to laugh and encouraged her strength. She observed the Indian couple one last time. The couple raised their hands in unison toward her. Laura raised her hand in return and smiled, "Unbelievable."

"No," Wil said. "Believe it. For whatever this is, believe it with all of your heart."

Laura turned toward the bonfire. "Don't be too long."

"I won't. And tell Elise thank you. I hope she understands."

"I will." Laura approached the fire. She exhaled and whispered, "Believe." She closed her eyes and stepped through the flames.

* * * * * * *

Wichita Mountains Wildlife Refuge Manager Russell Riley sat at his office desk staring through the window. Fatigue buffered his concern for anything capable of disturbing his quiet moment. The sleepless night ended with the rising sun ushering in a new day. The radio chatter subsided, quickly becoming replaced by an endless barrage of updates. His deputies traveled in and out of the refuge headquarters working their shifts and providing constant reports. Officer Riley leaned back in the chair and closed his eyes for a hopeful escape.

The distinct sound of heavy-soled boots echoed across the front entry floor. Officer Riley heard the approach pause at his office door. It flung open without warning as the patterned sound continued toward his desk. Officer Riley opened his eyes to see Sheriff Ken Stockton collapse in a chair across from him.

"If it had been anyone else, I'd have you cuffed and thrown out," Russell said and closed his eyes again.

Ken yawned and rubbed his face. "I'd welcome it if it would get me out of this infernal paperwork." The two men enjoyed the silence before surrendering to the inevitable. "I'm done. I finished my part of this ordeal earlier this morning. They towed my car back to Cache, and I filed my report with one of your officers. Pending any follow-up, you should have all you need from me."

"Thanks Ken. I'm sorry you got involved in this," Russell said.

"No, you're not," Ken replied. "Your part in this isn't over yet. Any word on those two missing men?"

"We arrested them out by the west entrance an hour ago," Russell replied. "They said they were supposed to meet their accomplices there at sunup. I heard they surrendered quite willingly. They kept going on about some guys dressed in black that attacked them. They got in a tangle with someone out there. They were badly wounded.

I'm not sure what to pursue on that one yet. One of my officers is working on it."

"What about the idiot that hit my car?" Ken asked.

"Oklahoma Highway Patrol picked up him and his son in Altus. They stopped at a pharmacy and tried to get some meds and bandages. The manager of the store got suspicious and called the police. Evidently, they pulled a switcher-roo and left their van as a drop car at Post Oak Lake. From what I hear, they aren't talking much. The son, Aaron, is scared to death and kept babbling on about some stalker. Al Silver was telling them that he has his own story for history. He was bleeding badly when they arrested him. One of the science team kids shot him in the leg. She said it was self-defense. Al Silver kept going on about some nonsense that now he will be famous when he writes his next book." Russell laughed. "I'll tell you, Ken, people are getting crazier every day."

"He will have plenty of writing time in prison," Ken said. "What about his brother, Ed Silver, and that treasure? Something about silver bars and gold coins? Any word on that?"

"Nothing. They checked the white van he was in, the one that hit you, and the entire area around Post Oak Lake. Not a trace of him or the treasure. Makes me wonder if he had his own transportation and pulled a fast one on his kinfolk."

Ken shifted in his seat. "You had better keep that treasure story quiet, or this place will be crawling with metal detectors." Ken cleared his throat. "I kept hearing talk about a ghost at the Charon's Garden area. What the heck is going on out here?"

"Folklore for all I know. Look, I've got enough trouble with the living. You can handle that one if you like. It's all yours."

Finding Sunset Peak

"Nope," Ken replied. "I'm headed to the house. Besides, there are enough ghost and treasure stories in these mountains to fill a library. What did you end up doing with that science team you let in here? The folks from Arizona? I had one of them in my car. He's the one that led me to this mess. A *Jeff* somebody."

"I chewed their backsides and escorted them off of the refuge. I figured they learned their lesson. Some of them were quite traumatized from their run-in with the Silvers. I could tell from their faces that they did not expect that level of drama. We've got their statements. I'm glad none of them got hurt," Russell said.

"What a night." Ken stretched and looked at the clock. "You get some rest. The weekend's coming. You've got to be ready for the tourists." Ken stood and approached the door. "Say, I was told I had two Cache citizens involved with this too. You might remember them, Wil and Laura Brooks? They were the same folks we rescued out here ten years ago."

Russell checked his phone messages. "I think we picked her up coming off of Sunset Peak this morning. I haven't heard much on those two. She asked to meet with that science team. She said she got split up from her father and thought he may already be at home. She didn't seem too worried about it. The stories on her and her father didn't agree very well from what the witnesses said. Most of them claimed it was too dark to see what happened with them."

"Did you know she left her white truck out there?" Ken asked. Russell shook his head. "Didn't we have the same kind of nonsense with those two ten years ago?"

"I remember something like that."

Ken watched Russell with a snide expression. "Russ, I know this is your refuge, and you don't need any advice from me. But this is getting rather obvious. I don't want to see you played by an old man and his daughter. You might want to consider that plan we talked about for the drop car the Silvers left behind. Apply it to this and see what you find out. If anything, they will get a wake-up call for who is in charge around here," Ken said.

"That's not a bad idea. Thanks, Ken. And don't worry, I'll keep an eye on things out here. There's not much that happens that I don't know about," Russell replied.

"It's your call. Either way, keep me posted if you would, in case they show up on my radar in the future." Ken grabbed his hat. "I'm out of here. Holler if you need anything. I'll be at home asleep," Ken walked out of the office.

Russell chuckled, "One of my officers will bring the final report to your house around midnight."

"I'll make sure my dogs are out and hungry," Ken replied.

* * * * * *

The sun began to set behind Mount Scott, casting a faint shadow across the small town of Medicine Park. The long-awaited end to the tiresome day arrived. The team finished packing their vehicles and prepared for their last night's sleep in Oklahoma. The events of the previous night lingered with them. The agonizing hours of providing statements and answering questions to the local authorities exhausted them. The weariness was evident as they assembled in the cabin living room. Cots were scattered throughout the room for a welcomed slumber. The team waited for the last member to arrive before departing for dinner. Some drifted in and out of sleep as a knock on the front door captured their attention.

"Look who I found," Elise said from the opened door. Laura Brooks entered behind her. The team rushed to hug Laura and escorted her in. They talked about the previous night, sharing individual depictions of the adventures shared between them. Moments of seriousness isolated their emotions with various perspectives and clarity that some provided more than others. The dialogue began to diminish, leaving the team staring at Laura for the question everyone wanted to ask. "Where's Wil?" Elise asked. Laura's face became tense. Everyone waited for her answer. Elise noticed her hesitation and alleviated the moment. "I'll bet he's at home asleep. Is he okay?"

Laura expressed her appreciation to Elise. "He's doing fine. He had quite the adventure too." Elise nodded in acknowledgment while the group turned their attention to more stories.

Jeff sat at the back of the room, observing the situation. He kept a noticeable distance from the group and casually approached Laura. "I'm glad you and Wil got out of there. Tell him hello for me."

"I will. I heard you had a change of heart and came back to save everyone?" Laura asked.

"I couldn't stay mad at these degenerates. No matter how irritating they can be." Jeff leaned against Elise, prodding her for acceptance.

"I see," Laura said.

"I know I'm probably not the guy you want to give a second chance to, but would you consider it over dinner tonight?" Jeff took a step closer toward Laura.

Laura confronted him. "You may have had a change of heart, but I didn't."

Jeff nodded and strolled away. Laura exhibited a prideful gleam. She glanced around the room and noticed Karen Farris watching her.

She sat with Mike holding his hand. Karen overheard Laura's statement to Jeff and winked at her with a supportive grin.

Elise stood by Laura. "My, haven't you become the feisty one! Come on, let me save you from this bunch." Elise led Laura outside. "I'm glad you came to see us. I figured I would never see you again."

"I wanted to. You mean a lot to us. I know Wil didn't show it, but he cares about you. He told me to say thank you," Laura said.

"I don't know what for. I didn't do much. He did everything for us." Elise waited before continuing. "Is he happy now?"

"Yes, he is. He found the connection that you mentioned—the one about the Indians and the fire. You were right. There was that and more."

"Good."

"Don't you want to know what it is?" Laura asked.

"No." Elise became stern. "That is for the two of you. Protect it. Don't tell anyone. You have something special. Keep it that way."

"Are you sure?" Laura asked.

"I've already told the team that it was inconclusive. And after the interference of the Silvers, we may never know anyway. Besides, after all that has happened, I told them it was another ghost sighting," Elise said.

"I thought you didn't pursue ghosts?"

"I don't. But it shut Jeff up and steered everyone else away from the topic. We have enough to analyze with Jeff's watch passing through the window, our Tombstone evidence and everything we captured here," Elise replied. "That is more than enough to keep us busy. We have some regrets, but losing the treasure is the one that really hurts. Besides, we have Fort Huachuca to look forward to when we get back to Arizona."

"What about the science? Aren't you curious?" Laura asked.

Elise put her arm around Laura. "If there is one thing your father has taught me is that some things cannot be explained. Whether you two have found a window or a door or some other crazy term we have yet to identify, I've learned not to let science get in the way of what may simply be a wonderful mystery of life." Laura nodded. "But I am curious," she looked at Laura. "Your people, the fire, everything was there. But in my dreams, there was something that I kept seeing vaguely every time. It wasn't until we found it that I realized what this could be about. I feel like it is the reason for all of it, but we never really confirmed it."

"Sunset Peak," Laura said. "The fire and the people have the connection, but the mountain is the reason. Sunset Peak is the real mystery. There is no other way to explain it. I guess you just have to…"

"Believe," Elise stated. Laura was stunned. She yearned to ask Elise how she knew to say that word but allowed her the confirmation she received from Laura's reaction. They appreciated the fervent bond between them and let the topic subside with their shared moment. "There is one last item I am curious about." Elise walked her toward her car. "Did you get accepted to Oklahoma University?"

"I did! How did you know about that?" Laura asked.

Elise laughed. "I may have had another dream or two." They embraced and said goodbye. "Hey, and one other thing. You will find love, Laura. Real love. Just make sure you give it a chance."

"Is this another one of your dreams?" Laura asked. "How will I know who he is?"

Elise waved and approached the door of the cabin. "You won't. But your dad will."

* * * * * * *

The stars glistened through the night sky. Wil sat near the bonfire, watching the day come to an end. A warm satisfaction filled his heart as he observed a wallet photo of his late wife, Ayita. He caressed the edges of the picture, viewing her face by the firelight. He tucked the picture in his wallet and stood. The fire burned with a fresh supply of wood and branches. Wil checked the small enclosure tucked between high walls of granite and large boulders. Convinced the location was well hidden, he departed through the west valley of Sunset Peak.

He hiked carefully through the darkness, avoiding the dense forest along the base of the mountain. The open grassland of the western side allowed him to see shadows more clearly in the night. A wandering herd of bison caught his attention. The massive animals continued their evening graze with no regard for Wil. Distant coyotes howled their presence. Their unison cry echoed as the emblematic tone of the wild west. A lone barred owl called from the trees waiting for a response from the darkness. Wil enjoyed the natural symphonic performance with every step. The peace of the refuge was his refuge from life's ordeals. With every sound and sight, he knew this was home.

Wil followed the contour of the creek bed and hiked up a rising slope. He ventured through a sparse forest and stopped behind an oak. A refuge highway glowed before him. He looked both ways for any interference of traffic. Confident it was clear, he hurried across the pavement to the gravel parking area. His distinct white truck remained where Laura parked it. He took his keys and opened the passenger door. A sudden display of red and blue lights flickered in the darkness of the parking area. Wil turned to see a police car in the tree line across the road. The car started and slowly approached him with no headlights. Wil remained motionless as the police car stopped near his truck. He watched the driver exit the car and approach him. He stared in disbelief at the recognition of Refuge Manager Russell Riley.

"Hello, Wil. I'm glad to see you are alive. I was wondering about you," Russel said with his hands on his hips.

Wil noticed he was dressed in full uniform and armed. "Officer Riley. What can I do for you?"

Russell chuckled with a displeased manner. "That's an odd thing to say way out here at night. But, since you're asking, what you could have done is respect the fact that there were teams of search and rescue out here looking for you and your daughter last night. Thankfully, she showed up okay too."

"Good. I'm glad she is safe. I didn't mean to cause any problem. I was already out here helping that group of scientists and thought I'd watch the sun come up," Wil replied.

Russell stared at him. "Do you expect me to believe that?"

Wil became unsettled. He panicked as anxiety began to cloud his judgment for words. "I'm not sure I understand?"

Russell remained entranced with Wil before leaning against his car with his arms crossed. "Wil, for all intent and purpose, this is my refuge. I'm charged with keeping it orderly and peaceful. That's hard to do if I have people out here that I can't trust." Wil remained stationary as Russell continued. "I need to know if you and your daughter are people that I can trust?"

Wil's anxiety became curiosity. "Yes sir. I don't know why you couldn't."

"Hiding out here at night when people are looking for you is one example."

Wil nodded. "Yes, I guess it is."

"If I'm to trust you, why would you do that?"

"Um," Wil rubbed his boot in the gravel. His nerves began to overwhelm him. "I'm not sure I have an answer for you, Officer Riley. Not one that you would believe anyway."

Russell laughed again. "Believe? It takes a lot to believe in something. Especially if that something is hard to believe. Wouldn't you agree, Wil?"

"I'm not sure I follow you," Wil replied.

Russell allowed a moment of silence to accentuate the conversation. "Wil, I've been refuge manager here a long time. I've seen a lot of things. I've heard a lot of things, too. Some I could believe and others, well, they seemed quite unbelievable." He stood from his car. "There are some unbelievable stories out here that I could tell you."

"I'm sure you could," Wil said.

"Hmm," Russell walked next to Wil and peered in his truck. "There's this one story that I know about. I don't share it with anyone, because quite frankly, I don't think anyone would believe it. Did you know that at any given time, day or night, there is always a fire burning somewhere on Sunset Peak?" Wil stared at him without reply. "No kidding." Russell backed away and pointed toward the slope. "Somewhere, always hidden, there is a fire – a big one, the size of a bonfire, always burning somewhere on that mountain. But here's the thing, no one can ever find it. It's as if someone runs around out here building fires in hidden areas on Sunset Peak. Nowhere else, just this mountain. It's hard to believe in something that can't be found, wouldn't you agree?"

Wil contemplated Russell's words. "Yes, I guess I would agree if you put it like that."

Russell stepped slowly toward Wil. "I mean, a fire like that, if it were true, would be better left unfound. That way, the fire would not, shall we say, get out? That could become a problem if it got out. Then others would have to get involved. Nobody wants that, do we, Wil?" Wil nodded again, becoming increasingly perplexed by Russell's insinuation. "Good! We have an understanding then." Russell walked around his vehicle and opened the driver's side door. "And Wil, one other thing, belief and trust go hand in hand. I expect that starting tonight, I have both with you and your daughter."

"Yes sir, you do." Wil hurried to address him, "Officer Riley, I've been curious for some time now, and if you don't mind me asking, do you have any American Indian ancestry in your family?"

Russell leaned against the roof of his car with an admiring observation of Wil. "My mother was an assortment of ancestries from the Great Plains. But my father was Wichita." Russell noticed Wil's reaction and expressed a slight grin. "Enjoy your evening, Wil." Russell started his car and drove away. Wil watched him depart with subtle intrigue and renewed curiosity.

Russell clicked his handheld radio and sped along the refuge highway. "Headquarters, this is Riley. Call Sheriff Stockton and inform him that his person of interest has been located. The matter is resolved. Case closed, over."

"Will do, Officer Riley," the radio operator replied.

"And headquarters, if you have to, send an officer to his residence. Knock till the sheriff answers. And watch out for any dogs, over," Russell smirked.

"Roger. Anything else to report?"

Russell glanced through the passenger side window as he passed the darkened rise of Sunset Peak. He noticed a pair of slanted, glowing eyes watching him from the forest. He held the receiver near his mouth and replied, "Nope, nothing unexpected. Have a good night."

CPSIA information can be obtained
at www.ICGtesting.com
Printed in the USA
BVHW070940221021
619495BV00001B/1